Fragmented

KATE BATTRICK

Fragmented
Published by The Conrad Press Ltd. in the United Kingdom 2025

Tel: +44(0)1227 472 874
www.theconradpress.com
info@theconradpress.com

ISBN 978-1-917673-51-8

Typesetting and Cover Design by: James Sadlier, jamessadlier@me.com
The Conrad Press logo was designed by Maria Priestley.

Printed and bound in Great Britain by Clays Ltd, Elcograf S.p.A

For family & friends

PROLOGUE

At the end of a garden two figures pressed against each other, a father and daughter. The father had his arm tight around his daughter's waist. Her head was nestled deep into his neck, almost pressing his head hard to the other side.

'Dad! Olivia!'

The voice came from the open kitchen door. They both turned. The man waved and took the female's hand.

'Come on, love, we'd better go back in. We can't leave Amy to do all the clearing up.' He gave a sigh.

'Don't sigh, Dad, it will get better. We are only more sad today because it's all over. There is nothing more to do for Mum now.'

'We'll always hold her in our hearts.'

'Of course we will, but Dad, you know what Mum said, we have to keep grasping at life and live it fully.' She squeezed his hand.

'You've got a wise head on you, Olivia.' He smiled at his daughter, who seemed to have become taller in the last few moments. 'I swear you are still growing! Have we been stood in manure?'

Olivia laughed.

'She who grows last, grows longest, that's what Mum always said when I used to cry about being the shortest at school.'

'Oh, I miss her so much, Liv.' His broad shoulders seemed to crumple and his torso concaved briefly with an involuntary spasm.

'Dad, I love you and I'm going to be here at home, but you promised Mum to be happy, and we need you to carry on, otherwise Amy will become the boss and that will be very annoying.' She gave him a quick playful dig in the ribs. He regained his posture.

'I'll try. Honestly, I will try, and if anything comes along to make my heart leap, then I will grab it, promise. Meanwhile, the drudgery of my demanding job is enough to wade through. Talking of which, I need your brother to drop me off there in the morning, so I'd better remind him.'

They ambled hand in hand back to the house. Both treading carefully, both deep in sorrow, but each step forward returned a modicum of hope.

URSULA

ONE

The trouble with the name Ursula is that people expect great things of you. I'd never discovered this greatness, nor had any expectation of it. Ursula from *ursa*, the Latin word for bear. I'm definitely more minor than major when it comes to bear territory, possessing more fortitude over strength and distinctly average in stature. I'm not very huggable and only have the ability to give good bear hugs when slightly sozzled. Yet, here I am, once again in a situation where my name defines me, not the moment at hand.

'Ursula, an unusual name.'

Ah yes, always a statement. Sometimes an inflection as if it were a question, for which they weren't really expecting an answer. Just as well, because the answer in my head was typically sweary and not befitting of an Ursula. On this occasion, I was blithely nodding my head, mainly because I didn't quite know how I was going to force the words out.

'And how can I help you?'

'Well, I'd like to report a body.'

The police officer sat opposite me at the town hall desk, separated by a screen, in a space accommodating two booths in a very public area. I assumed he was the desk sergeant, but didn't dare ask him. He was out of place, seated on a chair on the other side of the booth in a town hall. His tall but portly structure would have aced his occupancy if stood at a police station front desk. Hence, he merely raised an eyebrow at my statement.

The body in question was in a garden. The morning of the discovery still haunts me. It was the type of scream that tells you straight away something is dreadfully wrong. It was coming from Caroline. Both Fiona and I dropped the plants we were carrying and ran to the other end of the garden.

It was a huge garden, beautifully divided by paths, trees, and shrubs, each area providing outdoor rooms. The owner, Mr Etheridge, a man in his seventies, had developed his garden over forty years and had always refused to move despite having outgrown the need for such a large home. It was in this vast private idyll that we now faced a crisis. Out of breath, with an explosive heart rate, I stood next to Caroline's hunched body.

'Oh my God, I'll call the police.'

'No, Ursula, I'll do that, you see to Caro,' Fiona said, using the pet name we reserved for emotional moments. I lifted Caroline's half-crumpled body and drew her away from where she'd been digging.

'Sorry, so sorry,' she was muttering over and over as if it were somehow her fault. We were attempting to put in new plants, ready for the summer, in the spot she had been digging. It was a shaded, damp part at the end of the garden that was perfect for hostas and ferns. They could happily grow next to the line of trees and not mind the shade caused by the high dividing fence. It was a lovely, cool area in the summer heat for Mr Etheridge to sit and look back, in part, towards his house and contemplate. Now, in a large dug-out hole, we could see what looked like a skull and maybe a shoulder. It was hard to know if it was just a skeleton or whether there were traces of skin and hair. I had no stomach to investigate further.

There were no flowers in this part of the garden and the only smell was the dense woody bark. The end of the garden backed onto woods nestled behind the row of detached houses on the main road. It was an area rich in woodland, open fields, and ruddy great big houses. Today, the smell was accompanied by the unfamiliar and horrid stench of decomposition. It was awful, Caroline was shaking in my arms.

'It's okay, don't worry,' was my lame attempt to deal with the inadvertent digging up of a dead body. Fiona, meanwhile, was wandering elsewhere in the garden, phoning the police. Caroline, thankfully, began to compose herself after what seemed an age, and then Fiona reappeared.

'Well?' I said.

'Well what?'

'Oh, for God's sake, Fiona, how long will they take?' I was tense. The whole thing was beginning to stress me out now, and I felt a bit sick.

'Um, well, um, they're not coming.' There were some moments of silence, then surprisingly, Caroline spoke in quite a sarcastic manner, I recall.

'What, they've given up on dealing with dead bodies, have they?'

'Not exactly, I just think we need to think about this before we do anything,' Fiona said.

'Fiona! Are you mad?' I exclaimed. 'What exactly is there to think about? We've found a body and the police need to know.'

'They don't need to know yet,' was her reply.

Now there really was a tremendous length of stunned silence. I was particularly speechless. I don't remember if it was me or Caroline who asked why. I can't quite believe we asked why, instead of bloody phoning the police ourselves. Fiona had this effect, we seemed to take orders from her like we were twelve and needed a gang leader.

'Look, this garden currently represents our one and only client. Think what this will do for business!'

And that was that. We didn't phone the police, and somehow it was me who ended up reburying a body by chucking soil over the top, with Caroline raking the area and adding the leaves we cleared. Not my finest moment.

'No, really, I need to report a body found in a garden,' I said once again, staring back at a man the other side of the booth window.

'You didn't think to call us then?'

For a moment, I was awash with shame, but Fiona had prepped me on the script in her kitchen, so I stuck to it.

'Dreadful signal, no mobile phone coverage. It is in a garden where I work. The person wasn't in. He's elderly, and I panicked. I covered it back up with the earth and drove straight here to tell you.' I was almost triumphant at this point. I'd got it all out word-perfect. Me, the procrastinator, the muddler of sentences and words in general. Perfectly pitched.

'And why would you cover it up?' His face looked quite cross. I gulped.

'We didn't want to worry Mr Etheridge as he's in his seventies and there are a lot of foxes around who come into the garden. They could disturb it.' Again triumphant. A raised eyebrow met me.

'Well, it looks like you've done the disturbing already.' Drat. I was physically squirming now whilst trying to keep my composure. Bloody Fiona.

'I'm sorry, it was all a shock, and, and, I'm really still quite shaken to be honest.' My bottom lip quivered, and I felt tears welling up, mainly because I was genuinely quite scared now.

'You mentioned we?'

'Ah yes, well, there are three of us and it is our gardening business. We're friends.'

'None of them had a phone?' Again, the raised eyebrow! What was it with his eyebrow-raising capabilities?

'Oh, no, I was there on my own, well sort of, and anyway,

no coverage, literally couldn't get a signal.' It was getting too detailed now for my liking. 'Look, the body is in Malden Rushett, and the address is Foster Wright Villa, Rushett Road.' I was keen to move the conversation on.

'Malden Rushett?' he said.

'Yes.'

'Not us then, it is the Met. Malden Rushett is Metropolitan Police territory, not Surrey.'

In my head, I was thinking, *what the heck has this to do with me? How would I know such matters, he logistics of who deals with dead bodies?* This is beyond now. Fiona should have come. She could have stared him into action, regardless. I had nothing else to say. My mouth had reached involuntary jaw dropping as I frantically tried to remember my lines. Then, to my surprise, a chair, with a person sat on it, rolled into my view. Another man appeared by the intransient, large, booth-filling police officer's side, albeit backwards.

'Mike, sorry to intrude, but I couldn't help overhearing the conversation given the proximity of our desks and the lack of privacy. Might I ask where you live, Madam? I didn't catch your name.' That made a change. No comment on my name, although I did bristle a bit at Madam. I know it is polite, but when you are older, it makes you feel, well, old. *Fifty is the new thirty*, I thought, as I paused before answering.

'Here. Well, Ashtead, but this is the nearest police station.'

'Okay, well here is in Surrey, and as the area in question is on the border between Surrey and London, plus it is a body, I'm going to have to pinpoint the correct location to make a final decision, as some of the houses are in Surrey, but most are Greater London, therefore the Met. Wait here.' God, he was handsome. And not a youngster, middle-aged I guessed, like me.

TWO

Twenty minutes later, I find myself shifting my cake tin off the passenger seat of the van to make way for someone who seems in charge of examining the dead body residing at Mr Etheridge's house.

'We haven't been formally introduced, despite flashing my lanyard at you as proof of something.' He smiled at me and I smiled back, trying not to look too much at his lovely blue eyes. 'I'm DCI John Smith, and you are officially?'

'Ursula Edmondson.'

'Ah, that makes my name very ordinary in comparison. Which it is. The most common surname in London at the time of my birth, and my parents added one of the most popular, boring boys' names. Not that I'm bitter.' He smiled but also seemed to sigh. He carried on talking to me whilst I concentrated on my driving. I found it soothing. 'Anyway, thank you for the lift and being accommodating. I'll want to ask you some questions in a moment, but I need to make a few calls on the way. Apologies for the brusque nature of Mike. We've not always collaborated, the Met and Surrey police that is. Still a few raw nerves over older cases where toes have been stepped on. But we are much better these days due to county lines initiatives. Anyway, the property is in Surrey, just.'

With that, he went quiet and started making calls. The sudden lack of direct communication made me wonder how on earth I was driving a detective in the gardening van. It wasn't far to go from the town hall to the house in Malden Rushett, but there were a few traffic lights to navigate on the way, and every single one was on red; providing me with more time to feel the panic building inside me. Fiona hadn't mentioned this in our role play. She had decidedly not factored in the 'when you've got the detective in the van' element of the scenario when deciding to finally report our discovery. From what I recall, we'd stopped at the reporting bit. Oh heavens!

We'd reached the traffic lights before turning onto the main Rushett road when DCI Smith finished making his calls. My hands were gripped on the steering wheel. My adrenaline was rising rapidly.

'Would you mind pulling into the garage? I could do with a caffeine injection. Do you fancy a coffee?'

'No, I'm fine, thanks.' If I had coffee, I might explode, and I wasn't entirely sure how that would manifest. Pulling into the garage, I was relieved to see a space straight ahead. My concentration skills had become myopic. I was fixated on not blurting out the truth.

When he got out of the car and I could see he'd walked into the garage shop, I flopped forward on the steering wheel. My head rested on the back of my hands. I felt sick. I couldn't risk phoning Fiona or Caroline. What an utter mess. It wasn't as if we'd killed whoever it was buried at the end of the garden, but now we were complicit in the whole blooming shenanigans. It was only Wednesday, I couldn't legitimately hit the gin or wine in a gung-ho Friday feeling way, but I was going to need to.

'Oh Christ!'

'Sorry, you okay? I didn't mean to scare you.'

'No, no, of course not. No, yes, I mean yes, I'm fine. I was just miles away and forgot why I was here. I just wasn't expecting you. Back. Back in the car.' Geez, my verbal diarrhoea had set in. I needed to shut up. DCI Smith gave me a sideways glance. I couldn't tell what he was thinking.

'Right, ready to go.' My cheery mum voice came into action,

and I think he almost laughed at me. The ruddy van lurched rather than glided into reverse. We sort of stuttered backwards out of the parking space before I managed to compose myself and my driving. DCI Smith was gripping his takeaway coffee.

We'd arrived at the house. Somehow, I found some inner composure. My thoughts had turned to Mr Etheridge. This was going to come as a shock to him, and he was a quiet and dignified gentleman. Not someone who was used to drama and unexpected situations. He'd be taken aback to see me again as I had, per instructions from Fiona, popped round earlier to drop off some composted garden mulch as part of her plan. DCI Smith knocked on the door. After what seemed an age, the door opened, and Mr Etheridge stood there staring at the pair of us.

'Hello, Mr Etheridge, I'm DCI Smith and this, as you know, is Mrs Edmondson.' He was also showing him his badge as he spoke.

'Hello,' Mr Etheridge replied, although I could tell he was puzzled as he immediately asked, 'What is your business?'

'Of course.' The detective cleared his throat. 'Unfortunately, it appears Mrs Edmondson has, during the course of her gardening, potentially discovered the remains of a human skeleton. And in the case of finding a body or human remains in your garden, it is the police people rightly turn to. I'm with CID in Surrey.' DCI Smith paused. 'Can I just confirm with you your property is in Surrey and not the adjoining London borough? I have checked, but would like to confirm who you pay your council tax to?'

'It is. But only just. Mine and two other properties are an anomaly on this road, being in Surrey and the local borough council.'

'Would it be alright if Mrs Edmondson and me take a look

at the area where the body was found please, Mr Etheridge?'

'Yes, of course. Please follow me.' However polite he was being, he looked visibly shaken. I felt dreadful.

He led us through his house, which I'd never entered, as I'd always used the side gate. It was surprisingly modern inside, and I'd assumed from its exterior that it would be all chintz and heavy old furniture. Once through the hall, the back of the house was an incredible open-plan kitchen, dining and living area. It stunned me. I realised I'd not even so much as looked at the back elevation of the house. There was a mix of olive and bay trees dotted outside an almost concealed courtyard area. All three of us stepped out onto beautiful grey flagstones through the open part of anthracite grey bi-folding doors, and I almost gasped at the obviously expensive outdoor furniture in this hidden cosy area. I wasn't quite sure if DCI Smith gently shoved me onwards as I was so taken with the upmarket luxury feast of garden furniture. Arriving at the spot at the end corner of the garden, I hesitated as it had been a few days or more, and gingerly pointed my finger at an area.

'Mrs Edmondson, is this it?' DCI Smith asked, pointing.

I merely nodded my head. My throat felt tense. Both men peered at the area and the detective kneeled and started to scrape at the dirt.

'Can I borrow a spade, please? I'd like to take a look.'

'Are you meant to do that?' All of a sudden I was thinking of all the crime dramas I'd ever watched.

'Ursula, it's not Vera. I do need to verify this really is human remains. I'm going to take a look without being too intrusive and disruptive before I make further calls.'

Oh, he called me Ursula, and how did he know I watched Vera? I went and grabbed my spade, which I had left with the fork and a few other gardening tools on the nearby wheelbarrow from earlier. I passed the spade to him. Once we were stood on the same spot as Caroline had been, he poked the earth around and revealed the same skull and maybe the shoulder we'd seen. He squatted down and stared at the remains, and then stood back up.

'Right, I'm satisfied it *is* human remains. The skull is obviously the giveaway, but the rest of the body seems to be attached intact. I'll need to make a few calls now.' He looked at both me and Mr Etheridge and wandered off.

THREE

Mr Etheridge excused himself to go to the bathroom and I was left alone, stood next to the spot while DCI Smith was still pacing around the garden on his mobile phone. I was unsure what to do. I felt hot and bothered as now I was stood here, I realised how ridiculous Fiona's plan had been. It felt like I had struck a deal with the devil. My mind had been working overtime ever since I'd said yes to Fiona's madcap idea. Even my husband had shoved me away from him at night, muttering about me disturbing him as I tossed and turned, trying to settle the thoughts. Then DCI Smith was there by my side.

'Right, all calls made. Someone should be here within the hour. They said 30 minutes, but bound to be longer. Let's see if we can get ourselves a coffee or tea, shall we? Maybe we can sit out on the furniture you were so admiring.'

Did he wink? All I could offer was a lame, 'Okay.'

Actually, Mr Etheridge was on his way to offer us refreshments. We all walked back to the house and he indicated for us to sit outside in a lovely secluded outdoor area. DCI Smith was extremely cheeky and said he'd have a coffee if he had a Nespresso machine, if not, then tea. Mr Etheridge was quite jolly in response and assured him he could have a Nespresso. We sat outside together, and Mr Etheridge joined us with the requested coffees. I had a cappuccino and noticed he'd sprinkled chocolate on top. Maybe being in your seventies is the new forties. I felt so relaxed. It was a lovely spring day and I was outdoors with a cup of coffee, not made by me. Then I recalled why I was there. I think Mr Etheridge broke the ice with chat.

'Detective Smith, are you a homicide specialist?' he asked.

What! Where did that come from? How had he mentioned the word homicide? I couldn't even think about thinking the word murder, let alone saying it.

'Homicide, I always think, is so American. I still prefer the term murder. Although all our stats and reports reference it as homicide,' he replied.

I found myself nodding along to his words. Although I wanted him off this subject, he carried on. 'But no, I wouldn't say I was a specialist. I certainly don't belong to a specialised unit as such. However, my main gigs are murder, criminal gangs, missing persons, and supporting others where necessary.' He actually said 'gig'.

'I didn't realise policing was part of the gig economy,' Mr Etheridge said. What? Mr Etheridge was not only serving coffee like a hipster, but talking like one.

'Not yet. As far as I'm aware, you can't dial for Uber Emergency or Crimeroo yet,' DCI Smith retorted.

Oh crap, this was hopeless. I knew I was younger than both of them, but now I felt bloody ancient. How had Fiona made Caroline and me think Mr Etheridge was old? He most certainly wasn't old and doddery. Very sprightly, poised, and well, not elderly. He was slim, seemingly muscular given his poise and straight back, and he was well dressed, very European with his well-cut shirt and trousers. His hair was white, but he still had it all and he was faintly tanned. He really was elegant. I shook my head as I observed him and the detective chatting.

DCI Smith was really handsome with his aquiline nose. I tried to stop the thoughts, but his hair was thick and a variety pack of grey. I knew he was quite tall, but sat there, I could see he had broad shoulders, and now he'd taken his jacket off, his white shirt was tight on his biceps and... I had to stop there.

This was ridiculous, here I was sat checking out two men.

'What's county lines?' I asked, eager to interject to stop my mind.

They both looked at me.

'You mentioned it at the town hall,' I carried on.

'Yes, I did,' replied the detective. 'We use the term 'County Lines' to describe criminal activity across different police authorities, or basically when criminal gangs from big cities expand their operations to smaller towns. It is very enterprising, a good logistics operation from a big place like London out to smaller locations. Modern day crimes modelled on Amazon, mainly drugs but trafficking as well. This whole thing of policing via geography with our old, fixed police services means policing is hampered by old-fashioned structures,' he added. 'My view anyway.'

'But haven't drugs always come from bigger places?' I asked. This time, DCI Smith raised an eyebrow at me.

'Possibly, certainly cities are the main hub of drugs, but now it's the gang element. The county lines element is the fact they run it all by mobile phones. They'll drive out soft, old-school type local dealers, often with violence. Then they'll start exploiting children and vulnerable people to sell drugs. I've got a fifteen-year-old on my patch in a flat who is the main supplier to others. He was put there, probably trafficked, but isn't reported missing and is kept there by a gang. I can't touch him, or rather help him, despite safeguarding issues. His flat is paid for and he's getting money. I've not got the resources to put a twenty-four-hour watch on him. We'll only get him when something happens and he gets caught up in it, or someone mentions him in a statement,' he said.

'Why don't social services get involved?' I replied.

'They try, but there are children younger than him with

phones as part of the pickup and supply chain. You might have spotted them on their electric scooters with a hoody up, or balaclava, no visible features. We call them drugaroo deliveries. All of us, even schools and children's charities, are working together to help, but honestly, it's really complicated. My boy rarely leaves his flat. I presume he's got Netflix on tap and a Deliveroo or Just Eats account for supplies, and he's probably on something.' His face contorted. I could hear the genuine concern in his voice. Gosh, it was a nice, handsome face.

My attempt at conversation had somewhat taken the shine out of us sitting outside. We all fell into silence, I felt sad, as well as naïve. I was pondering what I'd just heard and wondering why Fiona wasn't here. She'd have steered the conversation onto totally unrelated matters and had them both eating out of the palm of her hand. Mr Etheridge must have understood my discomfort, which prompted him to say, 'This is why finding a deceased body in the back gardens is not the desired event one hopes for.'

As I contemplated the unfolding circumstances, Mr Etheridge struck up a conversation with DCI Smith on cricket. I must have missed the point where they established a shared interest, given I felt so out of sorts. John, I found myself calling him John in my thoughts, was unsettling me in lots of ways, and I had no idea why. Fiona would later refer to my musings on this matter as lust. All I knew at that very moment, the three of us were sat on expensive outdoor furniture waiting for a person to arrive to assess human remains, and I would have quite liked to be holding John's hand. He gave no indication of this, to be clear. All in my head, a head which hadn't until today entertained any such thoughts like this. I shook it.

My thoughts were interrupted by the sound of the doorbell. Actually, it was from Mr Etheridge's phone. 'I've got Ring so I don't always have to answer the door.'

Mr Etheridge was some serious modern-day gadget guy. I was really reappraising my belief he was some quiet, newspaper-reading-only old man. He showed me his phone, and there, outside, was a rather dumpy man with a couple of quite large holdalls. I'd expected more than one person.

John jumped up and said, 'I'll get him through the side gate if that is alright with you, Mr Etheridge, rather than traipsing through the house.'

Mr Etheridge gestured with his hand towards the side gate, and John left us to get the guy with the holdall.

'Mr Etheridge, Mrs Edmondson,' he said upon his return with the dumpy man. There was a pause.

'Please call me Ursula.' I interjected.

There was a brief smile before he carried on. Mr Etheridge said nothing.

'Harry Russell here is a scenes of crime officer, we call them SOCOs. He's one of the best we have for such forensic moments, namely bodies buried in gardens,' Detective Smith glanced in my direction. Did he look sternly at me? He seemed quite stern.

'Not so sure about one of the best, but I'm going to make a preliminary assessment before we go nuclear and bring a team in to excavate,' the man called Harry Russell said.

Mr Etheridge still said nothing. It was as if the arrival of this Harry Russell had brought the enormity of the situation into focus. I wished I could give him a hug. I found myself yet again walking to the corner of the garden where Caroline had made her unfortunate discovery. Mr Etheridge stayed behind, leaving us to it. If only we hadn't decided to plant ferns and hostas there, I couldn't help but think. I stood back as the two men examined and discussed the area. DCI Smith walked back to stand with me while the scenes of crime investigator continued his work. We didn't talk. After a while, the SOCO turned to DCI Smith.

'My initial view is the area has been tampered with before. See this bit of earth, well, it is less compacted than the wider area. It is damper below the surface, suggesting digging or turning of this section of soil. I obviously can't put a timeframe on it, but certainly within the last week is my best estimate.'

'Not today then? Because you know both Mrs Edmondson and I've dug this bit.' I heard DCI Smith ask Mr Russell.

'No. Definitely not. I can see the earth you've dug, but even so, this smaller patch is not as compacted as the other undisturbed ground. Where it has been disturbed, the leaves and other natural elements haven't layered in the same way as everywhere else. These are recent leaves but more decomposed than if they had just lain on the ground. They've been dug into this area, but not today. Hence my view it was dug up previously, but roughly about five to seven days ago.'

It was very quiet as the two men pondered this information. I might have wriggled a little. I certainly wanted the ground to open and swallow me up. DCI Smith was staring at the area. His eyes went from the patch outlined by the SOCO to the rest of the garden. The SOCO pulled out a camera and started to take photos of the area I'd led them to. My brain was suddenly shattered by seven words. DCI Smith walked over to me and gently led me back towards the house.

'Ursula, I think we need to talk.'

FOUR

It was Fiona's idea. Of course it was. She's usually the ideas person.

'The girls gardening gang! What sort of cheese-riddled name is that?' I exclaimed.

'The name is aimed at our potential clients, mainly elderly, in need of a gardener, and totally paranoid about dubious people stealing their life savings. I think a name implying female-only gardeners will seem more trustworthy and gentile.'

'Great, so let's get this straight, we pretend it's 1930s Britain, all ginger ale and Just William? Then the target market, the wrinklies, will buy into it because of our name?' Although why I was even discussing her ludicrous suggestion was beyond me.

'Look, we've got nothing to lose,' Fiona said. 'There are no overheads, and since I've given up the corporate world, we need to do something practical.' There she was again with the 'we' when Fiona always meant her.

'Fiona,' I said lamely, not quite the right tactics. 'Caroline and I work. We happen to like our work. You however, got bored of your job and pulled off a great result with your redundancy deal. I'm pretty sure your years of high earnings mean you don't have to work.'

Fiona pondered this for a moment and swiftly retorted, 'Yes, I know, but a classroom assistant and part-time charity press assistant wage isn't that difficult to match.'

Caroline sighed, before bravely saying, 'It's not only about the money, I actually like the children. It suits me to work the hours, and you know I need the holiday time to look after the children.'

'Oh, for fuck's sake Caroline, Jack is at university and Ruby is seventeen!'

Not liking where this was going, I attempted to get her to listen, 'Fiona, Caroline is only making the point because you need to appreciate we have commitments. I work for a charitable organisation and I know it's not well paid, but I do it because I want to. Also, there are other considerations to factor in, like PAYE, National Insurance, pension contributions, and sickness pay.'

'Ursula, don't tell me you haven't thought about working somewhere that doesn't smell of dead people's castoff clothes!'

Fiona's words sprayed out at me like stingy juice from an orange. She was infuriating. I busied myself making coffee and offered more to Caroline. Here we were again, sat around my kitchen island basically 'chatting shit' as my eldest Dan liked to point out. There are three of us, Fiona (natural leader and bossy), Caroline (steadfast with bouncy hair), and me, Ursula (baker of cakes). Hmm, baker of cakes makes me sound rather housewifely, which in a way I am, I suppose. Fiona frequently points out that I rustle up a cake without fail for any crisis, event, and birthday if I possibly can. It's true, any old excuse to while away time absorbed in a recipe. I do like to bake every Saturday, making the cake, biscuit and flapjack supplies for the week as I refuse to buy shop-bought anything. I can't buy anything from a supermarket that has more than five ingredients on the label. The baking started when we moved out of London.

When the children were primary school age, we moved to the suburbs. Easy commute, easy access to M25, Heathrow and Gatwick, you can imagine the estate agent blurb. I was loathe to leave the city behind. I knew I'd miss the hustle and edge of city life. But Ed insisted we got a detached house with a garden, a dog and a frigging Aga. I drew the line at the Aga. Luckily, the dog never happened either. The move unsettled me and I started baking cakes. Recipes bring order and require a plan. Ed and I have survived the years of marriage due to my planning. We absolutely love and adore each other, but without a plan in mind, I'm sure things could have gone very wrong. I have strategies for every eventuality. I rehearse them, just in case. Fiona says it's an issue about trust, but trust is not the reason. Ed works in the media. It's not him I'm worried about, it is the lifestyle. I think about him being led down a cocaine-fuelled path. I keep an eye on whether he drinks too much or parties too hard. I like to be prepared; having a plan is handy. I'm quite ruthless in keeping my world in order.

Proverbs are equally useful. My favourite one is 'there's no point closing the stable door after the horse has bolted'. It took me years to work it out. It really did. I asked for endless explanations, but finally the meaning came to me and I learnt from it. When I met Edmond Edmondson, I was merely twenty-four to his twenty-eight, and I knew I needed to look after the stable door. He was everything I wanted, funny, handsome, and an assistant radio producer. He seduced me with his talk of faders and programme timings. Ed loved his job and still does, though now he is the head honcho of a massive media group.

I've got two boys. Both technically adult men now. It still seems like only yesterday – when two years later, after meeting and being boyfriend, girlfriend – Ed and I got married. A further fun-filled four years passed until I was pregnant with Dan. I wanted to call him Dennis. I had some childlike obsession with re-reading my Beano annuals at the time. Ed pointed out that we would only have to go and change his name by deed poll some six weeks later when I got fed up with saying, 'this is baby Dennis'. He had a point. Two years later, we were faced with the same problem. Baby Stanley. Except he never was baby Stanley, not even Stan for short, just James. Ed objected to my fantasy gritty northern mentality that was dictating my name choices, which was a bit rich given his parents' choice of Edmond if you ask me. Naturally, my career in journalism, okay, writing for women's magazines, came to an untimely end with the children and the aforementioned move out of London. I didn't want both of us to be commuting. Fiona, of course, just hired a nanny; she didn't give a moment's thought about it. In fact, I'm not entirely sure she stopped working at any point. Of course, I missed the mess of the magazine office I worked at in Soho, tucked away in a side street off Carnaby Street, and the end-of-the-week, after-work carnage we called drinks. I loved being part of a team, but the children came first and I settled for being at home. The odd bit of freelance writing popped my way, and eventually, as Dan and James got older, I went back to part-time work, slipping into PR work for a local charity and hospice.

Still, I love them both, and I feel privileged to have reached my fifties with my family intact and my own set of teeth. Now James has joined his brother in heading off to university, I feel somewhat displaced. The house is quieter, and as lovely as it is to not be in a whirlwind of demands, my days seem more plodding, less structured. I don't think it's empty nest syndrome, more freefall. I've fantasised for years about Ed and me skipping off again without a care in the world. I've imagined Santorini, Seville and Stockholm as differing destination options. It was a bit of fun to plot breaks based on the alphabet, and the letter S turned out to be the most fruitful. I could add San Sebastian and Sorrento, but to achieve my top three would be a miracle as Ed is always too busy. It is never the right time. If it's not a presenter crisis at one of the stations, it's a takeover or merger to sort out. The demands of commercial radio and a media empire rule our lives. Fiona rolls her eyes at me constantly. Her view is 'get on the plane and go'. Caroline is more empathetic and understands the desire for companionship and time together. I always jolly myself with the fact there is plenty of time ahead of us. Ed promises me it will happen soon. When I think back to the time we had before the children, it's like someone else is telling me a story about their experiences. It's all very far away now. Ashtead village hasn't the same buzz as our old haunt in downtown Bermondsey. Still, I met Caroline when James went to primary school, and then I had the pleasure of meeting her mad, bad friend Fiona, who's now my very own infuriating friend too.

Poor Caroline. When I say poor Caroline, I don't mean money. Caroline is without love in her life. She loves and adores Jack and Ruby but has no man to love, or to be loved by. Which is a bit of a shame and waste, because she's such a good friend and company. Caroline is the opposite of me and my strategised life. She is fiercely organised but loves to suddenly drop everything and have an adventure. She seeks out fun and prefers a Saturday lunch to my weekend baking, especially if it involves wine. She left school at sixteen, went to a secretarial college, and then travelled and worked in mainland Europe. It helped she was fluent in French, and it goes in part to explain how she found love with and married an Italian cocaine addict at the age of twenty-two. It wasn't the wisest of connections. He was handsome, his family was wealthy, and at the start the coke was an occasional weekend encounter. Funnily, it was drink that killed him, not the drugs.

We had to go to Exeter many years ago when she received a call from the local police to say they'd found Paulo dead in a house and would Caroline come and identify the body as she was his ex-wife. It sealed our threesome. We'd always helped each other out with picking up the children or having one round when necessary, but this required a couple of days of solid support. After that, we settled into our weekly evening catch-up without fail, except holidays when it might just be two of us and sending annoying texts to the absent friend.

Paulo nearly got a swift pauper's cremation paid for by the local authority after the coroner's inquest, but his family paid for the body to go back to Italy for a family funeral. Caroline had kept in touch with his mother, Francesca, for the sake of the children, and whilst Paulo's family had washed their hands of him, they hadn't done the same with his wife and children. Caroline divorced him because when Ruby was two, she never saw him again. He disappeared. Despite filing a missing person report, no information came to light until he died. His father, Antonio, died when Ruby was five, as the family liked to say, through worry and a broken heart. His only son was lost to him. It took her over a year to tell Jack and Ruby the truth about their father passing away and the reasons why. She didn't have much choice when the money came through. Paulo's inheritance was an enormous sum, which was used to upgrade her cosy two-bedroom Victorian terrace into a lovely detached house in a leafier part of Epsom. The move required an honest chat. Yet she hasn't found love again after pouring all her energy and time into the children.

The past several years have been spent in unrequited love, apparently with a divorcee called Joe. If there were a section for this in the Guinness Book of Records, she would clearly be the winner. Fiona and I don't even bother to disguise our amazement anymore, nor does Caroline. We have thrown every type of man imaginable in her path. I think Fiona might have even paid someone once. Nothing. And I mean absolutely nothing. I also recall someone who was smitten with her attempting to force their lips on her as we left a party. I even walked quickly up the road, but she was by my side in seconds. She has made it clear that if she can't have this Joe, whom we've never met, then she won't have anyone. Surprisingly, Caroline, who is very easy-going ninety percent of the time, will quite happily fall out with anyone. She has a feisty streak and stands for no nonsense except when she has an emotional connection with someone. With her amazing, perfectly dyed, blonde, thick curly hair and a great backside, Caroline truly wears her heart on her sleeve for this Joe.

This is compared to Fiona, who'll happily do whatever she wants, regardless of anything. Her partner, Rob, who is only a forty percent stakeholder in their relationship, once found a note on the kitchen table in the morning with no explanation, 'I'll be late home tonight'. She went to Barcelona for the day. Drove really, really early to Heathrow. Got a flight and bought some espadrilles. Had a lovely coffee too. Mad. Fiona gets an idea and does something. Poor Rob is the only guy we know who has begged to get married. He's tried every trick in the book. Even getting Fiona knocked up twice failed to get a result other than Alice and Henry. Fiona holds no truck with ceremony or status. She really doesn't care. Caroline and I never enquire about her values on anything because we don't need to, we know.

We refer to her as 'successful'. Essentially, she terrorised her way to the top in the city as a commodities trader. Her view was, and remains having once been offered a job, the least the employer could do is promote her within three months or else it was their loss. Fiona, with her long legs and natural ebony hair, always looks determined. Her ice-blue eyes hook people in, and then they do what she wants. When she got to 'the top' at the age of thirty-four, she gave in to Rob and had Alice.

Her stay at the top was maintained and extended even when, at thirty-eight, she added Henry to the family. This happened with the minimal of fuss, to all of our amazement. Apparently, it was a good conversation topic with the important wives of corporate-dom-hood. Then she got bored. Thankfully, no one suffered, except the poor young city lads she ate for breakfast for a few months over their performances, until she decided it was work that had to go. Even Rob would have thrown her fellow co-workers in her path to prevent fallout at home when she was at her worst. And a very nice detached home in Oxshott it is as well. Though not on the Crown Estate, Fiona is slightly republican, shall we say. She loves the finer things in life and loves to live well, but there is something about her childhood and upbringing that means she has a passion for helping the most in need. To my eternal shame, I can't ask her what or why, but I'm never surprised when I get a food bank donation demand from her. She runs wild, our Fiona, although wild doesn't really describe her. But she is also great fun and always has ideas, and insists she is only friends with Caroline and me because our initials spell fuc. Without a k.

And it was her latest idea that we were discussing. Did I say discussing?

'Okay, I give in and will announce it all to Ed, and we all live happily ever after with tomatoes and cucumber salad for tea.'

'Great, glad you're agreed.'

'Fiona, I was taking the piss. Why would I want to sign up to a girls gang?It's not right, and you'll have me in a dodgy uniform before I know it.'

'Ursula's right Fiona, we do have to think about it.'

'Oh, come on Caroline, when has Ursula been right about thinking about it Too much thinking about it has let Ed rule the roost.'

'Fuck off, Fiona.'

Now I had her full attention and respect.

'What are you both afraid of?'

That was the second we gave up. Fiona's blue eyes glinted. She knew it. She'd won.

'Okay, this is the plan. I'm going to get a van, some essential tools, and produce leaflets. All you two must do is help me to leaflet and hand your notices in at work. Because believe me, we've got a name for the business and it does what it says on the tin, which is the most important ingredient in business.'

I muttered something about Enid Blyton under my breath as I thought nothing would move Fiona on from the stupid name. And after all, it was Fiona's idea. I fully admit the three of us had such great fun together, and Fiona always had ideas for keeping our friendship interesting. I don't know who first said two's company, three's a crowd, or why. In my opinion, probably more a reference to bedroom etiquette than friendship. However, something galled me about the name, and I found my inner voice for once.

'Ahem'

'Yes, Ursula?'

'Let's choose a better name. We are not jolly hockey stick types.' I cocked my head at her.

'The three hoes!' Caroline exclaimed. We burst out laughing.

'We can't call ourselves that,' I said.

'Hmm, I wanted alliteration, but you're right, we don't want pervy pensioners thinking they are getting a gaggle of young girls round to sort out their weeds and beds. Which means no to the three hoes, Caroline.' Fiona deliberated.

I quite liked the obvious gardening reference to a garden hoe.

We sat thinking.

'How about Hoes and Co? You know, like Top of the Pops, Legs and Co,' I volunteered. Fiona rolled her eyes again. Caroline and I were cracking up.

'Can you two take this seriously? I like the and Co. bit, so how about Cultivating and Co. Gardening?' We both nodded through our laughter.

And that is how our gardening company came to be. With our first and only client at the time being Mr Etheridge. Then we unearthed a dead body. Fabulous!

FIVE

'We'll go to the garden centre café,' DCI Smith said.

I felt a sense of immediate relief as I had anticipated I'd be put in a cell. Although judging by his expression, DCI Smith wasn't thinking of a coffee and cake type cosy chat. After he'd had a few words with the team, who were now fully in situ in the garden, we said goodbye to Mr Etheridge. I felt guilty leaving him alone with a young police officer taking a statement, however, it was in his splendid kitchen.

Once again, I was in the driving seat, although obviously, DCI Smith was really in the driving seat. I was merely the guilty partner in a collective cover-up. Although it wasn't as if we'd committed a crime.

'You do realise you've committed a crime.' The first words out of his mouth as I pulled off from Foster Wright Villa.

'Err, no.'

'Forgive me if I can't quote the exact statute book number and specific title of the crime, but I'm not in the habit of coming across a group of women who dig up a body, rebury it, and then report it a week or so later.'

I wanted to say something, but the idea of saying anything to further incriminate me at this particular moment seemed futile. Granted, I might have muttered 'not all of the body'.

We sat at the traffic lights in silence. The silence continued until I pulled up my car in the car park of the garden centre. We entered in more silence. We reached the coffee shop section and queued behind a remarkable number of elderly people, all getting cake. Neither of us looked at the cake selection.

'Coffee?'

'Yes, a black Americano, please.'

'Do you want milk with that?' The woman making the coffee said.

'No thanks,' I murmured.

I queued again at the till to pay for my coffee and found a table by the window. DCI Smith joined me. He'd been momentarily distracted by a meeting of uniformed police officers at a table.

'They always come here. It's what happens when you close police stations. That lot are all Met Police.'

I raised my chin and tilted my head to one side to peer at them. Great, surrounded by pensioners and police. Seemed to be my lot in life now. Fiona had the cheek to belittle my charitable work, but we were a more diverse cross-section of society than this current garden centre café lot. How was I going to explain this to Ed?

'Ursula.'

That got my attention. I quite liked his voice. Clear, with a velvety depth. Oh god no, he's going to arrest me if I don't watch myself.

'Yes?'

'What exactly happened? And please do not give me any more flannel or even attempt to fail to mention anyone involved. Got it?'

'Got it,' I said, slightly like a teenager speaking to their parents. I needed gin, not coffee to loosen my lips. 'Okay, I'll give it to you from the top, but believe me, it wasn't planned, it was just stupidity,' I said.

I then took a deep breath and proceeded to tell him how Caroline had been digging holes for planting and found the remains of the body. How Fiona had unintentionally panicked over our business. Well, I had to make her seem more ditsy female than she was. How stupid we'd been, but that it was all a bit of a shock, and of course, we came to our senses, and here I was. Which was more or less the truth anyway. I left out the coaching I'd received for reporting the body and said I'd popped in when I had a free moment.

'Glad you prioritised a moment to report a body, Ursula.'

Was he being sarcastic?

'No, honestly, it was obviously pressing, but equally, having hesitated, it became more difficult to report it because we hadn't called you immediately. Which, of course, we bitterly regret. As well as regretting finding the body.'

A period of silence ensued between us again. As uncomfortable as it was, I quite liked just sitting here, not in my usual habitual routine. John seemed to be staring into the middle distance. There it was again, John. I found myself studying his hands. Looking at his face would have been too uncomfortable. They seemed well-kept and nice, with clean, short nails. Fiona would ask me later if they were hairy. I assured her they weren't. I mean, there might have been hair on his arms, but no sign of werewolf hands.

'Okay, I don't really see much point raking over the fact you didn't report it immediately. However, you and your two gardening pals will have to come separately to provide formal statements. I'll make appointments at convenient times, but it will be sooner rather than later.'

'Right, that is fine, I'm sure.'

'I'll need full names and contact details please, Ursula.'

I nodded and started to get up, thinking that was it.

'Getting me a coffee to keep me sweet, are you?' said DCI Smith

'Yes, why not?'

I think I might have had a bit of a grin walking back to the counter for two more coffees. Although this time I was going decaffeinated, otherwise I'd be buzzing all night. Sitting back down after what seemed an interminable wait for coffee, I was surprised to see he'd taken his jacket off and was leaning back in the chair.

'Thank you.'

'You're welcome.'

'Not keeping you, am I?'

'No, nothing to rush back for. School runs are behind me.'

'Me too. More concerned as you are unofficially my chauffeur today.'

'Oh yes, I am, aren't I!'

We both smiled.

'Why am I, out of interest, your unofficial chauffeur?'

'Do you want the long story or the edited version?'

'Go edited first, and if the headline is grabbing, I'll do an interview.'

'I think that is my department.'

'Speaking as an ex-journalist, it is also mine.'

'An ex-journalist, hey?'

'Back to you matey.' Gosh, I was getting quite brazen now.

'Fair enough.' He took a huge deep breath. 'I'm banned from driving.'

I hope I didn't let my eyes pop out of my head, but I was completely taken aback. I had to think of the right question because I really wanted to know the full story now. I might have tapped my fingers on the table in concentration. If I did, he didn't say anything.

'An unusual position to be in isn't it, for a detective?'

'Not exactly. It is my fault and yes, I was speeding.' He looked momentarily cross.

'Speeding?'

'I already had nine points, and then I ran a speed camera on a job, and boom.'

'But don't you have immunity from speed cameras?'

'Yes and no. I was off duty on two of the four occasions. You still get tickets when on a job, but there is a process to it. The other two incidents I wasn't authorised to attend, which meant I didn't have eligibility to be exempt from speed limits. Don't look so shocked, I've been hauled over the coals by HR on this.'

I really wanted to know the full story but wasn't sure if now was the right moment. 'All sounds a bit dramatic,' I said. 'What do you mean by the fact you weren't authorised to attend?'

'I'm doing police jargon, aren't I? I can tell by how you constructed that question.' DCI Smith was grinning at me across the table and I'm afraid my stomach fluttered. I had completely forgotten what that sensation was like. In fairness, the last time was nearly thirty years ago. This was not good. 'Anyway, I've had my knuckles rapped, and I've only got a few weeks to go now before I'm back behind the wheel of a car.'

I felt he had more to tell me, but the moment had passed and I didn't attempt to pursue finding out anymore. We found ourselves once again in contemplative silence. I've no idea what he was thinking, but I inadvertently touched my face and discovered a chin hair. I was consumed by blind panic. Finding a dead body and hushing it up was one thing, but sporting a chin hair in a garden centre café was a catastrophe. I leant on my right hand. I now looked bored, which was not my intention. I was, in fairness, trying to contain my angst.

'I'm keeping you now, sorry, would you give me a lift back to the town hall please?'

'Of course. No worries. I was just thinking, sorry, didn't mean to make you think I was itching to escape.' I bloody well was. I needed tweezers.

'Ah, glad I wasn't boring you, but I really do need to get

back now to progress matters. I'm afraid I will be calling you to do a formal interview in the next few days,' he said firmly.

I had the decency to nod a bit in embarrassment at the reminder of why we were together. I went a bit red as I banished the inappropriate thought of him arresting me. I seriously needed to get a grip. I had no idea where this person was coming from. The fact it was me was shocking. I had Fiona in my head telling me I'd be watching Loose Women next. I stood up and took my khaki jacket off the back of the chair.

'Right, ready to go.'

Which came out in my best rounding-the-children-up voice. He smiled at me and got up. It was over. I took a deep breath and relaxed. I was Ursula Edmondson again. A woman in control of her facilities, laundry, and family. Somehow, I knew DCI Smith needed a hug. Not anything inappropriate, but a warm, caring one. Me, the non-hugger, wanted to give him a hug. Obviously, given his status and the reason for our chat, I couldn't anyway, but I felt a moment of sadness worn across his shoulders, which again I noted looked in decent shape. I quickly motioned that I was going to the toilet and scurried in. I ran the tap and splashed cold water over my face. This made my mascara smudge and reminded me of the chin hair, but it took the heat out of my body and gave my senses a chance to sharpen.

When we finally got back in my car and pulled out of the garden centre, heading back to the town centre, our reason for meeting came back into focus.

'I wonder how the SOCO is getting on?' he said. I wasn't wondering that at all, but felt I needed to respond.

'Do you think you'll find out who it is?'

'I have no idea. I'm not sure what we are looking at yet, to be truthful. There are all sorts of scenarios. A known missing person, a disappearance, or even a cold case, although that is unlikely. It is also likely we might never know, depending on so many factors.'

'Why is that?'

'To be brutally honest, there might not be the available budget or personnel to pursue this.'

'That is terrible!' I was quite stunned this might not be fully investigated. Not that I had any knowledge of policing, but I thought all crimes where dead bodies were concerned would be a top priority.

'Have I shocked you?' DCI Smith said.

'Yes, you have.'

'Well, you shocked me with your dead body cover-up nonsense.'

'Are you going to drop that?'

'What? The charges?'

'You haven't charged me!'

'Yet.'

Luckily, I caught him grinning again as I glanced in the mirror. I might have positioned it a bit more towards him than the rear window. Then my mobile phone went off. It was James, my youngest. Thank goodness it was Bluetoothed into the car so I could answer safely.

'Hello, darling. Sorry, I'm in the car with someone, can I call you later?'

'Okay Mum, I might be out, but yeah, speak to you later.'

'Love you.' But he'd gone anyway.

'What was that tune?' DCI Smith said.

'Oh, The Style Council's *Walls Come Tumbling Down.* Had a total teenage crush on Paul Weller. Saw them about ten times when I was in sixth form, then university.'

'I thought I recognised it. I also had a man-crush on Paul

Weller. Loved The Jam. Was that your lad then?'

'Yes, my youngest who is now at university. I have no idea how the time passed so quickly. I'm still the same now as I was aged twenty-four in my head.'

'Know that feeling.' It seemed to be followed by the tiniest hint of a sigh. I couldn't take a proper look at him to read his face as I was pulling the car up into the town hall car park. Then I realised he knew my battery wasn't dead as I may have mentioned earlier.

'Right, here we are. Many thanks for the lift, Mrs Edmondson.'

'You're welcome, DCI Smith.'

'I do need you to accompany me into the office area to take your details and to arrange an interview time. I might as well do that now rather than ringing. Get things rolling.'

Crikey, it was real. It wasn't some nice chit chat after all. He was truly back in full-on official mode. The teenage reversion happened again as I walked behind him in a stroppy exasperation mode. When we got to the desk, I sat down and waited for the questions.

'Right, let me find a notebook so I can get your full details.'

He went off and I glanced into the open-plan office. It was obvious the area I was sat in was zoned for the police. How could they work in a seemingly hot-desk fashion and not in a proper police station? I was most perplexed. Oh heck, he was walking back towards me, notebook at the ready.

'Let's get on with this,' he said from behind the screen. He wasn't messing around. 'Name, date of birth, address and contact number please.'

'Full name?'

'Yes.'

'Ursula Briony Edmondson, 11.5.70. Beechcroft, Farthing

Way, Ashtead, and can I call you on your phone as it's a new number and I can't remember it?'

He passed me a piece of paper with his number on it, and I dialled it, then hung up when mine appeared.

'Can I write mine down, please? I must learn it off by heart. I had my last number for over ten years but it got published by mistake. Well, I mean my number was used in an advert by mistake, and I got bombarded. I got a new phone out of it and my bills paid for a year.'

I was waffling now. I shut up and looked down at my boots. I felt like I was irritating him. His face was deadpan. I was actually irritating myself.

'Thank you, Ursula. I need the details of...'

'Fiona and Caroline?'

'Yes, and can you do next Wednesday at eleven? I've got a meeting room I can book here. Otherwise, you'll have to come to Reigate or Guildford.'

I agreed to the time and date. It was all over. He busied himself at his desk and I slipped off, avoiding the gaze of Mike with the expressive eyebrows. There was one raised.

I felt exhausted when I got home. I knew I should phone Caroline and Fiona immediately, but I needed some time on my own. I took my boots and jacket off, made a cup of tea, and headed to the bathroom. I lifted my chin up to the light, and using the mirror, I located the hair and violently tweezered it out.

SIX

Once again, Caroline and Fiona were sat in my kitchen. They resembled Meerkats waiting for me to tell them everything.

'Too early for wine?' Fiona said.

'Yes, it's only four thirty,' Caroline answered.

'I've got an espresso and hazelnut cake if you'd like a slice?' I offered.

Fiona rolled her eyes and put her hand up.

'Oh, yes please, Ursula,' Caroline gushed. I loved her enthusiasm.

She was always so cheery and positive. Back home, on familiar territory with my gang, I felt grounded as I made us all a cup of tea and cut some cake. I was glad of my nap. I had been completely exhausted. The late afternoon light of spring pushed some warmth into the room, improving the general feel of the day.

'Well?' Fiona asked.

I gulped. Tears came up, but I quickly wiped them away. 'It was awful.'

Caroline immediately got off her chair and came and gave me a hug.

'It can't have been that bad,' ventured Fiona.

'It was. Fiona, it was a mistake to do what we did. We're in trouble and we all have to make a formal statement. The detective concerned will be calling you both to arrange a convenient time.' It was quite satisfying to see Fiona's jaw drop.

'I'm not surprised,' said Caroline. 'After all, we should have called them immediately. It will be okay, we've got nothing to hide other than stupidity.'

We all sat in silence, although I slurped my tea by accident.

'Edmondson!' laughed Caroline. Fiona was lost in her thoughts.

'I guess it will be alright,' I said aloud. 'The detective, DCI Smith, was pretty decent really. We went for coffee at the garden centre near Mr Etheridge's place.'

'Cosy chat, was it? Fiona said a bit too sharply for my liking.

'Gosh no,' I responded. 'Far from it. He read me the riot act. It's just the fact he can't drive and would have had to book a meeting room in the town hall to talk to me. There was a bunch of Met police in uniform having a team meeting in there, or a break.' I ignored the fact Fiona gave me a look and said, 'Men in uniform, hey.'

'Wine anyone? It's gone five o'clock now, and I'll happily rustle up some food if you fancy staying. Ed isn't back until later.'

'I thought you'd never offer!' Fiona went to my fridge and pulled out a bottle of white wine.

'Or were you thinking fizz?' She asked.

Caroline looked expectantly.

'Oh, bloody hell you two! Go on, there is some Cava or a nice crémant in there. I'll grab some olives and crisps to be going on with.'

We all relaxed. The tension I'd brought back with me began to dissipate. Although it was all Fiona's fault, I couldn't be cross with her. No one could be cross with her despite her being infuriating on occasions, correction, quite often. She was just straight, no nonsense, no guile, and always good company.

'You didn't tell us Mr Etheridge's house was amazing inside?'

'Really?' asked Caroline, 'In what way?'

'Oh my gosh, Caro, he has the most amazing open-plan

kitchen, dining and living space leading out onto the private outdoor area that only Fiona deals with.'

'Perks of being the boss.'

'The boss!!' Caroline and I uttered in unison. She shrugged her shoulders and tilted her head to one side with a grin.

'You're dreadful, Fiona. I'm your very willing pal and still you like to lord it.' Caroline tried to look stern but failed as she shoved some crisps into her mouth.

'I can't resist it. Can you imagine what fun I had at work when I was a proper boss?'

'Yes,' I retorted, 'I saw you at work first hand once, in a meeting. You were such a cat! Preening yourself, putting in a hair flick, and can I add a flutter of eyelashes, all as distraction techniques to lull people into a false sense of security before you pounced. All well-researched and reasoned decision making, of course. You didn't even hire the PR agency I was doing the presentation with.'

'Well, they were rubbish. Didn't understand basic financial regulation. I couldn't trust them to help launch an IPO.' Fiona rolled her blue eyes.

'They only hired me for the pitch because I knew you. I told them it wouldn't help, but they didn't believe me. They were idiots.' I took a hefty sip of my drink before carrying on. 'But DCI Smith isn't an idiot and nor is Mr Etheridge. We need to make amends and then all sit down to grow the business properly. No more preening, okay?'

Fiona always knew when she was in the wrong; despite the bravado, her inner warmth would arrive and concede. 'Fair point. More than fair point, I've been too bossy and in charge. I don't mean to be. I think the transition from my city job has been harder than I anticipated. I know I don't need to be as on top of my game anymore as I was, and I really should relax. Rob has pointed this out as well. I promise I will relax, eventually.'

As usual, Caroline took it upon herself to provide succour and moved again to dispense a hug to Fiona this time.

'We are all in this together, and we need to work together to get this business off the ground properly. Because I'm really enjoying it. I much prefer the fresh air without herding children at break time.' Her smile was as large as her amazing head of bouncy blonde hair, and the glory of her eyes were caressed by kindly creases. The alcohol was clearly taking effect.

'Alexa, play *Chilled Ibiza*. I'll make a start on supper. Do you fancy spaghetti carbonara with salad? I was a recipient of two nodding heads.

I clattered around the kitchen while Caroline and Fiona chatted. It wasn't such a bad life after all. Luckily, I noticed my phone flashing as it was on silent. It was James calling back from earlier, which made me feel guilty for not returning his call.

'Hello, lovely, sorry I didn't get back to you before but...' I decided better of telling him the truth. 'Anyway, what have you been up to?' Bless him, he proceeded to regale me with a list of transgressions committed by his fellow university halls flatmates. He clearly wasn't impressed or used to someone nicking your milk and not owning up to it. I happily listened to him blather on, then made my excuses due to guests and momentarily wished he was still at home.

I turned my attention back to cooking and refilling the glasses, although that seemed to have happened without me noticing or being refilled! I nipped out to the garden to my herb patch to get some parsley. Rather bedraggled looking, but no one would notice once it was chopped. Fiona was smiling when I got back and she looked more relaxed than I'd seen in ages.

'I forgot to tell you both, I have good news. We have six more clients after my recent efforts and a few recommendations from Mr Etheridge.'

Caroline exclaimed, 'Not sure he'll be recommending us anymore.'

'Come on, he'll be grand about it.' Fiona seemed unfazed by Caroline's remark.

I just shrugged my shoulders. It was good news, and I didn't think Mr Etheridge would be gossiping about a dead body. He seemed too private a person. On balance though, I felt maintaining a pleasant evening was preferable to debating the dead body situation.

'Oh, that is good news, and Fiona, did I detect a bit of County Cork then?' I said.

She raised her eyes as I knew she would. Having left Ireland as a small child, Fiona rarely sounded remotely Irish despite her mother's heavy accent, nor did she talk about anything very much when it came to family. Not even her own children. I was never sure if she was guarded or disinterested. Still, it was good news the fact we had a growing business and a distraction from our impending interrogation at the hands of DCI Smith. We happily continued chatting as we ate and drank. Finally, I forgot about the day and was back in the moment, enjoying the company.

SEVEN

The kitchen door swung open and there was Ed, back from work. He looked tired and deadpan. I jumped up to greet him, happy to see him. I wasn't greeted as enthusiastically as I hoped, but he'd had a long day, and I was probably a bit tipsy.

'Hi ladies. How's it going?' he said, but didn't wait for a response and was immediately on the hunt for food.

'Darling, here, let me sort you out some food.'

I began to heat up the remaining spaghetti carbonara. Whilst my back was turned, I heard Caroline laughing at something Ed said, but I could tell it was her polite, kind laugh. She was really raucous when genuinely amused. I wasn't sure if it bothered me, but I decided not to dwell on it. I often politely laughed at lots of men who thought they were being amusing. At least these days it wasn't the nervous giggle of youth, the moment you wish you could enact 'Beam me up, Scotty', rather than stand there like a lemon nodding.

'Ursula?' Ed's voice cut across my thoughts, and just as well, as I'd nearly burnt the dish in reheating it. I was also momentarily startled by his tone of voice. I'd never realised it had that element of sharpness before.

'What?' was my retort. Which seemed a bit unfair as he'd only just got home from work and maybe I had bristled too much.

'Did you pick up my suit from the dry cleaners? I need it for a meeting tomorrow.'

'No, sorry, I totally forgot, I had other things to do today.'

'Exactly what was so time-consuming?'

The room's atmosphere took a dive and I shoved the plate

of food at Ed. I decided to ignore his remark and got a glass out of the cupboard and poured some red wine into it for him. I knew he wanted to ask me again, but with Caroline and Fiona in our kitchen, he couldn't. One glance in Fiona's direction and I could sense trouble brewing. Why had Ed chosen tonight of all nights to come home in a foul mood? Caroline must have sensed something as well, because before I knew it, she was by my side helping me to tidy up and gave my hand a knowing squeeze in the process. As we busied ourselves, I could hear the exchange between Fiona and Ed.

'How come you ditched the office job, Fiona?'

'You know why, I used to come home just like you, all frazzled and wound up. It wasn't good for Rob or the children. Of course, I didn't realise how much until we went through lockdown and all the Covid shizzle. Time at home was a bit of a game changer.'

Ed shrugged his shoulders.

'I didn't really get that time off running the radio stations and our media outlets – we were almost 100% open all the time. So no option for introspection and life-changing eureka moments. Still like it now, we are completely full-on.'

'Well, just so you know Ed, you used to be fun. Don't want you to think there isn't an opportunity to reassess things regardless of situations.' Fiona went to take a swig from her empty glass and glanced over at us. I wanted to mouth stop, but Ed was also looking in my direction and I chose to look away instead.

'Do you think I should go and intervene?' I almost hissed at Caroline.

'No, let them work it out. Two alphas, leave them to it. It will only fester otherwise. I don't, or actually didn't, always stop my two fighting, because if I interfered, they'd turn on me.

Now, I wouldn't wish that on you right now.'

We both grinned and I instinctively opened the fridge, grabbed some fresh glasses, and a chilled bottle of white wine.

'Here we are,' I said to Fiona as I refilled her glass. She said thanks, and I asked Ed if he'd also like a refill – of course he did, although it didn't stop him talking as I'd hoped.

'I agree with you Fiona, but honestly, getting through each year always happens before I realise it.'

'That is actually my point. I was like a hamster on a treadmill. Okay, Rob worked from home before, but I thought it was essential one of us work in an office, and my job paid more, so it made sense it was me.'

'Well, it did buy you a fancy house.'

'It's not fancy.'

'For fuck's sake Fiona, Andy Murray is one of your neighbours.'

'He's not, he lives across the way on another road.'

'On the Crown Estate!'

'My house isn't on the Crown Estate, Ed, it's on the main road. You know what I think of royalty.'

'It's worth millions!'

'What? Well, I earnt it. And what are you on about? This house is easily a million pounds plus now. You and Ursula are hardly slumming it.'

'Guys, cut it out you two.' I couldn't help myself, I had to stop their bickering. I felt like I was talking to the boys.

'Ed, and Fiona, you are both incredibly successful people,' purred Caroline, 'and,' she paused as she liked to soothe the moment, 'you're a right pair.'

Both were scowling. How had it come to this? They used to get on quite well, I thought. Neither seemed to care I'm put in the middle of their bickering. I wasn't sure if Ed was jealous of Fiona or she wanted to niggle him. We all seemed to muddle along for a little while longer while Caroline discussed the fact she was thinking of undertaking a landscape designer course. It kept all arguments at bay until their taxis arrived.

After I shut the front door, I did the thing they do in the movies, which no one ever thinks they'll do – I leant my back on it. I leant into that door as it had been a long day. A really long day, and now I had a kitchen to tidy and a husband to face. The movie moment ended and I walked back down the hallway, past the door to the living room. A quick glance revealed Ed wasn't there, so I resigned myself to his company going back into the kitchen. He had moved off the island onto one of the sofas. He already managed to pile some stuff on the dining table, but I averted my eyes from it to avoid finding out what it was doing there.

'Darling, would you like another glass of wine?'

I was a bit high-pitched in my delivery, trying to feign lightness. He gave a cursory nod. I'd never known such tension between us. I realised we'd drifted apart, or rather, my sparse time spent with him was more apparent now the boys had left home. I'm not sure anything had changed for Ed.

'What is bothering you?' I asked. I suddenly felt it was important to acknowledge the anger I thought Ed was containing.

'Bothering?' he almost bellowed. 'It's a bit more than bothering Ursula, it's a fucking annoyance to come home to find you three sat here getting pissed.'

Okay, anger firmly acknowledged. I had to stop myself from laughing. I really shocked myself, but he sounded like a pompous idiot.

'Ed, come on, we were just catching up. It has been a bit of a day.'

'How? You three aren't exactly doing much.'

'Well, I had to report the discovery of a body to the police,' I said.

That sort of shocked him a bit. And I quickly decided not to give him the backstory. I felt I had the moral high ground at this point and I wasn't going to lose it. I carried on, as he failed to interject.

'Yes, slightly mucked up our day, but hey, at least we had each other to chat to about it. Caroline found it when planting some ferns at Mr Etheridge's. Our only client. Although we have a few more now, according to Fiona, so business is heading in the right direction.'

Ed just sat there, sort of stunned. I foolishly sipped some more wine. We sat there in silence for quite some time until Ed broke it.

'Look Ursula, I'm not going to deny I think your decision to go along with Fiona's new venture is ridiculous. You had a good, easy job, and this is, well, manual labour. But I'm sorry you found a body.'

I slinked over to him and plonked myself next to him.

'Oh, thanks darling. I know you don't like me being a gardener, but it is more fun and despite my reservations, I've found it easier now Dan and James are at university to be with Fiona and Caroline. I felt a bit empty at work and then coming home. I much prefer pottering and being outside. Although I'd never tell Fiona that or she'd lord it over me.'

Ed sat there and I knew his brain was ticking over, but he still looked frustrated. He never seemed relaxed or engaged with me anymore. Even now, as I sat next to him, he bristled a little.

'I don't understand why you'd give up a regular salary. It was a tough call the last couple of years, but we made it through.'

'I didn't want to at first, but admit it, my salary was pocket money. I still write press releases, mainly from requests of previous contacts. It's nice to go with the flow. Anyway, James called me today and he was moaning about house-sharing, which amused me.'

The change of subject didn't lighten the mood. Which annoyed me because James was our child, and he was a delight now after his difficult teenage years. He didn't do anything awful other than exist on his phone, laptop, and PS4 for years. I mean, who goes to the toilet with a phone?

'Ed, you could at least be interested in our son.'

'For God's sake, Ursula, I'm not disinterested, but they are adults and at university, and don't need me to read them bedtime stories anymore.'

The room descended into silence again and I wasn't sure how to break it. I found it painful. I was finding this situation extremely painful. We weren't a team anymore. I'm not sure why I reached this conclusion, but I just knew.

'What are we going to do, Ed?'

'What do you mean, what are we going to do? There is nothing to do. Other than to clean up in here and go to bed after watching a bit of telly or Netflix.'

'You seem so angry.'

'Ursula, I'm not angry. I've just had a long, demanding day, and sometimes I like to come home to an empty house not filled with your friends. Especially not Fiona. You know we always clash. She's so opinionated, and yes, if she were a bloke, I'd say arrogant.'

I had nothing to say back. I realised we'd been here before, quite a lot, and I hadn't appreciated this until now. There was a time when Ed and Fiona got along just fine. But Ed can, and does, overstep the mark at times. Anyway, goodness knows when or why the niggling started, but it did.

'Urs, don't be so dramatic either,' he added.

With a sigh as deep as the emotional pain in my head, I got up and began tidying up in the kitchen.

'Would you make me a cup of tea?' Ed asked as he came up behind me and attempted a conciliatory hug, 'I'm just going to shower.'

'Okay.'

Oh well, I thought, *I've made my bed. I can lie in it*. Plus, I had the boys to think of. Maybe a nice cake tomorrow. I carried on clearing up. 'Alexa, play *Solid Ground* by Michael Kiwanuka.

EIGHT

I arrived fifteen minutes before my allotted time for the interview, as requested. I had to sign in and be given a lanyard, and was then taken to a partitioned meeting room in the town hall police area. I was sat there for quite some time it seemed. I wondered what DCI Smith was going to ask me and how I would feel seeing him again.

Eventually, the door opened, and a fresh-faced, well, to me, youngish man came into the room with a clipboard balanced on one hand with some things piled on top. He had a pen in his mouth and he used his left foot to shut the door. He nearly dropped everything onto the table, but somehow managed to place them heavily without upsetting the pile. He sat down in the chair opposite me.

'Hello Mrs Edmondson, I'm DC Bennett, and I'm going to be taking your witness statement today. DCI Smith sends his apologies, but he's busy and this is a straightforward process.'

I was slightly lost for words. I just nodded instead. Tears pricked at the inside of my eyes and I bit my lip to quell their rise. What on earth was wrong with me?

'Right, I need to put this contraption on so I can record everything as well as write. Is that okay with you?'

Again, I nodded. He then stood up the tape machine that had been lying flat on the table and started it.

'Quarter past noon, on April 16th. My name is Detective Constable Duncan Bennett. For the tape, would you say your name please?'

A slightly strained 'Ursula Edmondson' escaped from my mouth.

'Great. Okay, Mrs Edmondson, in your own words, would you describe the events that took place on the 28th of March at the address, in Malden Rushett?'

I took a deep breath and repeated the moment Caroline found the body.

'Would you also explain why you didn't report the discovery on the same day?'

Again, I drew in air to steel myself for my response. I continued to feel crestfallen. Recalling the decision still caused untold shame. I wasn't sure I'd really forgiven Fiona yet. So far, it had contributed to a dreadful schism in my marriage that I couldn't even fathom myself, yet. Perhaps if DCI Smith had been conducting this interview, it wouldn't have been so shameful. Every time I repeat our heinous act to a stranger for the first time, I feel judged. And rightly so. I blurt it all out to DC Bennett. He seems quite cheery given our duplicity. After what seems an age, DC Bennett informs me the interview has concluded.

'What happens next?' I ask him.

'That is for the SCI to decide,' is his reply.

'The SCI?'

'DCI Smith, he is the senior crime investigator leading this case. I'm here to take your statement only, Mrs Edmondson, and we've completed that now, so I won't take up any more of your time.'

I realised that was my cue to leave. That was that. I might never hear from them again. Well, I probably would, but my brief flirtation with the law, albeit on almost the wrong side of it, was over. I felt quite sad. I liked DCI Smith. Oh goodness, I did. I banished this thought away at once and conjured up images of kittens. I couldn't achieve this. I looked at my feet instead.

'Mrs Edmondson, are you alright?' I heard DC Bennett say.

'Yes, sorry, I was thinking about what I need to do for the rest of the day. Do I hand this back at the counter?' I took the lanyard off over my head and clutched it in my left hand.

'I'll show you out and take this for you.' He was so polite but quite directional.

Back outside in the April light, I didn't feel so gloomy. After all, it was done now. I had a few things to pick up from the shops before I met Caroline and Fiona, as arranged, for a post-interview deconstruct. Although, why I'd agreed to the garden centre café, I don't know. Fiona was all about us being seen in there. We mainly got our plants, plus garden hardcore gravel and chippings from the wholesaler, then supplemented with bits, when necessary, from the garden centre. Mr Etheridge also liked us to use it as it was local to him and he'd supported them since they were a start-up in 1967 – not that businesses were referred to as start-ups back then. If I was being honest, I didn't want to revisit my last visit there a week ago.

When I finally arrived at the café, Fiona had her back to me, and Caroline, upon seeing me, did some dramatic hand waving, mouthy stuff, which I failed to comprehend. I put my hands into a T sign. It was met with a major shake of the head, followed by an eye roll. I gave up and bowled over.

'If you don't want a cup of tea, then what do you wan...' I was stopped in my flow by the sight of Fiona, hunched and sobbing. She didn't even look up. Caroline stood up.

'Ursula, go and get some napkins. I'll have a latte and get a glass of water for Fiona.'

I nodded, and bewildered, I retraced my steps back to the serving area. Waiting for coffee took an age. Meanwhile, Caroline had moved her chair round and was comforting Fiona. I gently lowered the tray. Caroline immediately grabbed a paper serviette and passed it to Fiona. She then gestured to me not to say a word. Having firmly mentally zipped my mouth closed, I sat there in silent expectation and speculation. Eventually, fifteen minutes must have passed, as well as a cohort of nosey old pensioners. A couple of them patted Fiona on her right shoulder as they passed. I mentally conjured up the shrug emoji at this point. I was almost fit to bursting when a muffled voice said, 'Tell Ursula.' By now, Fiona's head and shoulders were lying on Caroline's lap like a child. Caroline did not look comfortable, but she soothed Fiona by stroking her hair.

'It's okay Caroline, it can wait a bit longer. I'm okay sitting here. Do you need anything, Fiona?'

'I think she's fine, but would you come and take over as I really need the loo?'

Caroline gently sat Fiona up, and I held her while Caroline stood up. I sat down, and Fiona flopped into my lap. I wasn't as good as Caroline at hair stroking. I tried, then did the old person shoulder tap a few times.

'He's gone, Ursula, he's gone.'

Good grief, had Rob left her? I couldn't imagine why. I know she won't get married and is a complete handful, but they both, in their own way, given that Fiona is less demonstrative, dote on each other. Rob adores her. I couldn't ask why. Caroline plonked herself in my seat and mouthed 'No' when I appealed to her to resume her previous seat. Covering Fiona's right ear up, I quietly asked,

'When did Rob leave?'

'Rob, leave?' Caroline said too loudly for my liking. 'He hasn't gone anywhere. I'm wondering whether to give him a call.'

Fiona shot up from my lap. 'Don't call him.'

Her face was saturated with tears, her eyes all puffy and red, and her nose was swollen.

'It's not Rob, Ursula, it's Luke. Luke, my brother. He's been missing since he was sixteen. And I can't keep it in anymore.' She slumped forward, her elbows on the table with her hands holding her face.

Caroline took up the story. She explained that when DCI Smith was interviewing Fiona, she got stuck when he repeatedly asked her why she had made the decision to prevent anyone from knowing immediately when the body was discovered. It transpired that Fiona explained to him the facts of the disappearance of her brother Luke. He went out one day from the family home when he was sixteen years old, never to return. He was a few years older than her, so would be in his early fifties now if he were alive. Fiona couldn't bear to know about the body in case it was Luke. Every discovered body in the last thirty-plus years has made her heart miss a beat.

It shocked me to the core. I'd known Fiona for over fifteen years, and not once had I had any inkling of this family tragedy. She had kept this significant fact from me and Caroline. I couldn't comprehend how. I was stunned, but I don't know what shocked me the most. Caroline gave me a look, which rightly focused me back on Fiona. I held her hand tightly and stroked the back of her hair. She muffled a sob and squeezed my hand back. The three of us sat in silence for ages. Fiona's sobbing subsided, and our drinks became cold and looked a revolting grey. Our contemplation was limited to nothing. Nothing passed through my usual Piccadilly Circus of thoughts. Silence, a heavy pulsating silence. I didn't know someone else's pain could travel so deeply into you. I almost felt sick, and I began to grasp the suppressed agony for Fiona.

'I'm sorry, so sorry,' rasped from my mouth, her hand tightened around mine.

'It's why I haven't married Rob. I want Luke at my wedding.'

It was on the tip of my tongue to say, but what if he never turns up, but luckily I realised how insensitive it sounded before saying a word.

'Right, I'm taking these cold gubbings back and getting us fresh ones. Tea or coffee, anyone?' Caroline asked.

'Can I have a Diet Coke?' Fiona answered weakly.

'Tea for me please, Caroline.'

When she was out of earshot, Fiona gave me a look.

'What?'

'Don't let her mother me. She's grand at it, but don't let her. I'm shaken up because of that bloody cop, but I'm alright really. My own mother does it enough, and as for Rob's aunties, geez.'

I understood. Fiona being Fiona cheered me up a little.

'Which cop, I mean police officer?'

'Your one.'

'What do you mean, my one?'

'You know, DCI Smith. He was about to leave the room and go and interview you, but he gave me such a disappointed look, I cracked. Then he sent the sidekick to you and asked me to tell him everything.'

Ah, hence why I had DC Bennett.

'Oh my, Fiona, how was it? Telling him?'

'Actually, it killed me. Hence why I'm such a mess. He asked me all the questions nobody has ever asked me. He made really detailed notes and said he promised me he'd do some digging.'

We both sighed together. Caroline returned with a tray and the drinks.

'Here you go,' she said and duly plonked the drinks down.

'We were talking about DCI Smith,' I volunteered.

'He is such a lovely man!' exclaimed Caroline. 'He was very patient and gentle with me, considering how banal the situation was.'

Fiona actually looked guilty for once, but I was in no mood to gloat.

'Good. Especially now we know why,' I answered.

'Sorry.'

'No need to apologise, Fiona, but it did seem a bit rich, it was all about our potential clients,' I blurted out.

'Ursula.' Caroline glared at me.

'What I mean is it didn't seem a rational decision, and of course it wasn't.' Although the follow-up remark didn't sound much better, I decided to drop it. It didn't matter now. Fiona was all that I cared about. I brushed her hair off her face. She looked like a broken child. We had completely forgotten anyone was around us in the garden centre. Time had stopped at our table, and everything around us was in the distance. It was Fiona who eventually broke our second period of abject silence.

'I've got to get home.'

'Will you be okay to drive?' I asked her.

'Yes. I'm fine. It's not far, is it?' she smiled weakly.

'Course it isn't. You'll be fine,' Caroline said. 'Although you'll have to call us when you get home. Three rings remember.'

It was our long-standing joke. The old give three rings and your parents would come and pick you up from a night out. Caroline and I cleared the table and then escorted Fiona to her car. We waited for her to drive off.

'Oh, good grief!' Caroline broke first.

I was just shaking my head.

'How on earth did she keep that inside for so long?' Caroline continued.

'I have no idea. It's such a tragic situation. I always wondered why Fiona's mum looked so old and broken. You know she is a real sweetheart and has spoiled all our children for years. My mum hardly acknowledges other children exist other than her own and her grandchildren. I'd presumed it was an Irish thing. But now, well, I suppose it's heartbreak.'

We stood there next to our cars a bit longer, each contemplating the situation. Eventually, it was hugs and goodbye. I drove home, stunned and without my usual loud blaring music.

NINE

'I love this song.' I said to Caroline as the opening refrain and lyrics from Fleetwood Mac's *Go Your Own Way* entered the work van. Caroline turned up the volume and we belted out the words or did la la la together as I drove us both to Mr Etheridge's house. The sun was shining, and the warmth of the rays coming into the van made me smile. Things had started to feel a bit better over the last couple of weeks. The body drama seemed less of a shadow, although Fiona was not joining us today for reasons she wanted to keep to herself. We grabbed our trugs and slipped in through the side gate. After thirty minutes of preparation and tackling weeds, Mr Etheridge joined us in the garden.

'Hello ladies, how are we today?'

'Fine thanks, Mr Etheridge,' we chorused.

'I think the formalities are over, don't you? Please call me David.'

We nodded and smiled.

'How is the planting going?'

'Well, the weeding is the primary focus at the moment, otherwise it will run away with us over the next few months,' Caroline said to Mr Etheridge, sorry, David. Not sure either of us were on board with that yet. 'I'm also going to make sure we check the pots and cut back on any shoots coming through now to encourage more growth, but I'm afraid the fern and hosta planting is on hold still.'

We all looked over to the still-marked police excavated area.

'Yes, that is not going to change over the next month or so, according to DCI Smith.' David sighed as he imparted this information. We all remained silent, which seemed to be a frequent pastime these days.

'Right, don't let me keep you.' And with that, Mr Etheridge, David, started to wander back to the house.

'I'll be over shortly to check on the next few months' dates,' I called out to him. He turned, smiled, and raised his right hand in acknowledgement.

'Gosh, Caroline, you really are becoming the gardener de jour!'

'I know. I'm absolutely loving the courses I'm doing with RHS Gardening. I was reluctant to go along with Fiona initially, but I think I found my passion. Although not sure learning Latin names is my forte, *Salvia coccinea* anyone?'

I was so happy for her. My dear friend who'd struggled on, on her own. Caroline truly was one of life's joys. She didn't moan about being single; she was warm and lovely, and got on with things. Not sure the same could be said of me. I was at sea. If I'm honest, I've done everything over the years. Self-help books, counselling, yoga retreats and mindfulness. For what reason, I ask myself every time. My only conclusion is as a distraction. Even as I think of this right now, my throat is tight and I feel a bit sick.

'Caroline, you are always so calm and happy,' I blurted out.

She looked up at me and smiled.

'Because I've been on anti-depressants for years, Ursula.'

My jaw dropped. This really was a month of non-stop revelations. I wasn't sure I had the headspace for any more.

'Didn't you know?' Caroline asked.

'Well, no, no, I didn't.' I said, feeling slightly foolish.

'I must have told you. It was years ago when Paulo was found dead. I was already struggling a little bit, but that pushed me over the edge.'

'But Caroline...' I hesitated. 'You have always seemed the most sorted person I know. You appear effortless.'

'Do I? Everything is such a whirl, I have no time to think about anything. But I was lonely and heartbroken. Paulo's death brought it all back, and whilst I'm still lonely, whatever I take keeps the edge off.'

'I'm sorry.'

'Don't be silly, I'm fine, and being outside more is helping, my dose is already lower than it used to be.'

We carried on with the gardening, both absorbed in our own thoughts. Or maybe it was just me.

'Caroline, honestly, I feel awful that I didn't know. Especially on top of Fiona's revelation.'

'Oh gosh, come on. It is hardly something you shout from the rooftops. Look at me, I'm a bit crazy cat lady, I need some pills!'

We both started to laugh.

'I know, but I could have been more sensitive to things,' I said, half in despair at my own lack of awareness.

'I'm the same Ursula. I know nothing of what is going on in someone's life, as I've got enough on my plate. We are friends because we all rub along nicely together. You and Fiona were so supportive when I had to go to Exeter. Anyway, it's not as if I ask you anything about Ed.'

Why did she mention Ed? My brain did a quick spin. Was there anything to mention about Ed? I had a horrid, tight feeling in my throat. I had to push it down and away. Back to silence and focusing on the gardening.

'Caroline, would you like a coffee or tea? I need to see Mr Etheridge, I mean David, and book in the dates as Fiona usually does.'

'No, I'm fine. I'm going to start on the pots shortly, so take your time.'

I wandered over to his secluded area and found the opening. I could see him in the wonderful kitchen diner and waved when he looked up. He gestured for me to enter.

'David, I've got filthy wellies on. Do you want to sit outside?'

'No, take them off and come inside, I'm enjoying the warmth of this late spring light pouring in. At my age, my bones seem to feel any chill in the air.'

The room was a spectacle of light and airiness, and I wanted the warmth of the sun as well. I somehow managed to pull my wellies off without sitting down and stepped in, noticing a bit of a hole in my sock on my right big toe. I stood waiting for him to suggest where to sit.

'Ursula, come and pop yourself here at the island. Would you like a coffee? I can do a latte if you'd like.'

I nodded and hiked myself onto an industrial-looking bar stool and leant on the counter.

'Right Ursula, let's forget the diary planning and have a chat,' he said.

I was quite taken aback by this. I hadn't expected a chat.

'I've got Rossini's *The Barber of Seville* on in the background. Is that okay with you?'

'Of course.'

'I'm a big fan of opera and I haven't listened to this for a while. Opera aside, how have you been?'

'Fine.' I seem to have turned into a monosyllabic teenager.

'I was only asking as it was quite an event, wasn't it? I've found it most unsettling. It is awful to think the poor person had been there for so long. I'm waiting for an update from DCI Smith. Have you heard anything?'

'No,' I replied. 'Since giving my statement, I've no idea what is going on. Although I do want to know.'

'Yes, it is natural to be curious. I've too much time on my hands since my wife died to think about such matters. Especially now I've retired, reluctantly, in the last year.'

'You were still working?'

Mr Etheridge smiled. 'Yes, even old fossils can work.'

'I'm sorry, I thought you'd retired years ago.'

'Luckily, there is no real ceiling on working as an architect. However, I did reach a finite point a couple of years ago and wound down my existing projects, and that was that. We were all rather forced to work from home for a while, weren't we, and I decided not to resume my central London commute.'

'My husband is a fervent commuter. I'm not sure he could break the routine and habit.'

'My wife probably wishes I would have done the same once she'd stopped fostering.'

'You used to foster children?'

'Eleanor, my wife did. We only had our son, Charles, and he lives in Hong Kong now. Despite wanting more, it never happened, and she found herself helping in an emergency once and then never stopped. Lots of paperwork and training, but Eleanor was used to that from nursing. She preferred looking after children who needed a lot of support. She turned around quite a few lives, but a couple were lost causes.' He stared into the distance.

'Do you miss her?' I asked. It seemed appropriate to fill the silence.

'I miss who she was, but she suffered so much with acute onset myeloma, a rare blood cancer, I was relieved when it came to an end. Suffering changes the memories and relationship. Charles has barely come home since.' More silence, which I couldn't fill this time.

'Enough about me, what about Fiona? She gave me a brief

outline on the phone. How is she really?'

I felt a bit guilty and sheepish as I didn't really know.

'I don't know to be honest. I've not spoken to her, except briefly about the gardening business over the last week.'

'I expect she's a bit overwhelmed and drained. It must be hard reliving the same circumstances with no resolution. Especially now she has opened up about it all. We've all been through the mill a bit recently, haven't we? Although I did rather like the company of the forensics team when they were here for the week.'

I found myself gaping in wonderment at the compassion and understanding of Mr Etheridge. There was much to admire in a wise and agile mind. I needed some of his clarity. My head felt a mess of emotions and misaligned information I couldn't process. I wasn't sure how long we'd both sat in contemplation.

'How long ago did your wife pass away?' I suddenly needed to know more about this man and his life.

'Gosh, must have been five years ago now. A good while. I went to Hong Kong for a year until I'd outstayed my welcome. A marvellous place to lose yourself in the crowd and be distracted.'

'Didn't you want to meet anyone else?'

'No. What am I now, 74? I'm going to be honest, I would have wanted my wife again. Someone good-looking, lively, fun, and caring. No one would have satisfied. I like stylish things as you can see, and a lot of people my age are, well, how can I say this, are not.'

We both laughed.

'And if I'm going to be totally honest, unless Sigourney Weaver threw herself at me, I preferred to remain a widower. Netflix, Alexa, books and the odd traipse to the Tate Modern or theatre is my lot now.'

'Well, your house is lovely.'

'Yes, although I am tempted to sell up, especially since the body incident. But I'm torn between a London flat or a seaside demise.'

'Moving to the seaside isn't a demise anymore, everyone wants to do it.'

We carried on chatting, and I completely lost track of time. Caroline knocking on the open bi-folding doors interrupted us.

'Did you forget me?'

I pulled a sorry face at her.

'Come in, Caroline,' Mr Etheridge said.

'I would, but I need to get going, and Ursula drove us here.'

I thanked David for his coffee and company. He winked at me when I asked him to email Fiona the next few weeks' dates. After helping Caroline to carry the trugs to the car, we were on the road to her house.

'Sorry, I got chatting to David.'

'Oh, David, is it now?' she laughed.

'Stop it! Mind you, he is a handsome, engaging older man. I had thought of him as old, but of course, he isn't. He is elderly, but his outlook and mind aren't.'

'Good to know. There is hope for me yet!'

'He doesn't want to meet anyone else.'

'Damn.'

'No, Caroline, I didn't mean a no for you!'

'Don't worry, it is a no from me. If I were twenty years older, then yes, I get it, but right now I need someone my age or younger.'

I really wanted her to find someone. I could feel the loneliness vibe emitting from her. David had it as well, but his was of his loss, not what he didn't have. Who could I find for Caroline?

'I'm going to throw a party, I've decided,' I blurted out.

'Oh, good idea, we've not done anything for ages.

Now all I had to do was run it by Ed, who used to be always up for a party, but his recent moods had made me wary of being spontaneous. A party was much needed for us pals.

'Do you think Fiona will want to come?'

'Of course. She's not moping around, only collating all the stuff on her brother for the police. Let me know what you need me to do.'

It was settled, we could do with a bit of a gathering.

TEN

The day of the party had arrived. I announced this inside my head with what I perceived to be a Jane Austen voice. It motivated me to get out of bed and start tackling the to do list. Nothing was achieved without a to do list. Part way through my early morning double espresso and peanut butter on toast breakfast, my phone rang, and a picture of James appeared on the screen.

'Morning, lovely.'

'Hi Mum.'

'You're up early.'

'I know, got lots to do and a lecture in an hour.'

'Everything ok?'

'Yes, don't worry, I'm not calling to moan about someone taking my milk. I'm trying to get hold of Dad, and he hasn't called me back. Would you remind him, please? It is about tickets for an event.'

'Yes, sure lovely. We are having a party tonight, so I might forget, but message me to remind me.'

'Still throwing parties, Mum?' James laughed.

'Life is for living, young or old, cheeky! Talking of cheeky, can you remind your brother to call me? I'm assuming he is still alive as I got sent a photo from him of a bare backside with the caption 'bants not pants'.'

'Fuck, he's such a dick.'

'James!'

'He's my older brother and all he does is mess around and pull his mate's trousers or shorts down. Such a loser.'

'Anyway, if he does call you, please remind him to call me. I've got to go now as loads to do. Come home if you fancy a party.'

'No, it's fine, I'll pass, no offence.'

'No worries. Love you, James. Speak soon.'

'Love you.' And he hung up immediately. No chance of a long, drawn-out goodbye with James. Smiling to myself, basking in the delight of his phone call, I started to plan 'Operation Party'. If everyone turned up, we'd be about thirty or maybe more. Numbers didn't matter, but food, drink and the playlist did.

The problem was, I couldn't get into my stride. No matter which task I began, my mind was wandering. I was ticking off the list, but the usual pleasure and tingles of anticipation were not there. I love throwing a party, and half the fun for me was creating the environment for people to let their hair down, unwind, destress, and not having to be involved. No involvement was key to letting me create an event.

My theme for the party, not that anyone knew it had a theme, was sweet peas. They weren't quite in season, but I'd been growing them from seeds under instructions from Fiona. My everlasting mix of the branded 'delightful cottage garden' climber were a white, pink-hued and deep pink, almost fuchsia version. I had white plates, very pale pink paper napkins, and bright pink flowers arranged around the house. Outside, I had hung white and pink daisy flower fairy lights, really old ones from Habitat when it was a high street store. The booze stash was lots of white and rosé wine, Peroni red label lager and Magners rosé cider. For a brief moment, I felt a flush of joy. The anticipation of the evening. The next, I was in floods of tears. A proper sobbing, snotty nose and tons of tears moment.

What? What was going on? Why on earth was I crying? I

couldn't fathom it. I loved throwing a party. My favourite bit was about to begin, prepping the food. I grabbed some kitchen towel and mopped up the residue of my bodily fluid strewn face and all the tears in my mouth. How on earth had half the tears ended up in my mouth? Exhausted by this momentary relapse, I had to make a quick espresso and down it in one. Back to the to do list.

I fussed around for a few more minutes, not really knowing what to do until I got back into my stride. Right, make a start on the chilli, Ursula. I was back in familiar territory, delivering my easiest batch of food for guests. I rarely wandered from this tried and tested offering. On the occasions I have messed with it, people have complained. In disappointment, of course. However, I can't take credit for the ingenious simplicity of such fayre. Years ago, before we got married, Ed was indulging me in a much-needed seaside dip outing. On our way back to London, we popped in, invited, to old university friends. Their East Sussex country farm was idyllic, and everything was beautifully convenient after a dip in the sea. A warm invite, welcome, and a kitchen with the shiniest Aga you had ever seen. Dave and Paul were pre-Elton and David. They were smitten from day one. Dave worked at one of the university campus banks, and Paul was a hapless student whose overdraft brought them together.

When we arrived, their party was in full swing, and Paul kindly led me to the food. He knew me too well. Nestling in the top oven drawer of the Aga were beautifully warm, soft jacket potatoes, and on top was a huge pot of chilli.

'Help yourself, sweetie,' Paul said.

'This looks like a hug on a plate,' I replied.

'Oh, you know me, all heart and soul. If you ever catch me serving canapés, shoot me. I refuse to become a mincing parody of myself.'

We both laughed. Paul was so masculine and proud to be from Newcastle that he committed to a football shirt outing on every summer holiday, much to Dave's disgust. I carried on adding a beautifully prepared green salad to my plate.

'Darling,' Paul elongated the word to get my full attention, 'don't take this the wrong way but...'

I gave him a hard stare and raised my eyebrows.

'Mind you don't let Ed stifle you in any way.'

'Why do you say that?' I was curious and slightly taken aback.

'When did we finish university, four years or so ago?'

'Nearly six.' I said.

'Really? Okay, it seems like yesterday we were scouring for illegal raves.'

I giggled.

'Ursula, Ed is a nice guy, but he's a bit self-centred, so make sure you can deal with it, that is all I'm saying.

I found myself nodding. Mainly because I was fighting back the tears then as well as now. Was Paul right? Had I missed the chance to really evaluate what I was like and who I was marrying? How had twenty-six years passed by since? I did smile as I remembered the Aga. I'd forgotten that Ed had been so taken with us having one. Perhaps he was a bigger softie than I gave him credit for. We did have such a lovely time together, but life changes, and perhaps I'd not been sympathetic enough to how hard he worked. Also, maybe it was up to me to carve out my own fun. I mentally made a note to plan a night out together. I refused to use the term 'date night' as it suggests the novelty of new love or lust.

You can't recreate the feeling of newness. Relationships are like my party chilli, they provide succour and comfort. You know where you are. While I understand the need for frisson, it's not the be-all and end-all of a marriage. I set about making blueberry muffins with these thoughts rambling around inside me. I had a tightness in my throat, and heat was rising inside me. I poured myself a glass of water and took a sip. I felt like pouring it all over my head. I assumed the heat was the impending peak of menopause, despite the daily application of HRT. The life and joy sucker. I've noticed there isn't a day that goes past without someone or several people banging on about it. Maybe that's why I cried.

After catching up on myself, despite a brief call from Caroline asking if she could bring someone tonight, my timings were all good again. I was ready to get scrubbed up for the party. I checked my watch as Ed was later than expected, and he was normally very punctual, if not early, when we had a party. I wanted him to be here now. I wanted to embrace him and remind him of the trip to the cottage and our discovery of the much-tried and tested chilli offering. If I could have just this moment with him, then we'd be back on an even footing. Then my thoughts spiralled into what on earth was an even footing. Why was everything so confusing at the moment?

'Fuck! Fuck, fuck.' I stubbed my little toe on the corner of one of the kitchen island stools. My eyes welled up again, but this time in pain. Ed walked in as I was cursing and hobbling around.

'What's wrong with you?'

'I stubbed my little toe. It really hurts!'

'Okay, well, I'm going upstairs to shower and change.'

That is it? A shrug? A departure? No concern? Suddenly, I was fuming, and I still had a throbbing toe. It was lucky the plate of pink and white iced blueberry muffins was just out of reach as otherwise they'd have ended up on the wall, floor, and mixed in with the inevitable smashed plate. Bastard!

Three very deep breaths later, sprinkled with a barrage of swearing, the likes of which I'd not heard from any fifty-something woman ever, I stood, ice cold and steely in my kitchen. My refuge. My mind was racing, but over and over with clenched fists, I reminded myself this evening was for Fiona. It was a distraction. A moment of lightness before we got down to the task, as firm friends, of helping her however she needed. With this in mind, I went upstairs to also shower and get ready.

After thirty minutes, I was back downstairs. I'd dug out an old, flippy dress which was quite short but had long sleeves. I'd squeezed my ribs in with a belt to really make an accentuated waist. Faked tanned legs were adorned with an equally old pair of gold sandals from Dune. My usual nice, understated look, mainly tasteful purchases from the likes of Me+Em or an online boutique, had been ditched for this old flirty Oasis dress and a modern day Carmen look, resplendent with hoop earrings and all. I tried some red lipstick on, but it looked awful, and stuck with my Victoria Beckham Beauty posh lipstick in Pout.

Ed was in the kitchen, and at first, he barely glanced at me. Then, in slow motion, he looked. Properly looked.

'Wow! Ursula.'

'Yes,' I replied very haughtily

'Oh, babe, you look a million dollars.'

In my head, I said, 'What a complete million-dollar give you a blow job in the toilets type babe? Yeah sure'

'Thanks, hon,' I replied. I never said 'hon', I wanted to gag, but I was going through the motions. 'Is there any delicious ice-cold champagne in the fridge?' I asked. I often asked for champagne, but normally without the delicious. I had no idea where this was going, but I had his attention.

I continued with my small talk. 'The neighbours but one

will be here shortly, I bet. They are always first.' I playfully leant over the kitchen island as he passed me a glass of champagne.

'Oh Christ, you didn't invite them, did you?' Ed exclaimed.

'It was either invite them or have a mention on the road's WhatsApp group. They always put 'someone is having a party' with an exclamation mark at about 11pm. I'm never sure if it is a hint for said party to stop, or they are highlighting that they weren't invited.' I promptly slugged the champagne.

Ed rolled his eyes.

Sure enough, the doorbell rang and I dutifully went to open the door.

'Are we the first ones here?' Judy, the next door neighbour but one, exclaimed as soon as she entered the hallway.'

'Yes, Judy. Lovely to see you.' Air kisses. The only thing the coronavirus pandemic didn't manage to kill off. Judy glided through to the kitchen and Ed greeted her like a long-lost friend, which made me roll my eyes, forgetting her husband was standing next to me. Oh well, he was harmless and didn't notice. I led him by the elbow to the kitchen, and then went and grabbed myself a glass of rosé and put a ton of ice in it. I managed a big gulp before the door went again and more neighbours arrived. Then, finally, Fiona and Rob turned up, and I felt my door duties were over.

'Look at you, Mrs!' Fiona eyed me up and down. 'What happened to dreary Mrs Boden?' I ignored her and gave Rob a hug.

'Ursula, Lorena, and a friend of hers are just parking the car. They'll be here in a moment. You did say it would be fine,' Rob looked me in the eye as he said it.

'Of course, it will be lovely to see her, it's been ages,' I smiled back at him. He was such fun, but incredibly considerate and kind. 'Rob, you are always so polite,' I added.

'It's the Barbadian way. Talking of which, I've mixed up a rum punch as I'm not driving tonight. Where shall I put it?'

I took the ready-mixed rum punch in a bottle off Rob. I got him a glass and added some ice before letting him pour what he wanted. Ed immediately made a beeline for him, which made me thaw a little towards him. At least he was being a convivial and decent host. Fiona eyed me sideways and I ignored her as I went to open the door for Lorena.

'Hello sweetie, it has been ages!' There was the gorgeous Lorena, ex-pop star who'd famously and surprisingly divorced her equally famous footballer husband. I was happy to do air kisses with Lorena, and she looked glowing. She introduced me to a very handsome man who was so charming when he spoke to me, I went a bit giddy. I quickly took them both to Ed as Lorena and Ed had known each other for longer than Fiona. Fiona and Lorena had become friends from their children's primary school days. Ed had moved in the music scene for so long now I'd forgotten who he did and didn't know, and suddenly I realised I didn't care about any of it anymore. But seeing Lorena made me think there were things for me to consider. Could I be brave?

Somehow the music became louder, and Fiona, Lorena and I were outside chatting about various offspring-related issues, especially university. I realised Caroline still wasn't here and felt guilty for not noticing. I checked my phone and saw a text message in capitals: WE ARE OUTSIDE. As I dashed from the garden patio, Fiona shouted 'slapper' at me. I started laughing and was still laughing when I opened the door to Caroline and – I caught my breath – DCI Smith.

ELEVEN

Stunned. I just stared at them. I must have stood gawping for a few seconds, but in truth, it felt like a lifetime.

'Come in, you two. I'm surprised to see a copper at the door, eh, already,' I said, followed by a stupid 'laugh at my own joke' moment.

'Is this too awkward?' I heard him say.

'Nonsense,' Caroline said. 'She's a bit pissed.'

'No. No, I'm not! I am surprised, but yes, come in, come in.'

I beckoned him through the hall into the kitchen, and Caroline I suppose as well, but she knew her way around, and so she left me to close the door. I had to walk back and shut it, but he was standing, waiting for me.

'It's John tonight, Mrs Edmondson.'

Did he wink?

'Would you like a drink?'

'Yes, please. I'll have a beer, well, lager, any Peroni?'

He also handed me a bottle of wine. I grabbed it and plonked it down on the counter as I simultaneously opened the fridge door and stuck my head in. I needed the cool air of the fridge. Either I was having a hot flush, or the fire inside me was something else. I took longer than necessary, clanking the same bottles that were within easy reach. Of course they were in easy reach, I'd organised the fridge exactly for this reason, but now I needed time.

'Here we are.' I said in the lightest, brightest voice I could muster as I handed him the bottle.

'Do you need a glass? And the opener is just here.' I looked but couldn't see it.

'This what you are looking for, babe?'

Who the heck was babe? Oh, me.

Ed had appeared by my side with the wine and bottle opener. An arm went over my shoulder. I resisted the temptation to shake it off and quickly grabbed the implement to hand to John.

'Ed, this is Caroline's friend John.' Giving him the wide eye over this minimal introduction. Caroline had already dumped her date and had disappeared. He extended his right hand towards Ed.

'Ed, pleasure to meet you. Nice home you've got here.'

'Thanks, mate. The very reason I married Ursula, her good taste, and I count myself in that bracket.'

The sentence hung in the air. But that wasn't enough. John smiled at him, which gave Ed an opening to say more.

'Although the real reason I married her was to say in a Sean Connery voice, Ursula undress! Geddit?'

There. There it was. My Jane Eyre moment, courtesy of Charlotte Bronte, the immortal words, 'Reader, I married him'. I was propelled back to my wedding day, where he first uttered this banal 'joke' during his speech. My dad's face moved from blank, attentive father-in-law to utter dismay in a nanosecond, while my mother, for the first and last time, in my memory, mouthed 'I love you' at me. I'd put it down to nerves and drink then. But now, now it railroaded me. I walked off. I went in search of Caroline. Fiona was holding forth in the garden, and I grabbed Caroline from the group.

'Caroline, you left me. You left John.' I hurled this at her, in a complete accusation of her actions.

'Oh gosh, yes. Sorry, lovely, I got sidetracked. Needed the loo, and then you, Ed, and John were chatting. Where is he?'

'Who?'

'John, of course.'

'Why did you bring him?' I was still cross.

'He's a lovely bloke and because he lost his wife to cancer, it seemed a good idea to bring him out and maybe stop him feeling lonely.' Caroline shrugged her shoulders. I was stunned at this information.

'I had no idea. No idea about his wife. How did you find out?'

'I asked him after he interviewed me. I had to make small talk, and it somehow came out. I knew something was up. We've met for coffee a few times as I know first-hand how he feels. Different circumstances, but still a loss.'

Coffee! Coffee with John. The image of them both ran through my head, and it exploded.

'Are you an item?' This blasted out of my mouth.

'Good grief, no. I like him, but well, you know me, not really my bag.'

The relief was enormous, and then the guilt of my feelings overwhelmed me.

'Caroline, let me get you some more wine.' I didn't wait for the reply, I was off. Nor did I get any wine for her. I bolted to the end of the garden. My head was spinning. I seemed to be receiving a myriad of thoughts, none of which I could process. After a while, I realised I was sat on damp grass without even a glass of wine. I stood up and contemplated my next move.

There was a tap on my shoulder. I was so caught up in my thoughts, I nearly screamed and involuntarily gasped. There he was holding out a glass of wine for me.

'It is the pink stuff you are drinking?' John said.

'Oh my gosh, you made me jump!'

'Again, sorry about that. I seem to be making a habit of shocking you.'

'Well, the Ursula undress moment wasn't the best,' I grimaced as I said it.

'Ah yes, but at least it was nothing to do with me.'

We stood there in silence. I could feel him wanting to reach out, but instead, he asked how I was.

'I'll survive. After all, it seems stupidity isn't a crime. Although, would you arrest my husband for it, please?'

The tension lifted and I smiled at him.

'John, I'm really sorry I didn't know about your wife. Caroline is more observant and a better listener than I am.'

He sighed. His feet shuffled in the grass. It took all my willpower not to blurt out some needy nonsense. I wanted him to grab me and hold me. Instead, I took a huge gulp of wine.

'It was tough. It still is a bit tough, the loss, but it has been quite a few years now.'

His eyes looked directly at mine. I held his gaze briefly, then looked away, back towards the house. I wanted to walk away. Away from the danger. Walk back to the familiar, the known. I hesitated. I looked at him. With his greying hair and his blue eyes. He was wearing a white t-shirt, a light grey crew neck jumper over it, sleeves slightly pushed up, and a pair of dark blue jeans. I could see a slight paunch from the fold of the knit, but actually, he was in great shape.

My thoughts were uncontrollable, and I realised, whilst I had no idea he was coming tonight, I'd thought about nothing but him since we'd met. My outfit was a reflection of how vibrant and alive I felt. I needed to dampen this down. The silence between us seemed to linger for hours.

'Are you impressed with my sartorial off-duty style?' he said.

I laughed.

'Because it is completely borrowed from Pepe Guardiola and I do not deviate from the t-shirt, jumper, jeans combo. I want to be clear about this. In my head, it transforms me from dull, sad London detective type bloke to sexy, Spanish detective. Of course, on duty, I am strictly plain John Doe with shirt, tie, ill-fitting cheap suit, or worse, combat trousers and a fleece.'

I'm not sure if the wine or his chat was giving me such an inner glow. 'Dampen it down, Ursula' was my inner monologue. 'Don't look at him, look at the ground.'

'I'm glad you've got someone like Caroline to talk to.'

Of course, I didn't mean it, but the poor bloke didn't need my emotional fuck-wittage of a marriage and my current lust dumped on him. I knew he was being friendly, and my Jilly Cooper brain needed to shut the front door. More wine was gulped.

'Come on, Ursula. I've had plenty of people to talk to about losing Jean. My mad dash speeding, coupled with recklessness on duty, forced an intervention and tons of counselling. My chats with Caroline have been pleasant and quite pragmatic.' He drew breath. 'What I really want, is to kiss you, to hold you, and it is doing my head in. It's madness, this could even be unethical, and I've never blurted out my feelings ever.'

He took my hand. 'What do you want? He continued, 'I'm not a marriage wrecker, but I can sniff out unhappiness from a mile, and if you want me to walk away right now and forget this conversation, I will. But I am not going to miss an opportunity to tell you what I want.'

Stunned.

I am completely stunned.

I'm in my fifties, and some guy is propositioning me. Okay, he is not a random, but still a bona fide man is stood in front of me, declaring an interest, and my head, in fact my whole body, is exploding. The same person I was mentally undressing a moment ago.

'Fuck!' I put my left hand to my mouth.

'Yes please.'

And suddenly we were both laughing.

'It wasn't a question, it was an expletive,' I clarified.

'It's been a long time.'

It was the worst middle-aged flirting I could imagine, but I felt amazing and stepped towards him.

'There you are!' And there was Fiona, glass in hand, swaying in her heels as she walked.

'You two look like you are up to no good. Hashtag awks.' She giggled and grabbed my hand, pulling me back to my house.

'Thought I'd rescue you from Caroline's dreary detective date, although...' She paused and looked back, 'he's actually quite a silver fox, and yes, I would. Anyway, because I'm pissed, and before I forget, there is something I need to tell you.'

Ed joined us and stood very close to me. An arm went around my waist as he pulled me closer and tighter.

'You were saying, Fiona?'

'What?'

The next moment, Rob appeared, all smiles, and took Fiona's hand.

'Come on, one dance before I drag you home. Excuse us,' he said.

Fiona lolloped off, spilling wine. She really was pissed. It left Ed and me alone.

'Fancy a dance, a bit of a smooch like it was 1999?'

I had a choice, dance and step back into all I have been invested in for so many, many years, or decline. Only a few weeks ago, I bought my own view of my life, my sales pitch, but now, I hesitated. Next moment, I was propelled forward by sheer force, stumbling, almost falling flat on my face. I turned to see Judy, next door but one, flat on her back with red wine over her face and dress.

Everyone looked horrified. I fight an overwhelming urge to start laughing and rush to the utility room to grab a towel. I'm cracking up. Tears are rolling down my face, and I almost snort. I know it's not funny, but it really, really is. Did I not mention Judy was wearing some A-line kaftan-esque look, which had slightly revealed some lacy bright green knickers? She was obviously too drunk to have felt it, but there'll be some bruising over the next few days. I go back with a towel, and Caroline has her sat on a chair and is being super kind. I feel guilty about the giggles.

Somehow, Judy's moment sobered up everyone else, except for her husband. He's happily carried on holding forth without even a glance at the commotion. I set about checking on drinks for those who could not un-see the flat on the back moment. I open the door of the fridge and glance out into the garden to try and spot John, but what I see is Ed remonstrating with Fiona. It seems quite heated, and then there is John, stepping in before anyone other than me notices. I calmly walk outside as Fiona is on her way back to the house.

'Fiona, what is going on?'

'Ask your prick of a husband! He's always harassing me because he thinks I'll tell you about the time I saw him in a bar with a bit of stuff. So there. Now you know. And maybe he can stop being snarky with me and you can see him for what he really is, a selfish fucking idiot.'

I'm left standing there as Fiona walks into the kitchen. I'm stunned, totally stunned, but an enormous sense of relief washes over me. I glance over and both Ed and John are standing there looking at me. Of course, Ed looks furious and moves towards me. I put my hand up.

'Don't.' It is all I can say.

He stands there and his facial expression changes. Caroline glides next to me and puts her arm around me.

'Ursula, Fiona is sorry, but come with me and we can take five minutes, hey.'

She shakes her head at Ed, I sort of crumple into her arm, and she walks me through the house and upstairs to the bedroom. Fiona is already there, looking crestfallen.

'Don't worry,' I say. 'It doesn't matter.'

'Well, it sort of does because I never meant to say anything. I don't know why he thought I would. It was none of my business, but I couldn't be friends with him anymore. That is why we were always edgy with each other. I'm really sorry, Ursula. It was probably nothing anyway, but why didn't he tell you if it was nothing? Sorry,' she says.

I didn't care. It was as if all the effort of my brave, jolly face, and being baking Ursula was over. I was obviously shaken, but more from the drama than anything else, and oh yes, Judy's knickers. I sigh.

'Honestly, Fiona, I really don't care. I'm most certainly menopausal, and my head is exploding, but what I mostly feel right now is relief. I don't know why, but I do.'

Caroline ruffled my hair and gave me a hug. The three of us sat there in silence on my bed.

TWELVE

'I'm going away for a few days.'

'Where?'

'To Paul and Dave's. Their old farmhouse near Rye. They've got a converted outbuilding which they Airbnb and I've rented it for a week.'

'Do you have to go?'

'Under the circumstances, yes, I do. I need to think, and chat to the boys, and go from there.' I paused and dug deep. 'You also need to think, if you can, and understand why I need time. I think we both know it is probably the end of the road for us.'

'It doesn't have to be Ursula, that's up to you.'

'No, it isn't. We've come to this point. Come on, I've been fooling myself, and you, what do you want? It's not just about me or you, it's about Dan and James as well. We've got to do the best by them.'

Ed ran his hands through his thick mop of hair and shrugged his shoulders.

'I've got work to jog along to. You do what you have to.' Without a backwards glance, he grabbed his keys and walked out of the kitchen and into the hallway. I waited until the front door shut and picked up my mobile off the counter to call Fiona. I felt impatient for Fiona to answer. It seemed to ring for ages.

'Hi.'

'Fiona?'

'Yes, do I sound that bad?'

'Well, your voice is a bit croaky.'

'Yeah, well, too much booze the other night and a bit of shouty nonsense isn't a great combo,' she said.

I paused. Deep breath, Ursula, deep breath.

'Look, I'm going away for a few days, well, probably the week. I wanted to let you know.'

There was a moment of silence.

'Good call.'

'You sure?'

'Yes, of course. You need to get away from that prick for a bit. Sorry, don't mean to be rude or biased, but you know, he's really pissed me off. I want to say something neutral, like think about your options, but truly, work out your exit plan, and I've got the number of a top divorce lawyer who'll be worth every penny.'

'Thanks Fiona, I know, I'm not ruling anything in or out at the moment, but thank you.'

After finishing the conversation with Fiona, the enormity of what I was about to do hit me. Did I even know what I wanted? All I knew was I needed some space and a different location. With renewed impetus, I set about packing items to get on the road. The day was middling to fair. There was some summer warmth in the air, and the blue sky was dotted with clouds. No oomph or wow factor to grip and move me into a more buoyant mood. The car journey was equally mundane as I plodded along in the motorway traffic and along A roads. Finally, after nearly two hours, I turned the car onto a B road that led to a road which was essentially a single-track lane. Every corner felt like a dice with death. Hesitant and slow was all I could manage as I tentatively manoeuvred the car along the track while keeping my eyes peeled for Dave and Paul's place. How easy it had been when Ed drove me here. I hadn't a care in the world then, and he'd always been the driver, in charge and dependable. That was the good thing about Ed, he never once drank when he was driving, not even a half pint of anything. I smiled inwardly at this. It was nice to move back to more favourable thoughts of the marriage.

Finally, the entrance to the old farmhouse appeared in my eyeline. I happily swung the car off the track, pulled up, and jumped out to open a set of massive old wrought iron gates. The creaking of the gates must have alerted them in the house, as barely had one gate been pushed to the side when Paul rushed out of the front door, grinning.

'You made it, fairy,' he said.

'Yes, I did, although the track...' I made big, scared eyes.

'It's a lane! You city dweller, there's room for a bus.' Paul winked back.

'Only one! And where the heck does the car go if you meet one?'

'Backwards.' We both laughed and Paul grabbed a few of my bags, which were various French supermarket ones filled with swimming stuff and clothes.

'Don't you own a suitcase then, fairy?'

'Of course I do, for air travel, but I love the ease of these for packing what I need in compartments, great for the car, and using in general.'

Paul led the way from the drive and then turned down the side of the main house. I took in a breath of fresh country air and surveyed the landscape as we walked towards an amazing kitchen garden, which was not a traditional one. It was full of grand, splendid plants. Huge fennels and thistles interspersed with grasses, wild daisies, and other wild flowers. Each of the four sumptuous areas was perfectly framed by box hedge.

'Wow, what a display!'

'It is Dave. He has just had a huge coconut thing delivered.

He's created all of this. These beds.'

'They are amazing, really architectural, not what I expected at all.'

'Nothing to do with me. I just admire them. Come on, here is where you are staying.'

I almost skipped following Paul as he led me towards a converted outbuilding. It was a single storey which may have housed animals or machines before the conversion. The grey and weathered wooden door was flanked by two large pots of Cordyline palms. It opened into a lovely living space with a large, sumptuous sofa, a neat table with chairs by a window, and a kitchen area. Paul dropped my bags on the rug atop the stripped wooden floors.

'What are you doing here, Ursula?'

'I'm here to live my best Instagram life. You know, swimming in the sea, a bit of yoga, meditation. Finding myself.'

Paul looked at me. He couldn't hide his surprise at what I'd said.

'Really? I know it is good to step back and think a bit, but would you find some time to make Dave and me a cake?'

I laughed. 'Don't worry, I'm going to bake in that wonderful kitchen of yours. And drink lots of red wine, and probably cry a lot.'

'What a relief. I'm done with people being the best versions of themselves. Middle age these days is a curse!'

'I am going swimming in the sea, though. I promise I won't say wild swimming.'

'I should bloody hope not. Wild swimming is running into the Aegean at midnight with nothing on in expectation of a post swim shag.' Paul grinned as he said this.

It was my turn to look horrified for a moment before starting to laugh.

'Okay, that might be finding myself a bit too far. Especially in the freezing English Channel and then running out onto hard pebbles.'

'Imagine the bruises!' Paul exclaimed.

'Alright, Paul, stop thinking about it!'

'Your problem, Ursula, is you haven't thought about it enough, probably not since your twenties.'

I grabbed the nearest cushion and whacked him. This resulted in both of us messing about and hitting each other with very expensive cushions until Dave appeared in the doorway.

'What the... You two are how old?'

He was grinning from ear to ear and walked over to give me a massive bear hug. He held me very tight and I was surprised at how much I really wanted to cry. Fighting back the feeling, I bit my lip and held my breath. When Dave released me from his grasp, I was relieved I could manage a smile.

After more chit chat and concentrating on not feeling sorry for myself, I flopped onto the beautiful brass bed as soon as I was on my own. Lying on top of the fresh, crisp white cotton-covered duvet added emphasis to the predicament. I really wasn't at home, and for the first time in forever, it seemed I was really on my own.

My first move was to open the French doors and let the lace panels hanging from each door flutter in the slight warm breeze. I knew as I lay there looking up at the ceiling, my marriage was over. The detail was irrelevant. Every cell, muscle, and telomere in my body carried this information to my brain. Over. I sobbed. Half an hour later, snotty, red-eyed and worn out with the effort, I stopped. I got up and went to the bathroom and showered.

Wandering out of the outbuilding, I walked past the back of the main house and out onto a wide, expansive area overlooking a valley. There on the left was a huge table exposed to the elements, looking worn, weathered, and inviting despite its ramshackle appearance.

I sat down to take in the view, the openness before my eyes felt like expanding and unfolding thoughts. These thoughts were focused on my anger and foolishness. The benefit of hindsight as it rushed into the mind on full beam. Why had I not noticed how pompous and arrogant Ed was? I'd been so focused on preserving the marriage, I'd forgotten to look at the reality.

It was nothing dreadful, part of me still loved him, but recent actions and my change of circumstances had exposed the shell of a life of my own making. I was living off hopes and desires, not a solid, intertwined relationship. Not even a mediocre bumbling along together, there was a chasm. Weird how suddenly a marriage can drop off a cliff edge with no real drama.

'Penny for them?'

Paul had arrived with a bottle of red wine and three glasses.

'Can't believe I fooled myself for so long. It is not that I don't love him in some fond way, but the reality of my trying so hard for something that wasn't there has hit me. Hit me hard.'

'You had the children.'

'I know, but we didn't have each other. Cliché of clichés, hey,' I sighed and continued, 'I hadn't realised because I'd kept myself busy and focused, and it has nothing to do with the children having left home. We should be whooping it up down the pub and doing stuff as joyful empty nesters, but the truth is we are not.' I hesitate. 'Because... we are not a couple.'

Paul put his arm around my back and squeezed the top of my left arm.

'I know what you mean, fairy. Dave and me, well, we are solid, we have each other's backs and we rub along very well.

No one is perfect, no relationship is perfect, but we've got an enduring love that carries us through all the bleak moments.'

'I want to cry. That is lovely!'

'It is, but he bloody well annoys me as well, in case you think I've gone soft in me old age.'

We sat in silence again.

'My only worry is the boys. Having to tell them. Well, that and what all the next steps are, should I proceed with a divorce.'

My body heaved with the enormity.

'They'll be fine,' Paul said and shrugged his shoulders. 'At their age, they are not going to be impacted that much. They're older, getting on with their own lives, and plenty of their peers are in the same position.'

I nodded and he carried on.

'Not that I'm an expert on raising children or anything. Dave and me were very clear about that. We are totally old school selfish poofs. I do understand the ones who want to be parents, but we appreciate we can be a gay couple with no holds barred, and I never thought we'd see this day. Don't get me wrong, there is still prejudice, but no one can deny us a life, a marriage, or anything. Talking of which, we are finally getting married – which is a complete cliché.'

I screeched!

'Fantastic news! I love a wedding'

And then I ruined it all by pulling an ironic face, at which we both laughed. Dave joined us, a huge enamel baking tray of shepherd's pie in one hand and a bowl of salad in the other.

'Don't stand on ceremony. I'm going to fetch the plates and cutlery. The least you two can do is pour me a glass of wine.' He rolled his eyes at us.

We ate, chatted, and drank whilst watching the sun go down. It gave me some inner warmth and I noticed my lack of tension.

I felt de-stressed and enjoyed the dark and quiet with no urban sprawl of street lights and roads. The view really was darkness, shadows outlining the surrounding vista and the sky. The only light was from the main house, and as it was set slightly behind us, it didn't interfere with the descending night. A few glasses in, Dave offered to make mint tea.

'He's gone all Ottolenghi on us now,' Paul teased.

'It is why you are marrying me, for a feast of preserved lemons and black limes.'

I had no idea what they were talking about, but their ease and engagement elicited a fresh round of tears.

'Oh petal, don't you be getting upset on us now.' Dave put an arm around me.

'I can't help it,' I snorted. 'I feel a failure.'

'No one is a failure when relationships go wrong. It is life and change. If you don't mind, tell us a little about it.'

I hesitated but then began with the party, wound back a few years, and ended up mentioning the detective. There was silence. Dave went to make the mint tea.

'About bloody time if you ask me,' Paul said, finally breaking the silence. 'You know I always felt Ed stifled you but was willing to give him the benefit of the doubt. But ultimately, he has always been selfish and self-centred. Sorry, fairy, but it is what I think.'

'I know and we had lots of really good times, but I've realised there has been a huge gulf for years, and I don't know if what Fiona said has any significance, but the bottom line is it is over. I'm done.'

We all sat in silence, which I was grateful for. I didn't need to say anything else or hear more views on something I need to untangle and sort out. Dave handed me a cup of mint tea, and we all drank the warmth as the night chill began to grow.

THIRTEEN

A slight breeze from the open bedroom doors nudged me awake. I peered over the duvet to see that the day looked sunny, although the sun wasn't in my view from the room. I looked at my phone and saw two missed calls from both Fiona and Caroline. I made a cup of coffee and then called Fiona back first.

'Morning,' I said.

'Thought you were avoiding me,' she replied.

'No, don't be mental. I was having a lie-in after an evening of being wined and dined.'

'Oh, the detective?'

'No! With Paul and Dave, of course. Their place is beautiful. I am so glad I came.'

'Good for you, but what are you going to do about him? He's so up for it!'

'Stop it. I should never have told you about the garden incident at the party.'

Fiona laughed.

'No, seriously, you must text him,' she advised.

'I'll do no such thing!'

'What is the alternative? Writing an email to Fi and Jane on 'Fortunately' so they can dispense advice or discuss what to do when you need to make a move on a man in your fifties.'

It was my turn to laugh.

'Don't imagine the moment when Jane says she can only give advice on the best big knickers in M&S.'

We were both laughing now, and I couldn't remember when I'd laughed so freely without a glass of wine. I felt so relaxed.

'I'd love to squirm some more, Fiona, but I must call Caroline back as well.'

'Ah, you called me first, the more fun friend, hey!'

'No. The 'more likely to give it to me straight so might as well get it over with' friend.'

'Still first,' she repeated.

'First the worst, second the best. As the boys used to say.'

'Okay, I'll let you go, but I need updates, please.'

We agreed I'd call later because I knew at heart Fiona was looking out for me, and now I knew about her brother, it seemed she'd always been checking in on people, and I hadn't realised it.

'Hello?'

'Hi Caroline, it's Ursula'

'Oh, Ursula, sorry, one moment.'

She seemed to drop the phone and there was a bit of a clatter, an expletive, and what sounded like a man laughing.

'Sorry, sorry, was trying to get my dressing gown on.'

'Do you have a man there?'

'What? No, no, must be the telly. I think that is why I dozed off again. Anyway, how are you?'

'I'm fine. Had a lovely evening with Paul and Dave last night and am going to bake them a cake this morning before going off for an explore.'

'Oh, that sounds lovely. Glad you are okay.'

Caroline sounded distracted

'Have I called at a bad time?'

'Gosh, no. Sorry, but I was up late last night studying for my landscape design course and the Horticultural Society exam. It's always the same when Ruby is at a sleepover, I grab a lie-in.'

We carried on chatting for a bit longer, and then I needed to get on with the day. After showering, I crossed the garden to the main house, knocking on the kitchen door.

'Come in. Don't stand on ceremony.'

I pushed the ajar door open and stepped into their gorgeous kitchen.

'I'm here to bake a cake.'

'Hurry up then. Would you like coffee first?'

We enjoyed a pleasant morning chat and Paul gave me a map to scour and pointed out Petts beach for my swim later. I checked all the available ingredients and utensils and set about making a humble Victoria sponge. It was a different feeling from cooking at home. I realised I'd baked to control my feelings and my purpose. Now I felt free and starting afresh. The cake was so uncomplicated and basic. The fundamental base of cake making. The perfect proportions of ingredients. The four fours. Flour, butter, sugar, and eggs. With no food processor, it meant getting my muscles into gear. Dave came into the kitchen.

'Oh, look at sexy, is that sweat or perspiration?'

'Perspiration, of course,' I said, although I was tempted to check my armpits. It took me longer than intended to find what I needed and prep the oven for cooking. Once I put the cake tins in the oven, I went back over to my hideaway and sorted out my items for a swim.

With the cake layers out to cool, it left me free to jump in the car and prepare to face the cold sea of the English Channel. I followed the sat nav to Petts Beach and managed to find a parking spot. Picking my way over the pebbles, I selected a place to put my blanket and took in the breathtaking view to the left of Dungeness. I'd never seen it before except in magazines. It was in the distance, but its desolate look explained the captivation of the area. I felt I'd been wrapped up in my current life for too long. I knew I needed to take risks and explore places. It wasn't so much to broaden one's horizons, but to get out and about. Doing. Being. I shook myself and attempted to walk into the sea with some degree of confidence. I had on neoprene swimming socks to prevent the pain of walking over pebbles and keep my feet slightly warmer in the sea. My bathing costume didn't seem enough as I stood in the cold of the sea and tried to brave the idea of a swim. Eventually, I managed to get to the point where once my stomach was covered, I decided I might as well crack on with pathetic breaststroke attempts. It was freezing!

What seemed like an hour, but was actually only ten minutes, passed by, and then I was out of the sea. I plonked myself down on my blanket and wrapped a towel around me. I also put on the dry robe Fiona insisted I brought with me and drank from the flask of tea I'd made. Although it was a warm day, it was a bit overcast, and bit by bit, I managed to warm up. And yes, I did feel exhilarated and a little bit teary. The tears were always at the ready at the moment, but then I needed to let them out. I wasn't sure what I was crying about, really. It was a mix of trepidation about going home and facing Ed and dealing with it all, coupled with the sadness of everything ending.

Sitting at the beach, the fresh sea breeze and the wide vista, even though it wasn't a picture-postcard Cornish one, helped. The headland and the now defunct nuclear power stations were a different look against the sepia brown of the sea, but equally pleasant as the picturesque blue of the Atlantic. Once I'd stopped contemplating my life, I got dressed in an awkward, almost falling-over fashion in the zipped-up, roomy dry robe. Admittedly, it was three hundred times better than holding a towel with your teeth and trying to dress, but still awkward. Back in the car with the radio on loud, I felt a little bit better all round.

When I got back to the house, there was another car there

that I hadn't seen before. I dashed to my place and quickly showered as I wanted to finish the cake. Once I'd got dressed again, I nipped over to the farmhouse kitchen. I could hear voices laughing in the garden, but ignored the distraction and whipped the cream ready to put with the jam on the bottom cake layer. I found a lovely big plate and assembled my effort to present to Paul and Dave. As I approached the outside table, I nearly dropped it. There sat with his back to me was DCI John Smith. He was sat chatting with my hosts.

'Ah, here you are, fairy,' a cheerful, smiling Paul winked at me.

I was desperately trying to find a neutral face, but resting 'wtf' face with crazy fixed smile seemed to be my default instead of the bland look I was aiming for.

'Hi.'

John stood up.

'Hello, Ursula, lovely to see you,' he said.

'Er, yes, what are you doing here?'

'I'm going to make some tea,' Dave interjected before there was a response. 'Will be perfect for having with your cake. Come and help me, Paul.'

I sat down.

'I did call you if you check your phone, but apologies for the surprise. Fiona gave me the address. I've got a day of meetings here with other forces colleagues.'

'Oh, okay. Would you like some cake?'

'Yes, that would be great.'

I suddenly realised I had no knife, no plates or anything.

'Is that your car in the drive?'

'Yes, I'm allowed to get behind a steering wheel again, and I did stick to the speed limits, even on the motorway,' he said

We both smiled. Paul came back with plates and a knife to cut the cake.

'Dave is bringing the tea, unless anyone wants anything stronger?'

I really did. Instead, I smiled crazily. As if smiling could crush the rising joy. Paul couldn't resist carrying on with the conversation they'd been having before I'd got back.

'You were telling us about Ursula's dead body?'

The joy was crushed.

John smiled. 'It was how we met, but thankfully it isn't anything really to do with Ursula, otherwise I wouldn't be here. Not that Ursula is the reason I'm here, well,' he stumbled, 'I mean it's great to pop by, but my real purpose is a meeting with local force colleagues in the morning.'

'Where are you staying?' Paul asked.

'I'm in Hastings tonight, the usual Travelodge booking for serving police. I'd much rather be here. Not that I'm trying to invite myself.' He seemed quite flustered now, and I felt obliged to lessen his discomfort.

'I can imagine! This is the best option I found in the area. I can't believe my luck thanks to these two clever boys. Did they mention they are getting married?' I said.

'No. Congratulations. I hope you have a wonderful day. I lost my wife some time ago, but I still love our wedding day,' John said.

We all fell silent at this, and yet I warmed to him more at this revelation. His lovely words revealed more of his endearing nature.

Dave broke the silence, 'Mate, I'm sorry to hear that.'

'It was a blessing at the end as the cancer had ravaged her and she could only touch us, as talking was impossible, she was so weak.'

I wanted to cry. Instead, I reached for his hand and squeezed it.

‘Sorry, I didn’t mean to dampen the mood. It’s just I don’t like to hide or pretend it didn’t happen.’

Paul sighed, ‘I think you are right. It’s better to be open. You can’t deny or pretend nothing has happened. Much better to celebrate what you had, however sad the circumstances.’

We all fell silent again. The evening sun was dipping and a slight chill accompanied this.

Dave broke the silence with his customary good timing. ‘John, you must stay a little longer as I am about to serve a chicken curry and salad. It would be rude not to. We can’t let you suffer the culinary delights in Hastings all on your own.’

It was tough waiting for the answer. Part of me needed him to go, and the other wanted him to stay.

‘If it isn’t too much bother, I’d love to join you all. This view and company is the preferred option now you’ve mentioned it.’

It was ridiculous the way Paul and I grinned at each other as John got up and walked with Dave to the house. Once he was out of earshot, we were both back to our student ways.

‘You kept that very quiet in the reveal last night,’ he immediately said.

‘What?’

‘How hot and silver foxy he is, and yes, I would if he would.’

We creased up.

‘Stop it. I’m a married woman.’

‘Well, you can jog on with that, love’, Paul replied. ‘You need to make hay while the sun shines.’

I buried my head in my hands. I didn’t know whether to laugh or cry. Paul tapped me on my arm.

‘What now?’ I said, and then looked up to see John standing next to us with plates and a large jug of water.

‘Dave asked if we could help clear the table and bring fresh cutlery and glasses out.’

Paul and I immediately became sensible and polite.

'Gosh, yes.' I got up and found myself walking towards the kitchen door with John at my side.

'Your friends really do have the most perfect place,' he said.

'I know. I needed some time on my own and couldn't think of anywhere better.'

John put his hand on my arm and stopped before we went into the house.

'About that.' He looked down and then up into my eyes. 'I'm here because I want to see you. I am sorry I dumped my feelings on you. Especially with what happened, but I want to ask you to meet me tomorrow afternoon. I'd love to spend some time with you, and I'm not going to push my luck, but I am going to be clear. I'm not going to waste any time and want you to know I can't stop thinking about you at all.'

My stomach had a sensation I hadn't felt since my twenties. Not only did I feel sick with excitement but my knees went a bit wobbly as well. All I could do was nod my head.

'Is that a yes?'

'Yes.'

What the heck was I doing? It was thrilling.

'You staying?' Dave asked John as he walked out of the house and past us.

'Yes, please.'

'Fancy some wine?'

'No. Despite all my faults, I never drink and drive.'

I knew then he wasn't going to try and stay, which was a big relief as this was my space regardless of anything. I needed to keep my time here as mine and mine alone. I wouldn't be able to discuss matters properly with Ed if I got carried away while here with Paul and Dave.

The rest of the evening continued in a relaxed manner and

I absorbed the energy with utter delight. I had an inner glow. I could barely eat or drink, and the heady rush of emotions were swimming around me at a rate of knots. After John had left and I'd helped clear up, I lay on my bed, giddy. Of course, I texted Fiona

'I'm fucked'.

Beep.

'Literally?'

'No figuratively, in my head, doughnut!'

Beep.

'Call me, you eejit.'

I immediately rang her. We chatted for an hour until I finally began to feel tired. I had no energy to call Caroline.

FOURTEEN

A tap on the door woke me up.

'Room service.'

I grabbed my short linen dressing gown, flung my way into it, and managed to tie it before opening the door to Paul with a cup of coffee in his hand.

'Here you go, otherwise it will be midday before you are awake.'

'What time is it?'

'10 o'clock, sleepy head.'

'Oh no, John is picking me up at eleven thirty to go to Rye for lunch.'

'Well, drink this and then shower. Beautifying calls.'

I rolled my eyes and gratefully took the coffee.

One hour later, I was scrubbed, hair washed and dried, and the best sort of natural 'not too much eyeliner' make-up I could muster. I took a moment to breathe. I had no thoughts in my head and no desire to eat. I was a vibrating body of nervous energy.

He was on time. Punctual and equally well scrubbed. He also seemed nervous. We barely said hello. My body floated into his car, and off we drove. In the wing mirror, I could see Paul waving us off with a tea towel. John drove us to Rye.

As we walked together through the streets of Rye, John was chatting and pointing out buildings. I gazed at him incredulously.

'What?'

'Nothing,' I said.

'I talk too much, don't I?'

'Gosh, no, I'm a little taken aback, that is all.'

'My wife said I never shut up. I think I disturbed her peace and quiet.' For a moment John's face tightened, and I was at a loss for what to say next. I needn't have worried as he grabbed my hand and pulled me down a narrow street.

'This way,' he said. 'Fancy a walk to a castle?'

'How far is it?'

'Not far, but it's a nice vantage point to look out to sea.'

'How do you know so much about Rye?' I was intrigued by and somewhat taken with his taking charge. My stomach did a somersault and I immediately doubted the sensation, until I looked at him again and realised I really was smitten. Really, really smitten.

'An unhealthy obsession with Malcolm Saville books when I was younger,' I just about heard him say over my internal whirring thoughts.

'Who?' I said.

'Exactly, not many of us devoted fans exist. But his books were the best 25p I ever spent. I lost a whole year or so deep in his adventure books. You could write to him and he'd answer your letters. I told him I wanted to be a detective, and he was very encouraging. I loved the landscape he wrote about and the idea of smugglers and hidden treasure.'

The happiness of these memories were clearly etched on his face. Without missing a beat, he blurted out, 'Come and join me at Tillingham Winery tonight for dinner. I understand why you don't want me to come to where you are staying. I get it compromises your time on your own, but surely you can't resist my company for one evening?'

Silence.

'I thought you were staying in Hastings?' I managed to stutter out, still stunned by his invitation.

'That was on police time. I'm on my time now and I have every intention of living it up for one evening.'

We both stood still, waiting for my answer.

'Would you give me a little longer to think while we walk?'

'Of course, not a problem. Ursula, I'm being unfair, I know, but I want to know all about what you are thinking, and forgive me for the Love Island perspective, but I am backing myself here.'

'You watch Love Island?'

'Best antidote for grief, I'm telling you. The children and me were able to sit absorbed and fully focused on the banality of it all. It was the only time we weren't crying or unable to communicate after Jean died. Discussing stupidity and shouting at the television was one of our many therapies.'

'I am sorry about your loss. I've never communicated that to you.'

'Thank you, but please tell me to stop if I discuss it too much. I learnt, the hard way, to talk about it. Ursula, I've worked with some dreadful people in my career, on both sides, criminals and police officers. There is nothing I've been spared, but I want to assure you it doesn't stress me out. I did get stressed by Jean's breast cancer, hence the speeding, but it was because I felt helpless.'

We somehow stood holding hands in a street, oblivious to all passing by, and it was busy. I didn't feel the need to make things better for John. I knew silence and acknowledging the pain was all he required. I admired his straightforwardness and realised I no longer felt any such regard for Ed. I'd almost forgotten who he was. I knew I didn't know him anymore, or share much with him. We existed together, nothing more. John shook me out of my thoughts.

'Right, I'm done with maudlin, let's make it to the castle

and take in the view.'

I enjoyed looking out to sea, even if it was the murky English Channel. There was enough glistening sunshine on the water to elevate its grey brown to a tinge of blue. The expanse also filled my mind with hope and a little bit of courage for the next steps.

'You didn't give me an answer about tonight?'

'Yes.'

'A yes to dinner?'

'Yes.'

John punched the air, lifted me up, and swung me around. I felt slightly embarrassed but couldn't help laughing.

'Sorry, that was a bit dad dancing level, wasn't it? But Ursula, you've made me so happy.'

How could I mind really? We walked back to the car and drove to Camber Sands. Lunch was a picnic he'd prepared, well bought, but he'd made the effort and also had a blanket for us to sit on in the dunes.

'I'm not great with sand.' I said.

'Really?

'I love it, but then, like now, some of it has ended up in my mouth whilst eating and I have no idea how.'

He laughed at me. And then did the most surprising move ever. His hand was on my back and he wiped away a vestige of pretend crumbs. Before I knew it, we were lying down and kissing passionately on the blanket in the dunes. When I say passionately, I mean we were actually kissing, it felt like passion. We probably looked ridiculous, but I really didn't care. We were lying happily in each other's arms.

'You go first,' John said.

'About what?'

'Well, you are the married one.'

‘Unfair.’

‘I know, and if it helps, I didn’t mean to do it. Kiss you.’

‘I’m more worried about us being saddos.’

‘What do you mean, Mrs Edmondson? After all, you re-buried a dead body.’

‘Oh gosh, yes! I’d forgotten that.’

‘How can you forget?’

‘Well, it isn’t something I do every day, and it all seems a million miles away.’

‘Nearly three months ago, but you know, details.’

We both laughed.

‘John, I am the person who mutters ‘get a room’ at the middle-aged drunks snogging at Waterloo when they’ve had too much to drink. Yet here I am, mid-life, snogging in sand dunes.’

‘Standards. Less of an obvious location, don’t you think?’

‘I give up! You’re the police officer.’ I sat up.

‘It is not a crime.’ He managed to put his arm around my shoulders and pull me back down.

‘Stop it!’ I said, even though I was laughing.

He just stroked my head.

‘It’s okay Ursula, it was spontaneous before. I’m more than happy with only spending time in your company.’

We lay there a while, both absorbed in our thoughts, and I drifted off.

‘Come on.’ I heard the voice in my head. I tentatively opened my eyes and reached for my discarded sunglasses. John helped me to sit up.

‘We need to go back and get you changed for dinner tonight.’

I didn’t really want to move, but reluctantly, I got up and dusted off the sand that had moved with ease onto the blanket. Luckily, no one was around in our dune area, as I felt as if I’d done something highly questionable.

We hardly talked on the way back to the farmhouse. I kept grinning and could tell John was equally happy. It was absurd but intoxicating. Pulling into the driveway, I got out to open the wrought iron gates. As soon as John pulled in with the car, Paul was actually skipping out of the doorway.

'You're back!'

'You're camp,' I retorted.

'You're no fun,' was his reply.

'Where's your tea towel?'

'Darlinnnng, I have moved on to rearranging the study for a shoot tomorrow. Some magazine is coming to use it for a location shoot.'

'Fancy pants.'

John, bless him, was standing there like a bit of a spare part whilst we continued in this vein.

'I'm back to change for dinner,' I eventually announced grandly.

'Bit early for dinner, fairy, it is only late afternoon.'

'I'm taking Ursula to Tillingham wines. I'm staying there tonight. Is it very far from here for a taxi back?' John said.

'Not really, about ten miles or so.'

'Oh good.'

Paul leant his head very slightly to the left, which I knew meant let's chat.

'Look, I'll change, and why don't you guys have a cup of tea while I'm occupied?'

'I'll be delighted to look after DCI Smith here, but I'll need to bring you over fresh towels in a little bit as well.'

'Okay, Paul.'

After fifteen minutes of me deliberating what to wear from my meagre collection of clothes I had brought with me, Paul knocked on the door and walked in, towels in hand.

'Cover!' he said.

We were giggling straightaway.

'Oh my gosh, what am I going to do? We were actually snogging today in the sand dunes.'

Paul punched the air. 'Best news ever. This is it now!' he exclaimed.

'Don't say that I'm not sure what to do.'

'I am. Make sure you pack a toothbrush, some clean knickers and moisturiser.'

'No, no I can't!'

'What are you wearing?'

'I thought I'd wear this white shirt and my denim mini-ish skirt with tan sandals. I didn't bring anything dressy with me.'

'Tillingham is a laid-back place. Lots of slap and gold hoops, please. Look, this bag is perfect,' Paul grabbed my very old Prada hobo shoulder bag. 'Make sure you roll a t-shirt in here for the morning. In fact, give one to me and quickly clean your teeth so I can roll the toothbrush, pants, and moisturiser in here. You are too old not to need hydration in the morning.'

'Thanks mate.'

'Hurry up.'

I did as I was told, Paul dried the toothbrush, and before I knew it, my bag was packed.

'See no indication of anything here. All you need is your phone and lippy or whatever else you have, and it won't even be full.'

'I am coming back tonight, you know?'

'Options fairy, options. Right, I'm going back before suspicions are roused. I'll say you were dithering.'

Once again, I was showering, which got rid of the sand. There was a lot in my hair. With hair dried and make-up applied, I put on my white shirt and tucked it into my pants before putting on my denim skirt. Immediately, I had a hot flush and had to fan my face with my bedside book. I then stuck my face in the small fridge, which aided my cooldown. I had no heels with me, but at least my flat tan sandals were dressy with a gold interlocking hoop detail. I found my sunglasses, took a deep breath, and went outside. They were sitting at the big outside table, chatting. I was too excited and nervous to sit down. Part of me wanted to change my mind. The other was fully committed to the thrill of it all.

'I'm ready. Best I could muster with no foresight.'

John was smiling at me, and Paul had a ridiculous face on him. Luckily, Dave was steadfast.

'Well, you two have a lovely evening.'

John sprang into action and was patting his jean pockets pointlessly.

'Right, yes, um, we'll be off then. Thanks for the tea.'

Somehow, we eased our way to the car without me having another meltdown of heat coursing through every part of me and erupting through my pores. I made a mental note to revise my HRT dose and not to drink too much alcohol. That wasn't merely to stop the hot flushes, but to keep my head cool as well.

The location of Tillingham was glorious. Secluded in a small hillside, there were views over Romney Marsh and the surrounding area. It was, as Paul said, very casual. An obvious oasis of living off the land, mixed with tranquillity, coupled with the hipster vibe of minimalism and wood things. I actually couldn't care less where we were, but it made me feel more relaxed.

'Are you okay to sit in the bar while I check in and pop my bag up into the room?'

'I want to see it. I'm very nosey, you know?'

'Well, you can go to the bar while I shower and change, deal?'

'Deal.'

The check-in was very relaxed and not at all a five-star luxury hotel where they cross-examine you, so it seemed no one cared I was hovering like a groupie. In my head, I was saying 'I'm middle-aged, you know, and married.' Outwardly, I was attempting a nonchalant French starlet pose, which probably translated in reality to a bored teenager look. In the room, I flopped onto the bed.

'This is too hard,' I moaned. 'Oh, I'm not talking about the bed. I mean the place.'

John laughed.

'Don't get ideas, this is a treat for me, not my lifestyle.'

'It is a nice room.' I pointed out his view, one side of the room had a window looking out to the coast, and the other side over the front of the building. The furniture was mismatched. A mix of rustic and eclectic decadence, but very clean and spruced. 'I'll go to the bar now and get a drink. What do you want?'

'You choose and put it on the room please, Ursula.'

I happily wandered downstairs to the bar. After much deliberation and politeness, I settled on a lovely French bottle of white wine, and went and sat outside to breathe in yet more fresh country air. There was a definite smell of hops in the air. It was a heady mix of the smell of cut grass with floral notes. I'd nearly finished my first glass before John joined me.

'Sorry, I was longer than expected.'

'I've been enjoying the stillness of my own company and the pungent whiff of hops.'

'And the wine?'

'Obviously, although I did choose a traditional French number, not their own made orange wine stuff. Was a bit unsure to be honest.'

'Live a little!' was John's retort. He had a point.

'Okay, Mister My Life Is Sorted. Anymore top tips?'

He exhaled. 'I haven't got my life sorted yet, but I've come to accept it.'

I felt a little guilty as it must have been awful to lose his wife, and I'd not really asked him or thought about it much. Deep breath, and I asked the question.

'How long ago was it? And I'm sorry I've never asked about your wife.'

'Are you sure about this, Ursula? This is our evening out.'

'Absolutely. There is never a good time to rake over the past, but in this setting it seems more relaxed, natural even, to discuss warts and all.' I looked at the outbuildings and mentally prepared myself for what he wanted to tell me.

'It's over three years now since I lost Jean. She had been ill for four years. The first bout of cancer was treated successfully, or so we thought, but within nine months, it was back, and nothing worked. That's it pretty much, in a nutshell, without boring you with the treatment, and the time as a family we spent hoping against the odds. Cancer is a disease that some survive and some don't. I don't think anyone knows why. Her treatment and care were excellent, but it didn't work.'

We both sat contemplating. I poured us another glass. Just as I was going to ask another question, someone approached.

'Your table is ready now if you want to come upstairs to the restaurant?'

John looked at me. I couldn't shake my head, but my eyes must have conveyed the message.

'Can we come up in about twenty minutes? Would that be okay?'

'Certainly, there is no rush. Pop up when you are ready.'

'Thanks.'

John took a sip and carried on. 'Of course, I was angry and felt cheated and robbed. I had plenty of time to come to terms with the inevitable, but I couldn't accept it, although Jean made me. She pulled me gently along with her as she needed a peaceful conclusion. We did lots of lovely things together, including a final trip to New York. She had family and friends to say goodbye to before it was too late.'

I was surprised by this information.

'Jean was American?'

'Yes, from Queens in New York. We met when I was there on some work exchange in the late 80s. She was working in a diner we went to every morning in Rego Park before catching the subway into Manhattan if I wasn't getting a lift.'

'You lived in New York?' I was impressed and surprised.

'For nearly a year. It was a tough stint over there, but I needed to do it after completing my graduate training with the Met. We were behind the times then, and had no real experience of modern gangs of different ethnicity. New York was the capital of the world in terms of nationalities. Where I lived in Rego Park was a Russian Jewish enclave. No one would serve me in the shops. I had to hit Queens Boulevard or head over to Forest Hill to find a barber who would cut my hair. Jean was a great find. She was finishing her degree in history and completing her teaching preparation certificate. She worked so hard to fund herself through college and qualify. That is how we met.'

He paused. The memories were flooding back again

'Anyway, I persuaded her to come to the UK eventually, and felt very guilty because she struggled to get a job.'

'Didn't they want history teachers from the US?' I asked, puzzled.

'Maybe, but not necessarily African American ones.'

‘Oh. Was London so biased, so un-enlightened?’

‘Look, it was a strange time, equalities were beginning to happen, but discrimination was rife everywhere. Being black and being a woman caused her problems when it came to work in state schools at the time, but actually not in the private sector; so she settled into a niche of teaching American History in Surrey’s finest schools.’

‘Was she resilient? She sounds incredible. To move for you and get on with it takes a lot of strength and courage.’

‘Jean couldn’t give two hoots about anyone. She was steadfast and contained. She loved her close group of American friends in London. They found us British stuffy and navigated around us.’

‘Oh John, no wonder you miss her. She sounds wonderful.’

‘Ursula, she was. She made sure we were all ‘Team Meghan’ when she married Harry. I found myself finally understanding how brutal it was for her to integrate into the UK. It is why I’m obsessed with my vulnerable county line charge. Although he isn’t my charge, I do need to look out for him. He is about fifteen or sixteen, and he is still a boy. But because he’s mixed race, seen as a black youth, we treat him as if he is a man. Don’t get me started on it now. Apologies, work is off the table.’

It was a lot to take in and only the beginning of knowing more about John, but it explained a lot about how he conducted himself and why I found him so attractive. Ed was undoubtedly an alpha male, but he was demanding, loud, and full of himself. John was none of these things. I couldn’t place him in a category. No wonder I was more relaxed with him. Suddenly, the need for my lists, my internal pep talks, melted away.

‘Right, enough about me, let me take you upstairs and wine and dine you.’

He got up and took my hand as he moved my chair. The next thing, we were embracing. If it wasn't for the fact that other people were around us, it might have been more. The heat rose from my chest to my face, and my forehead broke with a sweat. I pulled away and grabbed a napkin from the table and dabbed it.

'Hot flush?' John said.

I was mortified.

'No idea,' I said, trying to style it out, then immediately thought of chin hairs and started laughing. 'Sorry, it probably is, and I don't know whether to laugh or cry.'

'Jean's treatment put her into menopause at a rapid rate. I'll make sure we are sitting by an open window or a fan.'

I pulled an awkward face at his kindness as I still felt slightly embarrassed. I was a married woman in the company of another man, and instead of looking cool, I was a hot mid-life mess. Luckily, our table was by a very open window, and the cool breeze of summer air helped me relax.

We were poured a glass of house wine and presented with a tasting menu. The person rambled on as far as we were both concerned. We seemed to nod and smile appropriately, but I couldn't care less about the food.

'Did you book this place for the food?' I asked.

'Not really, more for the location and the opportunity to ensnare you.'

'No!'

'Honestly, Ursula, I was hooked from the moment I met you. I was trying to keep my workload light as I wanted to take a sabbatical, but you, you were tantalising.'

I blushed, but not from heat.

'Really? I had no idea. I was relieved to get away from that desk sergeant.'

'Don't get me wrong, after the body backtrack, I did question if I was of sound body and mind given you'd been party to concealment and failing to report a body,' he said.

I blushed again, this time through sheer embarrassment of past misdemeanours.

'But,' John continued, 'who was I to judge after speeding violations and erratic behaviour during a period of personal stress?'

'Don't you judge criminals?' I was glad of the change in the conversation. I needed time to think and take in his declarations. I realised I found the utterings intoxicating, but did I truly have feelings towards him, or was I invested in this scenario due to my now obvious marriage fatigue? Yet here I was engrossed, delighted, and full of lust. Fuck.

'Sort of, because they've overstepped the mark.' He paused. 'I have to apply the law and make sure everything is done by the book, which is really frustrating sometimes, and probably why I don't have time to judge. I even like some of them, not the murderers, but the petty criminals. But most of them are pieces of work and I really enjoy getting them sent down.'

My turn to sigh.

He raised his eyebrows and looked at me.

'Well? What are you thinking?' John asked.

'About why I am here.'

'Why are you here?'

The question was interrupted by food and John declining more wine. I was glad about that and asked for some sparkling water.

'Well, I'm waiting for your answer.' He leant forward.

I was scrambling in my mind to find anything to say. The silence was overwhelming.

'I'm getting a divorce.' There, it was said. 'I am getting a fucking divorce to leave my husband because he is a cock and I've known it for years but I had the boys. I also had hope, but there are only so many cakes you can bake, and baking is not the solution. Nor is wine o'clock on my own, or with friends. I am done.'

John held my hand and I burst into tears. Luckily, in a very loud dining area. A hastily grabbed napkin was used to wipe away my tears and blow my nose before I started the next phase, which was laughing.

'I'm only going through all of this due to relief.' I tried to explain.

The sun had set by now, and the yellow and blue of dusk looked magical. The glow filled my eyes, and exhaustion washed over me.

'Come on Ursula, let's get you back.'

We were sat downstairs on a bench in the cool of the night, waiting for the taxi.

'I'm really sorry about ruining this evening.' I leant my head on his shoulder as he pulled me closer with his arm around me.

'Ursula, stop being harsh on yourself.' He stroked my hair. 'Accept the outcome. I fought against losing Jean, but it was pointless. Jean and me, we met and we were always in the same slipstream. It wasn't perfect, we had plenty of turbulence along the way, but actually, the warmth of us, carried us. Without the warmth, there is nothing.'

I shivered. He was right, there was no warmth between Ed and me. We existed alongside each other, and my existence was different to his. I snuggled in closer to John. To his warmth. Twenty minutes later, he was putting me into a taxi, and all I could think was, 'Why am I not in his bed?'

DECEMBER 2023

Nine months have passed since the discovery of human remains in the garden in Malden Rushett. The team of detectives, led by DCI John Smith, are no further forward with any of their lines of enquiry. They are tackling both the identity of the body and the disappearance of Fiona's brother, Luke Riley. amongst the daily demands of their work. Detectives Stuart Johnson and Duncan Bennett are putting in extra hours, with the tedious compiling of notes, information, and timelines. Data capturing and manual grafting are their lot at the moment.

DCI Smith is increasingly worried about the youngest on his patch and has had no luck with any safeguarding measures or breakthroughs on the gang. He is contemplating his next move. The lack of bodies to tackle this crime is frustrating him. Yet there is a new verve to him. He is enjoying his life again. He couldn't be happier.

FIONA

FIFTEEN

'You're a fucking ledge, mate,' his voice blasted down the phone at me. Firstly, I thought 'I'm not your mate' and secondly, I was glad I'd given up my effing job. Did I swear as much as this prick? Seemed I'd answered my own question.

'Kevin, thank you for being so misguided and forgetful. Your offer of a new position in mergers and acquisitions is flattering for an old commodities trader, but I'm one hundred percent committed to my new venture, my gardening business. If you ever need some garden maintenance or landscape design work, let me know. My team are fabulous and more importantly, we are reasonable.' I added the last bit for good measure.

'I will, I will Fiona, but are you sure you won't think about it? I will try and tempt you again. I'll make sure I find the right offer for you.'

'No worries Kevin, and thanks for your call.'

You bloody eejit was voiced in my head. Only twenty minutes of wasting my time to a recruitment knob. Ugh. I don't even know why I offered our services to him. Who wants to schlep over to North London? Mind you, Caroline might if she fancied some design work.

I was impressed how she'd really got into the gardening and landscape design course. I can hardly get hold of her these days. I never intended to study anything, this venture is purely business and about the liberation of the mind with manual graft.

After years stuck in the commute and office, I needed a change. I am relishing my new, toned and strong figure thanks to muscle improvement. Even Rob complemented me in a guarded fashion, but I received it in good grace. I am such a nightmare, or 'ledge', depending on your interaction with me.

Of course, I was one hundred percent the darling of the corporate world. I made a lot of money in a tough environment. No one likes dealing with a commodities trader, as we set contracts and influence prices in the market. My area was the glamorous world of wheat. Wheat is big bucks. More stable than most markets due to demand, but weather and war can impact the global market. Anyway, all behind me now. Time for family and friends. Time to find Luke.

Had it really been a year since I set up the gardening business and ten months since we dug up human remains in Mr Etheridge's garden? Life had changed drastically since that day. For me, for Caroline, and for Ursula. I've been struggling, weighed down with my endeavours and hopes to find Luke. Rob insisted on therapy, which I'd reluctantly agreed to, and it has helped me to navigate my emotions.

I'm sat here pretending to work, contemplating my next move, the interruption by Kevin disrupted my thoughts. DCI Smith has been extremely helpful, but I don't want to bother him. This is the new me. Less brash, less brittle, and not being too bossy. I'm not sure I like being away from the mega stress and tension of work, but I figured out Luke was more important than anything. I'm also not sure if Rob is one hundred percent comfortable with my more laid-back vibe. He keeps staring or laughing at me when I am counting to ten to avoid repeating my past learnt reactions on matters. Deep breaths and contemplation are not my natural default.

My mammy is delighted. She has the look of a woman whose daughter just polished the skirting boards and achieved satisfaction from doing so. I have not polished the skirting boards, but in her eyes, I now seem the sort of person that might. It is enough for her. This is the mother who once a year watches without fail John Wayne's *The Quiet Man* and gives me marital advice based on it.

What she doesn't know is I'm searching, really searching, for Luke. I was thirteen when he left. I threw myself into studying, then work. I pushed the massive ache and hole in my heart to the bottom of my heels. I have stomped my way through life often in four-inch heels, but I'm afraid. I'm afraid the demise of our daddy is not through love and concern but through guilt. What am I going to find out? It terrifies me. The moment I stopped working flat out in the office, the need grew. I could no longer suppress my thoughts. The police interview tipped me over. When John realised the pain was genuine and why I had it, he was unbelievable. I had no idea a police officer could be so compassionate and knowledgeable. For two hours, he talked to me and spelt out what he might be able to do, plus the limitations of searching thirty-five-plus years later for a missing person. No wonder Ursula is much happier. He really is a catch. Even Rob agrees, and he likes Ed.

I sip the cold coffee and think about how and when to tell Rob more about my plans. He knows my hopes, but I know he'll want to protect me from disappointment. I want to protect myself. The ache is unbearable.

'Fiona!'

My mother shouting my name from downstairs interrupts my thoughts. She moved in with us when the children were little. I didn't want her living on her own, miles away in Liverpool, and the second nanny sacking gave me the excuse to snatch her from her orderly life based around flower duties at the local Catholic church. I appealed to her emotions and won.

'Yes Mammy, what is it?'

'You've a gentleman caller.'

I started to laugh as I left the study and came onto the landing. Looking over the balustrade to the hall, I could see DCI Smith, or rather, John. What the heck was he doing here? I tried to walk down the stairs calmly, but my heart was racing and I could see my mother hovering in the kitchen doorway, which was luckily further down the corridor and I could position my back to her, hopefully obscuring the conversation.

'Are you here about...' I started to whisper, but he cut me off.

'No, no, not that. I wouldn't.' He was shaking his head and attempting to convey reassurance.

My shoulders dropped and I almost exhaled. I wasn't ready yet.

'Look, I know this is an imposition,' he continued, 'but I need a favour if I'm going to be honest. Is that your mother?'

'Yes.'

He raised a hand in her direction and I could hear her scuttling further into the kitchen. I raised my eyes.

'She's very nosey.'

'Don't worry about that, I'm used to people gawping.' He gave me a rueful smile. For a moment, we both did an awkward shuffle on the spot before I gathered myself.

'Right DCI Smith, let's go into the lounge.'

'John, please call me John.'

'I know, but it seems inappropriate sometimes.' I stopped myself from winking. 'Would you like coffee or tea? I'm sure my mammy would love to be able to nose a bit more.'

'I would, a coffee please, but what I have to say to you is in confidence. Is that okay?' He sounded serious.

I took him into the cosy lounge adjacent to our huge kitchen diner. I opened the separating glass doors between it and the kitchen. 'Yes, sure. Won't be a moment.' I walked to the kitchen.

'Mammy, you nosey so and so, could we both have a coffee. Forgot to ask if he took milk and sugar.'

'Fiona, I wasn't being nosey, a handsome gentleman caller is always something to appreciate.'

I was left slightly gobsmacked by her remark.

'Bernadette, say two Hail Marys to cleanse your thoughts,' I retorted.

She was laughing, and at that moment, I wanted to cry and tell her my mission, but I hardened immediately and went back to John.

There we were both sat slightly awkwardly despite our few missing person meetings over the months and social occasions. I knew he would wait until my mother brought in the coffee and had safely disappeared out of earshot. For double measure, I made sure the glass doors from the kitchen to this sitting room were shut. I could see her looking in cupboards. After a few minutes, I indicated we were safe.

'Look, Fiona, it is a big ask, but I've got a situation unfolding and I'm attempting to rope you and Mr Etheridge in to help.'

'Mr Etheridge!' The surprise was clear.

'Long story short, his wife used to foster vulnerable children. They were placed there by local authority guardians.'

I still looked very puzzled.

'Part of my investigation into the body you discovered.'

'Oh.' I still felt unsure why this was relevant or where this was going.

He then began to explain. We talked for over an hour. My mother popped in to offer us lunch, but we were far too absorbed in the specifics of his plan.

'My only concern is getting Rob on board, but he is really accommodating generally.'

'I completely understand. Let me know. This is all out of the ordinary and not at all sanctioned, but I can't let it end badly, and it is very much looking that way. Two of my team are going to give up time if you agree.'

My face must have caused him to continue.

'Not that I'm putting the decision on you, but this plan is my best option.'

'I know, I get it. I'm conscious I need to chat to Rob. All part of my post-city rehabilitation.' We both laughed.

He hesitated before saying, 'Did you wear the trousers at work? Dreadful thing to say, I know, but I'll rephrase, how tyrannical were you?'

I smiled.

'I most certainly did not figuratively or literally wear the trousers. It was more statement dresses and heels. At five foot ten, as well as working too hard, I was quite intimidating, which is why I never had to say anything. My actions spoke volumes, although I did and still do tend to make decisions on the hoof.'

John looked at me, waiting for me to say more. When I didn't, he said, 'Hence the dug up body scenario.'

Only a twinge of guilt. I hadn't killed the person.

'Do you have any more news on the body?'

'Nothing significant. Other than identifying the person as a young adult female. Forensics are still painstakingly reconstructing, and once they've completed the work, we'll have more idea of her exact age, rough date of demise, and any indications on cause. It's not top priority, but I'm hopeful we'll get some way towards finding out what happened.'

'Mr Etheridge isn't a suspect, is he?' I don't know why I asked this, but I wanted to know.

I could see John calculate whether to say anything.

'I doubt it. I think there is a link because of his wife fostering, and he's been helpful in trying to recall everyone, but I'm waiting on a full list from social services. Their records from twenty-plus years ago are all in storage in folders. Again, not top priority. He doesn't fit in the picture at all.'

I didn't want to ask John about background checks as I knew he would have done them on all of us. Only because of his help with Luke, he'd explained this to me already. Both of us sat in contemplation, momentarily. John stood up and smoothed his trousers around his knee. He pulled his jacket sleeves down as well. I thought he was going to say more, but he smiled and thanked me for my time. After I closed the front door, I went back to the kitchen

My mother was waiting for me. I knew I couldn't avoid giving her some explanation for John's visit. I attempted to stall.

'I've got to pick up Henry from school soon. Then Alice at five. Do you need anything as I can pop to the supermarket before or after?'

'No, we are all grand.'

Silence. I cracked first.

'He needs a favour.'

'Who?'

'Mammy! The detective who popped round, who you gawped at. I know you are dying to know what he wanted.'

'Now you come to mention it, I am curious. What I'm mostly curious about is, is he Ursula's fancy fellow?'

My lips cracked an askance smile. I couldn't fault my mother for her constant interest in everyone's love life, despite only being married to one man and only ever involved with that said one man, my father.

'He is her 'fancy fellow' as you put it. She did get divorced.'

'That must have been a super quick one?' She said.

'Yeah, well, Ed paid for it all, and it suited him in his job to have the least fuss possible. He was surprisingly practical and generous.'

'Didn't he fight for her?' My mother asked.

'He isn't John Wayne, Mammy. He's the head of a huge media group, wanted the least publicity he could muster and no impact on the share price. His only concern was his image. Ed pragmatically decided to opt for the grown apart, my ex-wife will always be my best friend, we will always have our two sons angle. Fair play, he pulled it off.'

'Why didn't you tell me this before, Fiona? I would have given her a card.'

'I don't think she needed a card, more a cold shower. The pair of them are horrific get-a-room material.'

'Her and the detective?'

'Yes. Luckily, Rob is as embarrassed as me so I feel no obligation to invite them over yet.'

'Fiona Riley, I've no idea how you are missing the romance gene handed down through generations.' She winked.

It was in jest, but also true. I came from a long line of women who adore the romance of life. My Auntie Kathleen had been the worst for prompting 'alliances' as she liked to refer to them. She inflicted every spotty eejit from Mass on me. Thankfully, I had Luke to scare them all off. Had. I felt tears welling up. My mother put her hand on mine.

'Are you thinking of him?'

I nodded. Not trusting myself to speak.

'He's still alive Fiona, I know it.'

I knew she would say that. She always does sporadically.

'But Daddy...' My voice trailed off.

'He tried everything, it broke his heart.'

'I don't really remember much, to be honest.'

'You put your head down and we didn't talk to you about anything. That was the way then. There was no help either. No charities or organisations to speak of really. We tried everything.'

This time we both sat in silence. I saw the time and made a move.

'You never did say what the detective wanted.'

'Oh, I'll explain it to you later when I can. It does mean we'll have to help. It's not dodgy but more, somewhat unorthodox.'

My mother surprised me by nodding and not prying further. Any thoughts of Luke tended to dampen us momentarily. I was glad I had the distraction of walking to get Henry from school. He'd probably moan I hadn't driven.

SIXTEEN

It was today. Rob was dropping Alice off at Saturday school and we had to get to the farm by 10am. When he got back, we drove and parked our car in the nearby pub car park across from Mr Etheridge's house. One of John's colleagues was waiting for us. We got into his car.

'Hi, I'm Stuart, Detective Constable Stuart Johnson, I'd normally show you my lanyard, but well, this is off duty, in fact probably truer to say more off piste.' He smiled at us both.

Rob and I introduced ourselves, but really didn't know what to say next. He started the engine and drove off. After a minute, he spoke.

'Right, I'm going to drop you off at the BP garage and then you can walk back up to the farm. Takes about ten minutes or so. When you get to the garage, go first to the shop and buy something small, like a chocolate bar. Start walking, and then check back after a few minutes to see if anyone is behind you. Precautionary. John has already shared my number with you, so text me if you need to. We'll all go into the garage shop, but don't say goodbye to me. I'll be staying there for a while to make sure no one is following, and you might spot me later. Again, don't acknowledge me. Is that all okay?'

'Yep, got that,' Rob said.

It wasn't far to the garage, but the traffic was building up, and then doing a right turn into it across a busy road made it feel like forever. Stuart parked up and we got out of the car while he stayed in it. Once we'd made a garage purchase of chocolate, we were on our way, leaving Stuart in there.

I was surprised to find myself shaking slightly. It was a cold

January day, but I was well wrapped up in my puffer coat and cosy bobble hat. Rob was in full stride. I was impressed with his acceptance of it all. Actually, he was loving it. I was scared knowing serious criminal gangs were involved, but as Rob pointed out, the bad guys only want the bad guys.

He left Barbados when he was thirteen but went back every year without fail. I know he's been dismayed at the rise in some of the violent crime because, like most Bajans, he's proud of the island and its independence, and how it's finally become a republic. I smiled, remembering our shared love of republicanism when we met. As we walked, I felt his hand grasp mine and tighten his grip. I saw him look over his shoulder, and then we eased into our jaunt.

'The things I do for you, Miss Riley.'

'Come on, you are loving this. I bet you think you are Idris Elba in Luther right now.'

He let go of my hand and poked me in the ribs.

'Don't tarnish me with an Arsenal supporter.'

'Fair point.'

We were both Liverpool supporters, our one area of complete harmony. When Rob arrived in London, aged thirteen, he had to pick a football team. Stockwell was a far cry from the ease of his life in Barbados, and he chose to do two things: disguise his purpose, which was wanting to go to university, and also stay true to his identity. His identity was bound up in his Caribbean life. John Barnes was the only footballer he knew who was from there, and on his arrival in 1988, Liverpool FC was known worldwide, so he reasoned it would be an ideal selection. The one benefit of where he lived was The Oval, he loved cricket. He spent as much time as possible getting into the ground for free by fair means (persuasion) or finding gaps to sneak through or over to watch the cricket. I copied my brother Luke. Luke was

Liverpool mad.

I always came back to Luke. It was why we were walking briskly towards a farm to help out John. He was firmly John now. He was the opposite of Ed. Kind, steadfast, and interested in you. Ed was only interested in himself and what you could do for him.

'You are thinking of Luke, aren't you?' Rob ventured. He always knew by the energy I gave off.

'Briefly, but mainly about John. How John is different in every sense to Ed. Ursula is much happier,' I replied.

Rob thought for a moment before he spoke. 'I like Ed, he is a prize cock I know, but he's good company on a social level. I'm sure Ursula is in a better place now, but he is what he is, and honestly, he is good company if you are a bloke. Selfish, I know. You forget how hard he worked for his family to become the global head of a media company.'

In my head, I could concede the good fun bloke thing, but he worked to get where he was for himself. His own ego. I decided to let it pass. Instead, I grabbed Rob's hand and squeezed it. I loved him so much, but I could never tell him. Since Luke went missing, I hoped for the best and always planned for the worst. Even with Alice and Henry. I let Rob name them after his grandparents. It's not that I don't love them, of course I do, in fact, they love to accuse me of suffocating them, but I can't do sentimentality. I have a few good friends and did okay with the school mums thanks to my mammy, but I have a loathing of Facebook and Instagram women warriors with their besties love fest, beaming children, and all-out life bragging. I love Alice because she swore she'd divorce me as her mother if I ever posted a picture of her, even when she was ten.

'We need to turn up here,' Rob's voice penetrated my thoughts as we reached the Rushett Farm sign. 'You okay,

Iona?'

I laughed. He was worried about me. I made him swear never to call me Fi. Too twee and all manner of wrong. I cannot abide 'hun' or any other such modern-day term of endearment. Although I have to confess to a tolerance of the Geordie 'pet' thanks to one of the young traders. He was in my team briefly and supported Newcastle. I know this because he actually had the temerity to wear a football top under his shirt one Friday. Sometimes I missed the fun of city life. Definitely no room for sentimentality there. Suited me to the ground. Hence Rob settling for a Hebridean island name as a term of endearment. Tough like marble and hardy, the isle of Iona, alone in the sea.

'Yes,' I replied. 'Are we doing the right thing?'

'Too late now. It will be fine. It's not ideal, but I agree with you, John is on a mission. A pretty futile one really, to save one lad out of many, but let's help him out. If it goes wrong, it goes wrong.'

It was enough to make me stand taller and feel more confident. We increased our purposeful stride towards the farm, navigating the outbuildings until we came to the back of it, where a field area accommodated a coffee van with pallets masquerading as seating and tables. A few potato and grain sacks acted as coverings for the exposed pallet seats, providing a modicum of rustic opulence. I sat down on a pallet and Rob queued for coffee. I kept a watchful eye on the path leading up from the common through a large wheat field to the back of the farm where we were.

After twenty minutes, I could see Ursula with a young woman and what must be the boy. As they came closer, I realised the woman with Ursula must be one of John's children. He had thought of everything, nothing looked out of place. The rescued youth did not look out of place with all our ethnic mixing on display. He looked petrified. I stood up and waved as they got closer. Ursula looked in charge, she directed them towards us.

'Hi Fiona,' she said. Ursula's pitch was a bit higher than usual, conveying some element of tension she must be feeling. 'This is Amelia, John's eldest, and this is Tyrel.'

I warmly shook Amelia's hand and introduced myself while Rob did a fist bump at Tyrel, who glared at him with the utmost suspicion and dislike. It wasn't returned. In fact, he shoved his hands further into his hoody pockets. He was wearing top to toe black with a small bag across his body, also black.

'Coffee, Amelia?' I asked.

'Call me Amy, please, everyone else does. I'd love a latte, please.' She turned to Tyrel, 'What you drinking, Ty?' He also glowered at Amy. This did not deter her. 'He'll have a Coke if they've got one, although looking at the van, I think an apple juice is the best option.' Nothing from Tyrel.

Rob volunteered to go for the drinks. I took in the beauty of Amelia with her corkscrew hair pulled up on top of her head. Her face was glowing, and I could see hints of freckles covered by foundation. Like all young women of her age, she was wearing extra lashes and a sheer tint of something on her lips.

'What lipstick are you wearing Amelia, sorry Amy?'

'It's a tinted one from Charlotte Tilbury, Pillow Talk, I think. I've not got it with me. It'll be removed once I drink some coffee.' She rolled her eyes. 'I should have texted Dad to bring it from the car.'

Ursula and I sneaked a wry smirk at the dad reference. If Amy hadn't been there, we would have cracked up. Rob came back with the coffees and a carton of apple juice for Tyrel, which surprisingly, he drank. I suddenly realised at either fifteen or sixteen, he was still a child. My heart melted a little. He was the same age as Luke when he disappeared.

Luke had developed that sullen, mistrustful look. Why hadn't I realised? I thought he was being angry at the time, but didn't understand it. Maybe he's been taking drugs. I didn't think so because he was so fit and healthy. He was still going to football training with Daddy, although more reluctantly. I pulled myself back to the here and now, aware we were being joined by John. He smiled at me and Rob.

'Let me introduce you both to Ethan, my middle one.'

Next to John was a tall, striking young man. This time, Rob's fist pump was returned, and with a grin. Ethan shook my hand, he was so self-assured, but not in an arrogant way. I felt pleased for Ursula, although John's youngest was a bit more of an issue, mainly because she was in her first year of a demanding work apprenticeship university degree and still living at home. Otherwise, their relationship was still flourishing. John looked so happy, and then, as if he realised, he changed into work mode. I offered to get the coffees this time as I knew what he was going to say, and Rob needed to absorb the details.

As I stood waiting, I could see him explaining the route we were going to take to Mr Etheridge's. I knew we would walk back with Ursula, Amy and Tyrel in a similar direction they had taken to get here. Then Rob and I would walk Tyrel through the edge of the common back onto the main Kingston Road, at the top, near the pub. John wanted us to stay on the Surrey side, so if there were any problems, the fallout would be limited to him only breaking protocol in his patch. This place, the coffee stop at The Barn, was the only point we were in London and therefore Met Police territory.

It was then I noticed Stuart again. He was leaning on a wall, sipping a cup of coffee. I immediately looked away. Adrenaline ran through me. I bought another apple juice carton, as well as the coffee for John and Ethan. There they all were laughing, and Ethan was putting an arm around Tyrel. Tyrel's shoulders hunched, but he didn't pull away. My eyes welled up. Returning, I forced a smile, handed out the drinks, and hastily brushed my right eye dry as I sat down.

It seemed conversation had returned to everyday life. Ethan was moaning about applying for a law conversion course, and John said, 'Well, don't go representing criminals.' There was a momentary pause, almost an intake of breath, which thankfully Ethan swiftly filled.

'Dad, how many times have I told you I'm only interested in working in a big commercial firm?'

'Like in the legal team?' I stumbled the words out badly.

'Probably, in a consultancy-type business. That is what Olivia is doing. My little sis. She's becoming an accountant and getting her university course all paid for, as well as being paid. Savvy move, but not as much fun as going away to university if you ask me. '

'I agree,' said Rob. 'I wouldn't have met this one otherwise.' He was pointing at me.

'Did you guys meet at uni?' Amy asked.

'Technically, yes, we did, but we were not an item at university. We met again a few years later at a mutual friend's wedding,' I replied. 'We took some of the same mathematics lectures. Other than that, I think it is fair for me to say I don't think you noticed me, Mr Clark.'

'Oh, I noticed you, okay, but let me say I would never have asked you for anything other than a pencil. Too scary and probably too haughty.'

'What's haughty?' A voice no one recognised spoke. I immediately realised it was Tyrel. He'd been listening. Everyone almost answered at once, but Rob held his gaze and answered.

'It sort of means stuck up and a bit arrogant, but I was wrong to use the word haughty. Fiona was distant, not stuck up. I was joking around and don't want you to get the wrong impression.'

Well, that killed the vibe. Tyrel retreated again.

'Prick,' I mouthed at Rob.

Ursula nudged me. This time, there was no attempt to start a new conversation. John stood up and suggested we 'got the show on the road.' The blokes were really batting it out of the park today with their words. I attempted to smile at Tyrel, but he was looking at the ground.

Ethan pulled him up by his elbow in a way that looked like an older brother bossing a younger sibling around. He didn't resist. There were quite a few people with dogs basking in the noon winter sunshine around us. We regrouped on the worn path on the field and ambled back towards the common area. John and Ethan hung back from us, and Rob was firmly setting the pace at the front. Amy was with Tyrel, so I dropped back to be alongside him on the other side. I knew Ursula guessed what I was doing as she strode to be next to Rob and allowed me to chat with Amy over Tyrel's head. He was a little shorter than me, not much, but he didn't look as if he was fully grown, and he didn't look too healthy. His skin, despite being typically lighter mixed-race, had a grey tinge to it.

Before long, we were all going our separate ways on the path. Ursula and Amy were on their own as John and Ethan were behind us, but we knew it was only for a short while as they planned to double back. No one was talking. I could hear Tyrel's mouth breathing.

'You okay?' I ventured.

He nodded.

Then it was the three of us. The last bit was longer than

we thought, and Tyrel was trying to keep up, but he looked shattered. We entered a path through a gate leading towards the main road. The whoosh of cars filled our silence. Rob guided Tyrel to the inside of the path on the main road and I walked behind them. I did look behind quickly, but there was no one. Then we turned down the drive to Mr Etheridge's house.

Later that evening, as we sat exhausted from our mission, and the children sat firmly in front of the television, I poured us a large glass of red wine each.

'Penny for them, Mr Clarke?' I said.

'The young lad, Tyrel, what are the next steps?'

'I'm not sure, I think John will have to place him with social services and that will mean care or fostering, I'm guessing.'

'Fiona, that was me. All alone and sent to England to live with my aunt. I was probably a bit younger, but it made me think. Can we help in any way?' Rob said.

We both sat in silence. He'd taken me aback. I hadn't thought much about the situation other than helping John out. But now Rob had mentioned it, was there a possibility we could help?

SEVENTEEN

It had been two long weeks since we'd left Tyrel with Mr Etheridge. He had been waiting for us after our forty-minute walk to his house, through the common, with a male nurse in tow. We were all relieved John's preparations had gone to plan. There was no sign of anyone following, not a hint of anything untoward. Tyrel was safe.

The reason for the nurse was based on John being unsure if Tyrel had been taking any of the drugs he was supplying. Apart from vaping and the odd joint, it appeared he'd been fairly clean, if a little malnourished, from a diet of highly processed takeaway foods and a lack of fresh air and vitamin D.

Each night, John, his son Ethan, or his work colleague Stuart had been staying as well. It seemed as if Tyrel was making progress. John's eldest daughter, Amy, was with Mr Etheridge, assessing his education. Amy had followed in her mother's footsteps and taught mathematics at secondary school.

Following Rob's views on helping the lad, I was getting legal advice without revealing too much to see how we could look after Tyrel. I knew it would involve some local authority interaction at some point, but we needed time to assess what danger he was in and what our story was going to be given the circumstances surrounding his potential arrival into our care.

I was also deep in the development of a business idea. Prompted by the conversation with obnoxious Kevin, I realised maybe I could make this a bigger offering than the three of us riding around in a van with our gardening tools. Oh heck, was that the time? I flew downstairs.

'Mammy, I'm off.'

Not stopping to hear a reply, I grabbed the van keys off the hall table and went out into the drive. The gates took ages to open, another item to check added to my mental to do list. Why had no one invented an app that read your thoughts and compiled the list in notes on your phone? Once on the road, I called Ursula.

'On my way. Can you call Caroline and say I'm running a bit late? I'll get to her first.'

'No probs, but why didn't you call her instead of me?'

'Ursula!'

'Oh, a Fiona dash, is it? Laters.' She hung up on me, at least the mind-reading app was working.

The bloody lights were red.

When I pulled up outside Caroline's, she was waiting outside. She bounced into the van.

'Morning.'

'Is it? I feel like I've been up for 24 hours.'

'I thought you'd swapped that lifestyle.'

'Caro, I seem to have swapped skin-of-my-teeth work decision making, for skin-of-my-teeth life decision making.'

She laughed. 'You are loving it really.'

'I thought I'd have more time to myself and for facials. I really thought I'd be getting facials,' I sighed.

'Well, we did have a few weeks of calm with one client before the body,' Caroline ventured.

'True. We've only got four clients now. We're not fully booked, but still, with everything else, I don't have enough hours in the day.'

'Welcome to my world.' It was Caroline's turn to exhale, and I did feel a bit guilty given she'd been a single parent with no family locally to offer support.

'You'll have to give me tips,' I replied, no need to mention my thoughtlessness. 'Especially on managing to fit in the studies.'

'It is easier now Jack is away at university and I've got into a routine with Ruby, both of us studying together. It keeps her on the straight and narrow when it comes to homework for her A levels. She is less inclined to be on top of everything like Jack. Too busy looking at TikTok.' She paused. 'And don't get me started on the new AI thing that writes for you. She is all over it, and the plagiarism checking app.'

We both laughed. Alice was the same. Any shortcut was her default mode of operation.

'I'm paying for the privilege of Alice to roll eyes at me and tell me everyone is doing it.'

'Ruby can't wait to leave school. Being at an all-girls school is not her favourite choice. I was glad to leave her moaning behind the other night when I went out.'

'What were you doing?'

'Nothing exciting, just a drink in Wimbledon. It was nice to have a change of scenery and...' Caroline stopped.

'And what?' I asked.

'Nothing, just catching up with an old friend, but we both had an early night. I'd hoped for more, but the timing isn't right.'

'Who is it? I'm presuming he, or are they they/them?'

Caroline pulled a face at me.

'Look, Ursula has a for sale notice outside her house.' She pointed at the sign as I pulled up in the van outside. 'Don't beep the horn, Fiona.'

I was tempted, but Ursula was coming out the front door. She walked down the drive to the van and got in.

'Budge up.'

We both looked at her.

'What?!'

I pointed at the sign.

'Oh yes, forgot.'

'Does Ed know?' Caroline asked.

'No. I've not mentioned it to him yet as the house is mine. I thought I wanted to stay here, but neither Dan nor James are bothered, and I'm ready to move on.'

I did a three point turn on the road and headed to our appointment.

'I reckon ready to move on is ready to move in with a certain detective, and if I were a betting person, I'd say it was a dead cert.' I winked at Ursula.

'Save your money. Nothing is settled on yet, but maybe,' was her reply.

'Definitely maybe?'

'No Caroline, maybe. Maybe. I'm unsure. I quite like my own space. It's not like we need to set up home together. Anyway, how's your secret fellow?'

'He's still secret,' I interjected.

'It's complicated,' Caroline said, and both Ursula and I thought better of saying anything else, so I changed the subject.

'Ursula, don't put the radio on. I need to talk to you both about taking our gardening company forward as a business.'

I started to explain the concept of packaging the name with operational delivery and solutions. They both stared blankly at me. We pulled up at our client's house, and as we were unloading the van, I carried on.

'I know I'm explaining it badly, but have you seen the dog walking vans. There are quite a few that are franchises. The person buys the business proposition with some ready-made customers, as the brand is established and they are known. You get to be the only franchise in certain geographical locations. Due to the name, the service is up and running almost immediately. There is a central website which defaults to the local provider, etc. We can meet up properly to run through it all, but I'm working on it now.'

They both looked a bit taken aback.

'This is sudden,' Ursula said.

'I know, but I was having one of my work smarter, not harder moments. I don't want to stop doing this, but there is no need for us to work all day every day in a garden.'

Caroline surprised me by saying, 'I think it is a good idea. It is about leveraging trust, isn't it? Everyone likes a brand they know.'

Ursula still looked unconvinced. I didn't want to dwell on it, but I added, 'We'd have a launch event and you can do more PR stuff, Ursula.'

Her face shifted. She gave me a sideways glance. For once, I decided not to get firm and left it. I knew she'd do it. Instead, I picked up a trug already filled with garden woodchip.

'Blimey, this is heavy.' I walked laden with the heavy trug to the side gate entrance to the garden.

Our three hours passed silently. We all seemed absorbed in our thoughts. I couldn't help but break the silence towards the end as we were gathering the various tools scattered around.

'Caro is in love, Ursula.'

'What? Who? Is it still Joe?'

Caroline looked stunned.

'I'm not, it's nothing,' she glowered as she spoke.

'Okay, I was exaggerating. You are still moping around after Mister Unobtainable, aren't you? They met for drinks.'

With that, Caroline threw down the spade and stormed off.

Ursula gave me her death stare. 'Fiona, don't, she's lonely, you know that. Don't tease her about whoever it is. It's been going on for years. Leave her be.'

'Sorry.'

'You said what?'

'I said sorry. I'll go after her. I didn't think, that's all. We've got Tyrel over for dinner tonight to meet Alice and Henry. I'm on edge and I don't know why.'

Ursula's face softened.

'It's because it is important to you. You and Rob are doing a good thing. How is your mum about it?' She asked.

'Oh, she's grand. She is never happier than when she's got someone to fuss over, and a waif and stray scenario is a dream come true for her. I'll go after Caroline, it's my fault.'

I walked out of the garden to the van, and Caroline was leaning against it. Her face was quite pale, and she looked a bit nauseous. I felt dreadful.

'Caroline, I'm so sorry I was messing around and...' I stumbled, 'honestly, I'm a dick.'

She didn't speak. I carried on. 'Whoever it is, he isn't worth it. You are worth one hundred of anyone.'

No smile. In fact. she looked worse. I thought she was going to say something, but instead she stifled a sob. Why had I been so thoughtless? What was wrong with me?

'Please Caro, call me an eejit, anything. I am an idiot.'

She grabbed my wrist.

'Stop, Fiona. Don't say another word. I'm not worth anything over anyone. I'm just besotted with someone I shouldn't be, so can we leave it at that? He's... he is unsuitable, that is all.'

'He's not a nonce?' The words were out of my mouth before I could stop them.

Caroline started to snort instead of cry.

'Oh my good God, Fiona, as if! Only you could leap to that conclusion. I'm not a weirdo.'

'What's so funny?' Ursula asked as she carried the spades to the van.

'Nothing,' Caroline said, 'Fiona's apology went from decent to stupid. Ignore me, bad timing. I'm feeling sorry for myself, and it is pointless.'

Ursula gave Caroline a hug.

'I'm sorry as well, we've all been a bit self-absorbed lately. I know I spend far too much time with John. We all need to go out for an evening. I'd say come round to mine, but I am swamped with the high maintenance of open day preparation. I need to tell Ed about the move and see if he wants anything else he hasn't taken already. A night out would be like a breather from all the events going on,' Ursula said.

This seemed to cheer us all back up and I felt relieved. I hadn't intended to upset Caroline, but we'd never met this Joe, and I wasn't sure if it was him she was still seeing. I didn't understand why she was so guarded, even if he was married. Once the van was fully loaded, I backed out of the drive to take us all home. Ursula immediately put the radio on, Suede's *Animal Nitrate* was playing, and we found ourselves 'oh-ing' a lot as they were the only words we knew.

'Will you drop me off first, Fiona? I need to meet up with Ruby. Town will be fine. Is that okay with you, Ursula?' Caroline asked.

'No problem,' Ursula replied.

I was a bit concerned about getting back home but thought better of saying anything.

'Fiona's got Tyrel coming over tonight,' Ursula added.

'Why didn't you mention it earlier?'

'Because I was too busy upsetting you.'

'Don't be daft, I love hearing about him. How is he doing?' Caroline perked up completely.

'Not sure really. He's been on a strict diet of protein, fruit, vegetables and other nice high-quality foods. Mr Etheridge has been a force of dietary guidance. We're no nearer knowing his background. He seems reluctant to talk.'

'Oh well, he will in time,' she replied.

We all seemed to nod our heads in unison on that. What the feck had I got myself into? Bloody John and his bright ideas. I dropped Caroline off and went back around the one-way system to get to Ursula's home. She turned the radio off.

'Don't take on too much Fiona, I know you've really helped John out here, you and Mr Etheridge. I still can't say David easily. No idea why, he is soooo lovely.'

'I won't, we won't, me and Rob. For some reason it's given us a shared purpose. Even Alice and Henry are on board. We did the whole giving back to society chat. My mother, of course, loves an opportunity to, well, mother.'

We both smiled ruefully, and I didn't add that we'd checked with John on his background, undertaken safeguarding training, and both Rob and I had debated the different options nearly every night.

'As long as it doesn't get disruptive, but from what John and Amy have said, he seems a nice lad. A dreadfully sad one,' Ursula said.

'Yes, he was lucky John cared enough to risk his job.'

'He does love a project, and I'm including myself in that analysis.'

I pulled up outside of Ursula's and pre-empted any offer of a cup of tea. 'I'm going to have to dash. Let's arrange drinks for next week.'

'Will do, and good luck for tonight. Text or call me later.'

Ursula high-fived me to diffuse the emotion I was omitting at a high frequency before getting out and waving me off. As

I drove home, I wanted to cry. I gave up work to find Luke, as pointless as it might be. Everything I have read and researched indicates my search is futile. The information on missing persons websites is now immense, as are the number of charities out there. But Luke went missing a long time ago. None of the networks existed then. He disappeared into a void along with all the other thousands who've done the same.

When I was working, I couldn't afford to think about it. Mammy, Rob and me have acted as if nothing had happened eighty percent of the time, particularly for Alice and Henry. The twenty percent was unavoidable, his birthday, Christmas, and the date he went missing. The days my mum disappeared to church, to the refugee of Mass, always on his baptism and first holy communion dates. Dates I had come to know.

Tyrel was our attempt to fill a void, and he needed to know this. I had to tell him about Luke so he would understand our decision to help was not random. Our altruism was not without fulfilment for ourselves. Was he too young to grasp or even care about our loss? Did he want to stay with us? I had more questions than answers in every area of my life at the moment. The gates were still so slow, so as I parked the van, and before I forgot, I called our handyman and left him a voicemail.

EIGHTEEN

'Hello. I'm back.'

There was no response. I checked the time, and mammy would have walked to get Henry. I grabbed some water in the kitchen and stuck my head in the fridge as I felt very flushed. I headed upstairs to shower.

By the time I came down, my mum and Henry were back, and it was time for me to go and pick Alice up from school. I ruffled Henry's hair as he sat at the kitchen island with a sandwich and a glass of milk, attempting to do his homework.

'How was school today, Henry?'

'Okay.' He didn't even look up.

'We've got Tyrel coming round for dinner soon. Dad is picking him up on his way home from a meeting he had today.'

'Uh huh.' He nodded his head and carried on scrawling in his school book.

'That's not very neat, Henry. How does your teacher read that?'

'Mum, it's fine. I'll type it up on the iPad. They just like to see some written stuff as well.'

I smiled. He had an answer for everything, and so did Alice.

'Where's Mamo?'

Before he had a chance to answer, my mother appeared.

'Was putting some washing on, Fiona dear.'

'Sorry Mammy, I meant to do that earlier but I dashed out and forgot.'

'Too much on your mind,' was her reply.

'A little. I'm going to get Alice now.' I gave her a hug. 'Be good, Henry.'

The electric mini was charging, but there was enough to get to school and back. I unplugged it and pinged the gates so I could get out without having to wait. I was a bit impatient and also on edge. When I got to the school turning, I wasn't sure how I'd driven there. I parked up to wait for Alice. She could have got the bus, but I wanted to make sure she got home on time, instead of dawdling with her friends.

'Do I have to have dinner with you tonight? Georgie wants us to do prep together, and we can order Domino's.' Alice's entrance to the car was not unexpected.

'Hello to you too,' I responded.

'Mum, please, come on!'

'No.'

I started the engine and pulled in behind the exiting cars that were snaking their way around marauding pupils and parked coaches. Alice put her AirPods in and our journey home was silent. When I pulled in, the gates were open, and Rob's car was there. My stomach lurched. I really did feel sick to the core. This could be disastrous. Alice got out and slammed the door. I knew she'd attempt to go straight to her room. Bad luck for her as Rob was waiting for us both. He made her give him a hug and her defiance began to melt.

'You alright, Iona?'

I nodded. Not trusting myself to speak. When he hugged me, I almost melted into his being. Love surged through me and I began to hope. I choked back the tears.

'We've got this,' he whispered in my ear.

There was Tyrel, my mother showing him where to put his coat and shoes. She seemed taller and in charge. I smiled.

'Hi.' I walked to him, unsure what to do next, but my mother interjected.

'He's going to help me lay the plates for dinner, aren't you

Tyrel?'

He nodded and returned my smile. Gosh, he looked different. More of a glow about him. A white Nike t-shirt and grey tracksuit bottoms had replaced the all black he'd been wearing when we walked him to Mr Etheridge's. My mammy turned and said, 'I've introduced him to Henry and Alice,' just as Alice skipped past to run upstairs.

'What you doing?'

'Getting changed. Oh my days Mum, he is fit! Jude Bellingham fit.' With that, she was charging up the stairs. Rob and I were left speechless, then we both started to laugh.

'What's so funny?' a still studious Henry asked as we came into the kitchen.

'Nothing, mate,' Rob said.

Before we knew it, we were all sat around the table tucking into a feast. Mammy had made lasagne, a salad of leaves, and a tomato and red onion one as well. Garlic bread, bread, and olives were also on the table.

'We don't always eat like this in the week,' Rob said to Tyrel as we ate.

'Hey mister, don't talk with your mouth full,' I darted at him.

'My Nana always said that,' said Tyrel. What to say back to him. My mind was whirring.

'Well, your Nana is a sensible lady,' my mammy said.

'She's dead,' Tyrel responded.

We were all silent.

'Our Grampo is dead,' Henry said. 'He died of a broken heart.'

'Henry!' I exclaimed

'It's true. My mum's brother, Luke, went missing and everyone was very sad.'

'Is that true?' Tyrel asked.

I took a deep breath.

'What do you want to know?'

He thought for a minute between mouthfuls of lasagne. We were all waiting on his response.

'Everything. I wanna know everything.'

'Okay,' I said, taking the chance to add, 'And we'd like to know about anything you want to tell us, but that really is up to you and we won't press you.'

'I'll tell you, but I don't want the fed to know. I mean, I like him, but I'm not a snake.'

Rob and I exchange glances, and from Rob's eyes I could decipher 'not got a scooby but let's leave it'.

I nodded. Suddenly, Mammy spoke. 'My Luke went missing when he was sixteen. Over thirty years ago, he'll be fifty now.'

Tyrel sucked in his cheeks. 'Man, that is a long time. You sure he's not dead?'

'No, he isn't, Mamo would know if he was,' Alice piped up.

I could have sworn she was just Snapchatting her friends, as I knew she had her phone on her lap, fully exploiting the circumstances. 'Mamo is my Nana, her,' she added and pointed.

'Yeah, I always knew my mum was dead, and I can't remember her. My dad was in the army and he got killed, and I don't remember much about him either. I was only four, I think.'

This was a lot to take in.

'I'm really sorry, Tyrel,' I said.

He shrugged his shoulders.

'I mind more about my Nana. She looked after me.'

I knew this was important. Think, think.

'What was her name?'

'Patricia.'

'Why, that is a grand name,' my mother said, and Tyrel smiled at her, and before we knew it, he'd told us everything.

He began by saying he had always lived with his grandparents, and then told us all about them. Patricia Charles was from Trinidad. His grandpa, Pedro Perera, had been Indian, from Goa. He was of Portuguese Catholic descent and had gone to Trinidad to work for a Venezuelan oil company, which is where he met Patricia before coming to the UK.

Mammy was all over the Catholic connection. Their story was fascinating. They had come to London because Patricia's sister, Cherelle, had moved here in the seventies to work as a nurse, and when the oil work dried up, they joined her. Tyrel couldn't remember which hospital she worked in. Pedro worked as a welder and did a lot of plumbing jobs for friends and neighbours.

His dad was called Anthony Charles Perera, and he joined the infantry as soon as he could leave school. He was killed in Afghanistan when the truck he was travelling in was hit by a rocket. It went a bit quiet at this point. Alice had long abandoned her messaging, was now as interested as the rest of us.

Tyrel told us how his Grandie, as Pedro was known, loved sardines and was always making him sardines on toast. He passed away not long before his nana as he had emphysema, a chronic pulmonary disease, where his lungs had been damaged over the years from his work and smoking. He gave up smoking a long time ago, but it was too late. His nana had a heart attack, and he was on his own.

'Didn't you have any other family?' Alice didn't hold back, but Tyrel wasn't offended.

'Nah. There was only my nana's neighbour who asked about me before they, the drug gang, took over the flat.'

Rob was sat next to Tyrel and put his hand on his shoulder.

'What did you do, Tyrel?'

'I did nothing. I was still going to school and all. I didn't have much money left when the gang spotted me and knew I was on my own.'

'Where was this?' I asked

'Croydon. We lived in an area called Fairfield. They followed me home, took over the flat and moved me to Epsom. Told me I owed them and to keep quiet.'

'Oh mate,' Rob exclaimed.

'I managed to grab some photos. That's what I had in my bag. Mr Etheridge is reframing them for me. He likes doing arty stuff, doesn't he?'

Who knew our first client would be such a find? I could feel the warm regard even Tyrel had for him.

'What a lovely man,' Mammy said, then she was up and clearing the dishes.

'Come on Alice, you help.' I pulled her chair back for extra emphasis. Of course, she scowled, but Tyrel got up as well, and suddenly she was '*Little Miss Helpful*'.

'Who's for pudding?'

'What is it, Mamo?' Henry was the most enthusiastic of us all.

'Whatever you want, love. I've made apple tart, and there is ice cream, or you can have custard,' she responded.

Everyone but me had apple tart with either custard or ice cream. The table was quiet for a while. It gave me time to think. I knew more details now, which should help if he came to live with us.

'I can't believe no one missed you, Tyrel?' It came out before I checked myself.

He shrugged his shoulders.

'I went to a school where people dropped out all the time. The gang would have used the flat until someone from the housing association came round. I dunno. You said your brother went missing. Same thing, isn't it?'

I didn't want to say we looked everywhere, the whole community, we called the police, we spoke to the school, and my mammy and daddy never stopped. It wasn't fair, he was only young.

'Tyrel, are you fifteen or sixteen?'

'Sixteen. I'm seventeen in September.'

'Okay, will you want to go back to school? Have you missed much?'

He groaned. 'I haven't been since last year. They moved me in July. But I watched loads of lessons on YouTube. Can I really go back to school?'

'Yes. I'll need to sort a few things, but I'm sure we can sort something out.'

'Mum, can he come to my school?' Alice asked.

I paused. This was awkward.

'I'm not sure. I'll find out, but it's probably unlikely as it's a private school and you have to pass exams to get in. It's not a question of money, more what the rules are for entry.'

Alice made a face and Tyrel laughed.

'I knew you went to a posh school.'

'How did you work that out?' She was being sarcastic.

They then settled back into eating their puddings while I thought about all the things we were going to need to sort out. I looked at us all sat around the table, a mash-up of everything, and felt pleasantly warm. It seemed as if a new phase really was beginning, and reading the silent joy in Mammy's eyes was enough to confirm it was the right thing to do.

Somehow, Rob turned the conversation to football, and I

helped my mother with clearing up, as I didn't want to burst the bubble quite yet of this seeming normality.

'He's a grand lad,' Mammy whispered to me as I put the plates in the dishwasher. 'It's a good thing to look after him. He's part of the family now.'

With that, Tyrel's fate was sealed. No amount of red tape would be insurmountable. No problem too much. He had a future here, and I needed to ask him if he wanted it. An hour later, we were in the car driving back to Mr Etheridge. Tyrel was quiet and looking out of the window, and although I hesitated, I knew from Alice, car journeys were a good opportunity to ask questions.

'Tyrel, would you like to come and live with us? We'd love you to, but I know it is a big decision, so no pressure.'

Nothing.

I concentrated on the road and resisted the temptation to look at him. At the lights, I knew it was only five minutes to go. I'd be dropping him off and saying goodbye.

'Yeah,' he said.

'What? Yes to coming to live at ours, or yes, it is a big decision?' I turned onto the main road and my heart was beating faster.

'To living at your gaff.'

Wow. Fiona do not gush, do not gush.

'Amazing! I mean, as my mammy would say, that'll be grand.' I glanced and saw nothing but sadness. 'But only if you are really sure.'

'I miss my nana and I like your mum.'

The magic of Bernadette Riley. The magic she stored in hope. I wanted to cry. It was becoming a habit. I pulled my thoughts back to Tyrel.

'We'll be really pleased to have you. I need to sort quite a lot of things out, but I will check and talk to you about everything.' We turned into the drive of Foster Wright Villa.

'How long will it be?' he asked.

I hesitated. Would what I was going to say upset Mr Etheridge? The reality was that he could come now. No one knew anything.

'Let's get you in and I'll have a quick chat with Mr Etheridge.'

Once inside, Tyrel, after a cursory hello to Mr Etheridge, went up the stairs to where he was staying.

'David, can I have a word?'

'Certainly Fiona, let's go into the sitting room. How was young Tyrel this evening?'

As I followed him to the room, I ventured, 'Well, that's what I want to speak to you about.'

'Fire away.'

'He told us everything. As much as he was able to at one sitting. I'm sure there is more, but he was very close to his grandmother, and he really likes my mum. She is ready to dote all over him. Can he come back with me now? If that is not too presumptuous. I'll call John to let him know, but I think he's ready to be with us.'

'Fantastic news!' Mr Etheridge's face lit up, 'I cannot emphasise how important it is for him to settle somewhere and soon. I'm a good stopgap for five minutes, but it was my wife who did the doting as you alluded to regarding your mother. It would be a pleasure to hand him over safely.'

I felt an inner glow which reminded me of warm sunshine and being at Bantry Beach with Luke when we went to stay on our annual summer holiday at Glengarriff in County Cork. It was more likely to be windy and cloudy, even in August, but when the sun shone, it was the best place to be. It's why our house is named Bantry House. I won the fight over Rob's wish to call it 'Speights', after Speightstown in Barbados. Not sure leafy Surrey was ready for a Bajan reference.

'I'm going to phone my mammy and John before I say anything to Tyrel. Can I go outside in the garden?'

'Of course, follow me.'

David led me through the wonderful modern rear extension into the private courtyard. I turned back and spoke to him as he was stepping back inside.

'Did you name your house?'

'Yes, we did when we bought it. It was called something like Sunnymead, I believe.'

'Why did you choose a new name?'

'I wanted to note my architectural inspirations, Frank Lloyd Wright and Norman Foster. I also worked at Foster's studio for many years. Hence, he gets the first mention.'

I had no architectural knowledge but smiled gracefully. A new move for me. My listening skills were improving. I was shaking as I called Mammy, and as I anticipated, she was overjoyed to be asked to make up a room for Tyrel immediately. I told her I hadn't spoken to him yet and needed to let John know, but she dismissed it all with 'He'll be coming back with you.' John's phone went to voicemail. I called Ursula.

'Howdy, Fiona.'

'Howdy!'

'I'm watching a Dolly Parton biopic.'

'Oh, okay, anyway, is John there?'

'No, he's working. Is that the only reason you are calling me? We don't live together. I'm still in my house, remember.'

Great Ursula was getting all defensive about her relationship. I didn't have the time, nor the inclination, to tell her to get over it.

'I'm at David's, Mr Etheridge's place. Tell him I'm taking

Tyrel home with me. He can call me tomorrow.'

'Wow! That's sudden.'

'Yes, well, he liked my mother, so what can I say? He needs some TLC.'

'Right. I'll tell him when I see him.'

'That'll be later then.' I couldn't resist.

Ursula laughed. 'Am I being a prig?'

'A tad.'

'I keep worrying I've jumped from one relationship to another, sorry,' Ursula stated.

'I haven't got time to chat now, but you were not in a relationship with Ed, you were his housekeeper and sex worker,' I retorted.

'Fiona!'

'Come on, give yourself a break. What does it matter? You are in your fifties. Live a little.'

Silence.

'That is exactly what John says to me. I will stop this now. I overthink and worry about everything,' she moaned.

'Good. Well, look, enjoy Dolly, and I'll see you at work later this week. Bye.'

I sort of waited before ending the call, but I needed to crack on. David had already called Tyrel down and was making him a drink in the kitchen. They both turned to me as I came back in from the courtyard.

'Fiona, would you like a cup of tea?' David offered.

I stopped myself from saying I needed something stiffer for Dutch courage. Tyrel was going to need my full focus. I guessed his nana didn't drink much other than tea, a bit like my mother.

'Tyrel, would you like to come back with me tonight and live at ours?'

He looked at Mr Etheridge, who smiled at him.

'Don't mind me. It's been a pleasure to have you, but I think Fiona's home is going to be more suitable for you, wouldn't you agree?'

'Yes,' Tyrel smiled.

NINETEEN

'Jesus Christ!'

'Who the heck is blaspheming?'

'Mammy, it is me. I'm having a fecking nightmare getting the three of them co-ordinated for school.'

'Fiona,' she said, her stern voice engaged. 'That does not require you to take the Lord's name in vain.'

I rolled my eyes safe in the knowledge she couldn't see me and muttered, 'Well the fecker never lends a hand.'

It was all the bags. I was checking they all had their sports kits sorted. Wednesdays were a universal nightmare if your children played sports, and Tyrel had taken up football again with gusto. Ah, located the shin pads.

'Come on, Alice and Tyrel. Henry, Mamo is taking you, so get a move on.'

Before long, I'd packed kits and kids in the car. Winning. On the journey, I checked they were both all clear regarding pick up and getting home instructions.

'Alice, you are getting the school bus home and I'll meet you off it, okay?'

No answer.

'Alice, comprende?'

'Si señora,' she eventually replied.

'Text me if anything changes, won't you?'

This time, all I got was a nod.

'Tyrel, I'll be picking you up at 4pm. Do not go into town with anyone. You know the score. It is too soon.'

'Yeah, I know.'

I didn't like to remind him of before, but his school was

close enough to walk into town. Thankfully, he always either went to football practice after school or was happily picked up. Today, they would be back a little late as they had an away match.

'I think John might be coming to watch you play,' I informed him.

'He'd better not wear his fed suit,' Tyrel responded.

'He hasn't got a fed suit and it will be fine. He won't be obvious,' I replied. but I could tell he didn't look convinced.

Once the two drop-offs were complete, I dashed to the new client's house to do some planning on layout and planting options. Caroline and Ursula were already there. Caroline had the van for the week as she had more work on with the landscape design. They were both already hard at work, digging and planting new flowers. I quickly joined in, grabbing my gloves and trowel, and getting stuck in.

'Thought you might have been doing more planning than planting?' I asked, trying to disguise that I was slightly miffed.

'No, I'd already agreed with Lucy, our client, what we would do in the borders, staying or not impacted by the proposed design. Which reminds me Fiona, we need some lads for hardcore work. We can't do it.'

Caroline was in charge on this project and I needed to let go. I was struggling with being a co-worker. Ursula glanced at me.

'Welcome to the world of juggling children and being unimportant at work,' she said and stared at me.

For one brief moment, a flash of myself striding into work with a camel Max Mara coat, a briefcase, Prada bag, and heels passed inside my head. I looked down at my torn jeans and my gardening boots.

'At least I'm not wearing Craghoppers,' I replied

Ursula winked at me.

'How's the brood, Mama Riley?' She asked.

'Do you mean me or my mother?'

'You, of course!'

I told them how Tyrel had settled into the secondary school. It had been easy to place him once the fostering papers were in place, as he had priority, but my concern was that it was too near the same area as the county lines flat. Even though the flat was no longer being used.

'John mentioned the school, but I'm sure he said Tyrel looks different and there has been enough time now.' Ursula tried to look as sympathetic as possible. I knew she wasn't being dismissive, but I still had a feeling of dread. I smiled back. I knew I wouldn't rest easy until I'd got him in the same school as Alice. I was working on it.

'Talking of school,' Caroline piped up, 'did you know my old school has asked about doing the gardening contract. I was out with them the other night as one of the teaching assistant colleagues is retiring and the head asked how work was going and whether we would be interested in tendering.'

'We really do need to do some recruitment Fiona, if we win that contract,' Ursula exclaimed.

I thought for a moment.

'You know I've already begun to look at expanding and developing the business. Think I'd better get a move on and share the plans. We officially need a team meeting.' I laughed, which seemed to be the first time I'd done that in a few weeks. I was laughing at the fact I'd upped the ante again. Not content with merely working, but building a business.

'You'll be listing us on the stock exchange next,' Caroline laughed.

'Don't encourage her!' Ursula exclaimed.

'I promise I won't, but I can't help wanting to improve

what we do. Mainly because you, Caroline, have been such a star with your horticultural and landscape design courses.' I was genuinely proud of her. She gave me a hug.

'Not so brittle now, hey Riley.'

I tried to ruefully accept the compliment, but I preferred the word steely. Let it go Fiona, let it go. Luckily, Ursula changed the subject.

'I've booked us a table at the cocktail place in Cobham for two weeks' time. We can have food as well.'

'Awesome.' I hoped I didn't sound too forced in my response. My mind was already wandering back to Tyrel.

'I'll text you both the time and date as I'm getting the feeling your minds are elsewhere,' Ursula added.

'Sorry, you are right. I'm thinking of Tyrel.'

'No idea what I was thinking of. Was I really not paying attention?' Caroline asked.

Ursula laughed. 'I'm only teasing. It's nice not to be the person being self-absorbed for a change.'

Ursula carried on planting in the one area we'd planned to do today, while Caroline and I checked the draft designs she'd drawn up and noted the feedback from the client. We agreed on the final look, and she said she'd send the updated version to the client. I couldn't help but take satisfaction from what we'd achieved. I knew Ursula only stuck with us out of loyalty, but Caroline and I had found something new.

'Your plans Fiona, are they realistic? Because you know it's a competitive market even where we are.' Caroline sounded weary. I looked at her and realised she looked tired and tense.

'You okay, Caro?'

'I'm fine. Perimenopause, it seems. I need to Botox my forehead and have a vitamin drip, otherwise I look and feel drab. It's not what I was expecting. Anyway, I'm HRT'd to the hilt now, so expect to see a new me in a few weeks.'

She smiled, although her chest heaved in a sigh. Mental note to self to go and get bloods done, plus go for a run this evening. I thought I'd also talk to my mum. However happily we'd rubbed along, I needed to have the chat I'd been putting off. I looked around the garden and held on to the moment, the space and the stillness. I took a deep breath and exhaled as slowly and quietly as I could manage.

Before long, we were all on our way. I drove into the town and parked in the shopping centre as I needed a sandwich. I'd totally forgotten to bring anything with me and was starving. I picked up some items I knew we needed and grabbed a coffee. I devoured the sandwich in the car while sat in the car park. A million miles from my desk lunches or out to lunch life of the city. I didn't miss or care about my previous job, but I was still adjusting to the past year. A lot had happened.

I checked myself in the car mirror and gave myself a fright. Caroline wasn't the only one in need of a pick-me-up. I added facial to my list of to dos. Unlikely, but I knew I needed to make more effort; my glossy exterior was fading. Yet my inner being was flourishing. For the first time in years, I felt content and less as Caroline would say 'brittle'. I still needed a bloody facial though. I started the car.

'How did it go?' I asked Tyrel when he got in the car. I hadn't heard from John.

'We lost,' he said and smacked his lips. 'We were shit.'

I left it. I'd learned the hard way with Alice. Whatever I said, she would contradict and disagree with me.

'Put some tunes on then,' was my helpful suggestion. Tyrel needed no encouragement, and he plugged his phone into the car system. Our drive was silent apart from some rap and grime music I had to grit my teeth through.

Home was the usual routine, a routine I'd avoided for years, of sorting bags, homework focus, dinner and TV. At half seven, I left all three of them slumped in front of the television, flicking through Netflix, Disney and Amazon Prime, trying to decide on a programme to watch. I quickly changed into my running clobber and let Mammy know I was going out. Rob was going to be late due to a work event. Still, a bit of me was on city work alert. The after-work drinks with colleagues or brokers. My rule of never to have more than one alcoholic drink. Strictly adhered to. No one ever noticed I was only drinking tonic. It was how I spotted Ed that night. I would never have noticed him if I'd been sloshed. I shook the image from my head.

Little by little, my feet and breathing took over from my thoughts, and the focus shifted from my mind to my body as a whole, co-operating to propel me along the path and into the woods. I had to concentrate on foot placement and avoiding branches. I had no truck for civilities with those ambling or walking their dog. Gradually, the tension eased. The rhythm took over, and for a brief moment, I thought about entering the London marathon. I was invincible.

Before I knew it, I was running back down the main road to the house. Panting in the drive and feeling momentarily sick from exertion, I knew the time had come. With trepidation, I went inside. No one had moved from the sofa, and for a moment, I breathed in the contentment of the three of them absorbed in whatever they were watching. I decided not to disturb them. I found my mother in the kitchen. She was emptying the dishwasher

'Mammy, you should make the kids do that.'

'Och, it's no bother Fiona, they are doing what they should be doing, nothing,' she replied.

'Bernie?' A voice said behind me.

'Yes, Tyrel?'

'Can I have a hot chocolate and take it to my room?'

'Of course you can, dear. I'll make it now.'

I stared at them both. Tyrel was calling her Bernie. I shook my head.

'I'm going to shower, then I'll be back down. What are you up to, Tyrel?'

'I've got a book to read for English. Well, it's a play,' he answered.

'Which one?' I asked.

'The Merchant of Venice. It's got lots of fighting and arguing. I need to learn about what they are arguing about for class tomorrow. We've got a discussion about it,' Tyrel explained.

'Do you like English?' I realised I'd not asked him anything much about school due to my worrying about his safety.

'No. But I want to go to Alice's school and need good grades.'

I knew I hadn't mentioned anything about grades to him.

'Who said that?'

'Alice. She said the school I go to isn't as good as hers. I'm going to show her anyone can get into hers,' he grinned.

Bloody Alice was such a madam. There was nothing wrong with his school.

'Tyrel, I went to a dreadful comprehensive school with half the windows missing. Your school is very good. I only want you to move for convenience.'

'Yeah, but they've got better facilities and smaller classes where Alice is. I reckon I could make the first team in football as well,' he added.

'Tyrel, here's your hot chocolate.' My mother handed him the mug.

'Thanks.' He went off to his room.

'Bernie? Since when have you been Bernie?' I waited until he was out of earshot.

'He's such a love, isn't he? I couldn't have such a poppet calling me Bernadette. I was always Bernie when I was his age, except when being told off.' Her eyes were sparkling, 'Now, let's be giving you your tea, shall we?'

It was after eight thirty, and Rob and I said supper these days, but I wasn't going to mention it.

'I'm going to tell Henry and Alice to get ready for bed now. Back in a mo.' I walked to the TV room and sat between them.

'Budge up. How's it going?'

Which was a bit pointless as both of them were absorbed on their phones. I gestured for them to hand them over. 'In a minute, Mum,' Alice wailed. Henry handed me his.

'Go up and get ready for bed. Lights out at nine thirty for you, young man.' He smiled and obliged. I probably had another year of his compliance. I sighed.

'Come on, madam,' I ventured to Alice.

I was met with a scowl.

'Don't make me snatch it off you, Alice.'

'It's so unfair, everyone else takes theirs to bed.'

'Well, good luck to their parents getting them up in the morning, and I really don't care what everyone else is doing. You are fourteen Alice, you need downtime and sleep.'

She gave in and handed her phone to me. She also allowed me to give her a hug.

'Don't say bad things about Tyrel's school, please. It's not very nice, Alice.'

She huffed.

'Well, why don't we go there?' was her retort.

'Because I worked really hard for years and wasn't at home,

so I sent you to a school with longer days and more after-school activities,' I explained.

'But Mamo always took us and picked us up.'

'Not always. There were a couple of nannies as well, but you won't remember them. Anyway, enough chatter miss, and get ready for bed.'

Alice gave me a hug and went upstairs.

Once I'd showered, changed and done last-minute chivvying, ensuring everyone was in bed. I knocked on Tyrel's door. He was sat reading on the comfy chair in his room.

'Come on mate, you need your sleep as well,' I picked up his mug off the floor.

'I won't be long.'

'Okay, well don't forget to clean your teeth.' I hesitated, half tempted to take his mobile, but didn't want to enforce my no mobiles in bedrooms on him. 'Your phone doesn't disturb you at night, does it?' I added.

'It's switched off. Otherwise I'd be on TikTok and not reading,' he replied

'You really do have a point to prove.' I smiled.

'Innit,' he replied and was also smiling.

On impulse, I ruffled his hair. He didn't flinch, and I then tiptoed out of the room. Shutting the door, I felt a wave of choked-up emotion. My throat was tight and my legs were wobbly. Downstairs, I plonked the mug on the counter next to the sink. I opened the fridge and poured myself a glass of white wine.

'You'll be needing food first, Fiona,' my mammy's voice said from behind.

'Geez Bernie! Making me jump.'

'Tch, you rascal. Here you are.' She produced a warm plate of colcannon with sausages and an extra garnish of spring onions. I tucked in. The first mouthful made me hungrier than I realised. I had a few mouthfuls before taking a sip of the wine. Before my next mouthful, I decided to speak.

'Mammy, I've something to tell you.'

She looked at me with her head slightly tilted to the left.

'Please don't be cross with me,' I continued.

'You've not decided to go back to the city, have you?' Her eyes widened in alarm. This caught me off guard, and I blurted it out instead of a softer preamble.

'No, I've been searching for Luke.'

Silence.

I gulped some wine. I didn't know what to say. I felt dreadful.

'You're your da's daughter, that's for sure. I wondered why you were so compliant with John. He's helping you, isn't he?' Her face gave nothing away.

More wine.

'He is Mammy, I couldn't help it. When we found the dead body and did the stupid covering up, I had to explain to him why. Why I reacted the way I did, and that it wasn't Caroline and Ursula's fault. Anyway, he's reopened the case. Since Luke went missing, there are a number of charities now, and also the Missing Persons Information Hub.' I stopped at this point, not sure what else to say.

'Any news?' She asked.

'No, not yet, but John and his colleague Stuart are still working on it. Stuart volunteered to help. They both do it in their spare time. John said he could only allocate a minimum of hours to it. He's tagged it onto the forensic case of the body in Mr Etheridge's garden. He used that allowance to send out information to other forces. But nothing back yet.'

'How long has it been?'

'Ten months, or is it nearly a year?' I wasn't sure, nor was I expecting these questions.

She huffed. I wanted to cry.

'Well, it is a good thing you are doing. Your daddy tried everything, but there was nothing.'

'There wasn't much then, in the mid 1990s, Missing People had only just been founded. Did he get any information?'

She shook her head.

'Oh Mammy, I'm sorry. I didn't want to upset you. I kept it quiet because I didn't want to raise your hopes. I'm not sure I'll get anywhere either.' I took another gulp of wine as it really hurt to admit I wasn't as confident as I had been.

'You've not upset me. I've dealt with all the disappointment of finding out nothing. Even your da felt he hit a brick wall. He kept trying to find out if anything had happened at football, but your uncle Pauley couldn't find out anything, then he moved to Chorley or Manchester, I think, a few years later.'

'I don't really remember him.'

'He was always round most weekends, He was your daddy's cousin. Their fathers were brothers. But he moved away, probably a few years after Luke disappeared. You always had your head in books or were with Auntie Kathleen, so maybe you'd not have paid much attention. They were all about the football. He helped run the team Luke was in when we lived on Hinton Street. I'm not sure if the club was linked with All Saints or the school, I can't remember because Luke got picked by the Liverpool Academy and only trained sometimes with the club,' my mother said, barely drawing breath.

'I honestly think I've blanked it all. I can barely remember our house.'

'That's trauma for you,' she stated.

It was my turn to look at my mammy again. She was far more composed than I was.

'Mammy, what do you mean by trauma?' I ventured.

'Fiona, it was a dreadful thing that visited us, Luke's disappearance. It turned our world upside down, and we lived in a city steeped in trauma, what with Hillsborough and the council, you know that chaotic man, Derek Hatton. We were all run ragged.' My mother looked tired from the memories. She was right, it was dreadful trauma, and there was so much tragedy when I was growing up; I hadn't thought of it like this.

'Mammy, you are a revelation. Or should I say Bernie?' I smiled at her and we both laughed.

'Would you like a small glass, Mammy?' I asked her as I went to pour another glass.

'Oh, go on.'

We sat chatting about Luke, Tyrel, and of course, Daddy.

'I wish he was here now, Mammy.'

'I know you do, but the stress of it all and his years of working at the docks took their toll on him. The doctor tried to get him to relax, but the stress was too much. He might not have got prostate cancer if he hadn't been so run down.'

I could see the love on her face when she talked about him. I suppose he, Luke and I were her world. She was of a background dedicated to her family. I felt touched by this. I put my hand on hers.

'They have better treatment now,' she carried on, 'I think the advances are all for the better, even for you and Alice. Less rigid, more opportunities.'

We both thought about this for a while. I heard the front door open and close.

'Oh hello, late night chez Riley's is it?' There was Rob in the doorway.

'I've told her.'

He walked into the kitchen and joined us at the island.

‘All okay?’ he asked.

‘We are grand, Rob,’ Bernadette said and smiled at him. ‘Will you be wanting anything? I’m going to turn in myself now.’

‘I’m all good, Bernadette. Had a nice meal and drinks, which was civilised.’

He put his arm around me and gave me a squeeze. My mother went to bed. I poured what was left of our wine down the sink and tidied up the kitchen. Rob helped.

‘Was it all good, Fiona?’ he tentatively asked.

‘I was a mess, but Mam was quite matter-of-fact. Of course, it was emotionally draining, but cathartic, not dreadful. I feel better that she knows, and I don’t have to hide anything from her.’

He gave me a hug, and suddenly I felt very tired. I got two glasses of water for us and went up to bed. The house was quiet, and I was out like a light.

TWENTY

The worst bit about going was sitting in the car and waiting for the exact time of the appointment to do the dash. In this case, the dash was in a residential street, into the house of a therapist. I had to switch my phone off and put it in the glove compartment. Are they still called glove compartments? I'd never used it before these sessions, and every time I use it, the ruddy car handbook falls out. It is a hefty tome of all the car's features and warning lights. I check my phone for the time. Switch it off, stuff the handbook back in, and shut the compartment before getting out of the car.

The suburban road was always quiet. Eerily so, and I kept thinking there was surely a curtain twitcher looking to see the comings and goings from the particular house at which I was about to knock.

Rob and Ursula had insisted, well, suggested, I have therapy about Luke. I hadn't even resisted. I knew they were right, but finding someone who didn't annoy me wasn't easy. Luckily, Tanya fitted the bill. Although I thought Tanya had to be the most unlikely name for a therapist. She specialised in Gestalt therapy, which I briefly read up on and immediately forgot the details of it all. She also didn't suggest I keep a journal, which sealed the deal. For the last four months, I'd been coming, initially once a week, and now once a fortnight.

Tanya opened the door, smiled and gestured for me to come in. I'd become used to the silent greeting and directing. The small room was at the front of the house, perfect for my imagined nosey neighbour, but with blinds, a net curtain, plus curtains. It felt private and cocooned from the world. The candle was lit and the room smelt faintly of the seaside. Fresh air and salt.

I sat down and immediately examined the permanent tissue box for any sign of heavy usage. I had never seen anyone else come or go. Ursula had dissuaded me from my threatened stakeout when I initially believed the whole thing was a scam. Now, now I didn't care. The ritual of these sessions had steadied my emotions. The varied explosions of grief, anger and sadness had ebbed.

'How are you?' And we were off.

Tanya never said much, but she guided me towards and through discussions I couldn't believe I was capable of articulating. I didn't know or recognise some of the thoughts I verbalised to her at the beginning. Today was different, I had something specific.

'Good,' I answered. 'I told my mother about looking for Luke. She was quite matter-of-fact about it, and she surprised me.' I drew breath and with Tanya's encouraging look, I continued. 'She said I'd experienced a lot of trauma. In fact, she specifically talked about living with trauma around us, when and where we lived in Liverpool. I hadn't expected her to be so aware of the notion of collective and lived trauma. I was about eleven, I think, when the Hillsborough disaster happened, and I was watching it with Luke and my daddy. We were transfixed. I remember Daddy shouting at the telly, telling people to do things, and asking why wasn't anyone helping. In the end, my mother came in and switched the telly off and said we were all going to church for the six o'clock evening Mass. The church was full, and people were crying. Luke and I just held hands. Then a few years later Luke was gone.'

'How did that make you feel watching the event unfold?'

'I was glad Luke and my father hadn't gone, as they had tried to get tickets. Then both of them were gone.' First tissue down.

'Where are you feeling this now?'

'In my throat. It is always in my throat.'

'Did you say anything that day, when you were watching the television?' Tanya asked.

'No, I don't think I did. I didn't really understand what was going on. I know everything about the disaster now. In Liverpool, people talked of little else for years. Liverpool was really cut off because we knew people had died needlessly, but for years it was made out to be the fans causing trouble and being drunk.' My voice became brittle.

'Close your eyes, Fiona. I want you to think back to sitting in front of the television and what you would like to say. You don't have to say it out loud, but talk to your younger self and get her to tell you what she was thinking.'

I closed my eyes and my mind went blank, but slowly I could picture myself in our old living room and looking at the Philips television. It took a while, but part of me was transported back, and all I wanted to do was touch my daddy and hug him. In the therapist's room, tears were streaming down my face, and I was gulping. In my head, I wanted to tell my dad not to leave me, to go to the doctors to have a check-up, and for him to know I loved him. I had an involuntary huge gasp and opened my eyes. Tanya gave me a moment. I could sense her patience.

'How do you feel?'

I felt lighter. My mouth had gone dry. I faltered as I spoke.

'I...' I paused, 'I was surprised. All I wanted was my daddy. I hadn't realised how much I missed him and how, if I could go back in time, it would be him I'd want to give my attention to. He was my daddy, and I've spent too long wondering what happened and not enough time just chatting and being with him. I still play The Cranberries' *Sunday* at least once a month because it has the lyrics about not being able to say I love you. For God's sake.'

'That is grief for you, Fiona. You've now expressed and released your hurt over missed time with your father. There is no answer to this. We look back on the past with our current perspective. What you do know is your father loved you very much, and you him. That is enough.' Her voice was warm and soothing. I was emotionally spent.

She guided me to a conclusion as I sat there with my eyes closed, my hands on my knee, and a few deep breaths in and out. With a gentle business manner, Tanya suggested I start to come every three weeks and see how I got on with that.

I got back into the car and was too dazed to look for curtain twitchers. My mind was completely spaced out, so I drove off, and when I was around the corner, I found a space and pulled over. I pushed back on the seat and tipped my head upwards to try and physically connect again with my body. After what seemed an age, but was probably only five minutes, I came to.

Feeling able to drive again, I took my phone out of the glove compartment, switched it on and then connected it to the car's audio system. I was about to use my WAZE app for the quickest route home when text messages and missed calls, plus a voicemail alert, screeched into the car. I quickly listened to the voicemail. It was John asking me to come to the town hall. I phoned him back.

'Hi John'

'Hi Fiona, are you free?'

'Yes.' I must have sounded anxious as he immediately said, 'Nothing to worry about, I would like to update you on some information.'

'Is it Luke?' The panic was amplified as I spoke.

'It is, but nothing to worry about, no news, just some

questions Stuart and I need to ask you.'

John's voice was calm and he spoke very softly. My panic abated. I took a moment and some deep breaths before I let him know I'd come now. Every traffic light was against me. Every car in front of me was a Sunday driver or incapable of indicating or pulling off when the lights went green. My blood pressure must have been through the roof by the time I pulled into a space in the car park. Paying for parking was all fingers and thumbs as well. My hand was shaking so much I could barely use the app. The reception area was quiet, but both screens were occupied for the police section. I called John on my phone.

'I'm here.'

'Give me five,' he said.

I sat down on the seat along a wall facing the council reception. I couldn't remember ever coming into a civic building before the body incident. I tried not to think about that. I looked at posters I couldn't read as my eyes wouldn't focus, and stared at people. Luckily, no one noticed my intense gaze. I wasn't really looking at them, but trying to distract myself by observing them.

'Fiona.'

John was in front of me with his lanyard visible.

'Come on, follow me.'

He guided me through a door, down a corridor, and into a very basic meeting room. Stuart was there and stood up and shook my hand before we all sat down. My heart was pounding. They both looked serious.

'Do you mind if we record this?' Stuart asked.

'No, not at all,' I replied.

'It's just we need to document everything for our end,' he continued.

'We might need this later,' John said. 'Okay, so there is some information which has come to light as part of our investigation into the disappearance of your brother.'

I shuffled on the uncomfortable blue plastic chair. Stuart showed me the recording application on his computer and then pointed the camera at us all sideways on. John spoke, giving his name and details, Stuart's and mine as well.

'Right Fiona, firstly I need to let you know that since your brother's disappearance in 1995, a lot has changed. Not only in policing, but organisations that assist families in this matter. Luke was never registered other than via the initial missing person's report. He was nearly sixteen at the time and was not at the age of majority. I believe your family received no support, and actually, it would be fair to say there was not a lot of investigation into his disappearance at the time.'

This felt brutal. I didn't know if I was meant to say anything. My mouth was really dry.

'Can I have a glass of water, please?'

Stuart jumped up.

'I'll go and get you one.'

John paused the recording. He put his hand on mine.

'Sorry about this Fiona, but I need to do this properly for lots of reasons.' He looked at me with genuine concern.

'I know, it's just I'm scared. Scared of what you are going to tell me.'

He nodded, and then Stuart was back in the room.

'I could only find this.' He handed me a small bottle of water.

'Thank you.' I opened the top and gulped some water.

The recording was back on, and John continued.

'As you know, Stuart, Detective Constable Johnson, and I have been looking back over the information and have opened a new investigation into his disappearance, albeit with limited resources and availability. However, we think we have been successful in locating where he is.'

At this point, my head exploded. I wasn't expecting him to say this. Before I had a chance to say anything, I heard his voice again.

'There are some questions I need to ask you before I provide further information to verify we have the correct person.'

Again, I nodded my head.

John asked, 'Are you okay for me to proceed?'

'Yes,' I managed to say.

Stuart pushed a piece of paper towards me.

'Is this your brother, Luke Anthony Riley?'

There was a picture of him in what looked like a brown shirt and a side profile shot as well. At the top, it said West Yorkshire Police and then all his details. Again, I nodded and somehow muttered yes.

'This is a document relating to the placing of Luke on remand in 1998. He was put on remand for six months in Leeds prison.'

'What did he do?' I asked.

'On the nineteenth of June 1998 he was charged with grievous bodily harm,' Stuart said.

I gasped.

'Does the name Paul O'Brien mean anything to you?' John asked.

'Well, yes and no. I mean, he was my dad's cousin apparently, according to my mother, but I don't really recollect him, to be honest. Vaguely maybe. Why?' My mind was whirring.

'It seems that Luke assaulted him in a pub in Leeds city centre on that date. It was a Friday night and Mr O'Brien was taken to hospital with broken ribs, a broken nose and substantial cuts and bruising to his body.'

I leapt to his defence. 'Why would he do that? He wasn't violent. He was never in trouble at school, even for fighting.'

'It's okay Fiona, no one is saying anything about Luke here, but this incident did take place, and you've answered with some vital information about Mr O'Brien. Did he ever coach Luke at football?'

'Yes. I know he did because my mother said that. I do know my dad always took him to football training, and before he disappeared, he didn't want to go. Not even to the Liverpool academy session, and Luke loved football.'

There was silence. I saw John and Stuart exchange looks.

Stuart spoke. 'As part of the investigation, I cross-checked records on Paul O'Brien, and it came to light he was cited in a number of allegations of sexual assault on minors as a football coach.'

Stunned. I felt sick to the core.

'With regard to Luke and the assault incident, for which he was being held on remand, it transpired before the matter came to trial, all proceedings were dropped and he was released without charge,' Stuart stated.

'There is more Fiona,' John added. 'Are you happy to continue?'

'Yes.' Although by now tears were streaming down my face. I wiped my nose with my hand. Stuart got up and went out of the room and came back with blue paper towels.

'Sorry, all we've got to hand.' He looked sheepish, but I attempted to smile with gratitude at him.

'I'm just stunned by this. Poor Luke. Why didn't he come home?' My question was rhetorical. I couldn't understand why he didn't reach out to us.

'I can answer that, Fiona. It seems one of the police officers dealing with the incident did link him to a missing person's file, but Luke obviously made it clear he did not want his whereabouts disclosed, and as he was an adult at this point, his wishes had to be respected. All the officer could do was file a report of the discussion. Also at this point, West Yorkshire police had no knowledge of the allegations facing O'Brien.'

'When were the allegations made?'

'The first one was in 1995 but nothing was done. There were a few more the following year, but by then he had moved to Manchester. He must have been on a night out in Leeds. Anyway, by 2003, due to a change in the law, there were multiple retrospective allegations made by adults who'd been coached by O'Brien. Unfortunately, before he was interviewed, he skipped the country, unsurprisingly to Thailand. There is a warrant for his arrest.'

I heard Stuart mutter, 'He's not the only one there.'

'He caused our family all of this.' I could feel the rage heating up inside of me, I knew my cheeks were flushed.

'Fiona, we don't know for sure,' John paused, 'but I agree the circumstantial evidence points towards his actions having a bearing on Luke's disappearance. This is something we need to talk to Luke about, as we will add any information he can give us to the file.'

I looked puzzled.

'Talk to him?'

Stuart looked at John and then at me.

'Fiona, I believe I've located your Luke, despite tracing several Luke Riley's,' Stuart said.

I was trembling, I could feel the pace of my heart quickening.

'Where? Where is he?' My voice was pinched.

Stuart hesitated.

'Lisbon, we believe he is in Lisbon, Portugal.'

He pushed another piece of paper to me with a photocopy

of an identification card. I couldn't read it, but there was his name and a photo of a man in, maybe his forties, who looked exactly as I would have imagined Luke to look. I pushed it away. My hands pushed me up out of the chair.

'STOP RECORDING!' I shouted.

Then I buckled. I screamed and I screamed. I heard chairs moving, felt an arm on my right shoulder and one under my left arm. I was being supported as I cried and wailed. I heard John's voice, 'Fiona, it is going to be okay.' Then a 'Fuck, I should have had Ursula here.'

Eventually, the noise I was making subsided, and I was manoeuvred back into the horrid plastic chair. Stuart was then kneeling beside me, propping me up with his left shoulder. John was also kneeling in front of me. They must have moved the chair. He was wiping my face. I took the blue paper towel and carried on wiping. My hands were weak.

'How are you feeling?' John asked.

I shook my head. I couldn't speak.

'Look, Stuart will get you a cup of tea and I'm here with you.' He gestured to Stuart, and by the tipping of his hand, I guessed he meant add sugar. This made me laugh.

'I'm not laughing,' I said. I wasn't really. Everything had become an involuntary action. I needed to get my thoughts back under control. I was a mess. A snotty, broken mess. My brother was alive. I was ecstatic and hurt.

'Thirty years,' was the next thing I said. Was it thirty or was it less or more? I didn't know anymore. With John patiently sitting on the floor next to me, saying nothing, my reaction to the news eventually subsided.

'How are you doing?'

'Grand,' was all I could muster.

He returned my 'grand' with an 'awesome'.

'Yes John, it is awesome, my brother has been alive all this time.' He winced as I said it.

Stuart came back with the cup of tea. I took a sip, and it did have sugar in it. I took in a deep breath and let out a massive sigh.

'I'm sorry John, I didn't mean that. I'm sorry. It is the shock. I thought I knew how I'd feel. All happy and elated, but actually it's been an almighty shock,' my voice dropped off.

Suddenly, Stuart took charge. He switched back on the recording.

'Fiona, everyone reacts differently, and it is never easy, but can you confirm please that the photo identification I've shown you, a Portuguese national card, is indeed, to the best of your knowledge, your missing brother Luke Riley.'

'Yes,' I replied.

'Good. I would like to say we are really pleased we have located him. However, we have no jurisdiction or ability to conduct further investigations. By this, I mean you will have to go to Lisbon to track down your brother. Do you want to do this?'

There it was. The reality. I had to go to Lisbon to see if it really was Luke.

'I do. I mean, I will. How did you find him?' I felt composed now.

'By chance really. I'd exhausted all the known routes. Your brother certainly didn't leave the country on a British or Irish passport. In fact, he has only his Portuguese national card and a Portuguese passport. As you can appreciate, there are a lot of Irish citizens called Luke Riley living and working here and in Europe.' Stuart grinned.

I sort of smiled back as I was thinking how soon I could get on a plane to Lisbon.

'The breakthrough was his national insurance number and his release papers. He must have used them at some point in obtaining his Portuguese papers. I don't know how, but when I crossed-referenced his national insurance number, it came up on the Europol system, which we still have access to, and his information was on the system due to his release papers in 1999 and predated Brexit. The Portuguese police must have checked him out, and because he was of no concern, they put his Portuguese tax number against his name as a reference. I knew he was in Portugal at this point, so I could narrow the search,' Stuart explained. 'With this information, it was easy to ask some basic information without causing alarm. I'll confess we used the sexual assault allegations and asked the Portuguese police permission to, if necessary, make a phone call for a statement. They took ages to get back to us, but this week they did. With his name and work information only. No private address.' John explained.

'Are you going to call him?' I asked.

'No. We can't. We'd need authorisation from the Portuguese as they don't take kindly to any police, outside of their sovereignty, contacting citizens without permission, and especially now we are no longer in the European Union.' He sighed. 'We really can't do anything more as we are not actively on an open case on this end either. Merely tying up loose ends, really.'

'I can put you in touch with a charity who work on international missing cases if you'd like me to?' Stuart added.

'No, that's not necessary. I've read up on all the missing charity information and what they can do. I've got this. I'm going to Lisbon. It's what my daddy would have done.'

Both men glanced at each other, unsure what to say next.

'Fiona, Stuart will drive you home in your car and I'll follow to bring him back. Would that be acceptable for you? I don't want you driving now. It's been a huge upheaval, and we should have planned it better, but you know...' John didn't finish his sentence.

'I understand. I'm not sure there is any good way to do this.'

I raised my eyebrows in acknowledgement of the circumstances. I felt calmer. I also felt giddy with excitement and trepidation. He really was alive. I finished my cup of tea while both John and Stuart sorted themselves out. I was glad for some time on my own to process it all. I was still shaking and my legs were like jelly. I realised I only had my phone and car keys with me. I couldn't sort out my face. I must look a right state. Before I knew it, Stuart was driving me home. A quick glance in the passenger mirror revealed a blotchy face and very puffy eyes. Yikes.

'Sorry, there was no other way to do it,' Stuart said as we stopped at the traffic lights.

'Better than telling me he was dead,' I responded.

'True,' he replied ruefully. 'We, well, I want to say if you need me to come in with you when you get home, I will.'

'Thanks Stuart, but I think one wailing woman is enough for you in one day.'

He smiled. I smiled. The day suddenly looked brighter.

I waved them both off after being dropped off. I opened the front door and said a tentative 'Hello'. My watch said one-thirty. I realised I left the house at eight this morning. I took off my shoes and walked to the kitchen. The bi-fold doors were open and I could see my mother sat outside. I grabbed a glass of water and went out to join her.

'Budge up, Bernie,' I couldn't resist saying.

'You've been a while,' she said as she shuffled along the outside garden sofa.

'I know, Mammy,' I gulped.

I didn't know what to say to her. I took her hand. She gave me a quizzical look. The air became still.

'What is it, cherub?' Her voice tightened.

'Oh Mammy, it is Luke.' I started to sob.

'Fiona, I need to know! What is it?'

'They've found him. They have actually found him.'

'Is he alive? Tell me he is alive!' Her eyes beseeched me.

'He is, he really is.'

There I was crying all over again, holding her hand.

'Come here, you poor love.'

She pulled me to her, and my head was in her lap as she stroked my hair. We were like this for some time before I sat back up, unable to say anything. My mother hadn't even cried one tear. She was smiling.

'I knew he was alive. I never doubted it for one minute. You have no idea how happy this makes me feel.'

Her hand gripped mine tighter. Then the sobbing came. Quieter than mine, but a release nonetheless. It was my turn to hold her. Our moment had come. It took us a while to gather ourselves and to explain everything to her. We decided to pick the children up as normal, and I'd ask Rob to come home early. Over the next few hours, it took all of our mental focus not to mention anything and attempt to act as normal. How Mam managed to make a meal for us all, I do not know. I was all for ordering takeaway, but she insisted. Of course, I told Rob the gist of it when I called him. There was no way not to. By the time we were all sitting down, I felt utterly drained. It was the mix of anticipation and knowledge, not to mention the physical limitations of geography. I played with the food on my plate. My mouth was too dry to attempt to eat.

'Mum, you're not eating,' Alice said gleefully as she was always being chivvied along when eating food she didn't like or was 'off'.

'I'm not that hungry to be honest, love.'

'And you look sad, and come to think of it, why is Dad home early?'

I looked at Rob and Mam. Alice spotted the exchange.

'Well. Are you pregnant?' She exclaimed.

Do not burst into tears, Fiona. Do not burst into tears. Composure. At which point my mother did.

'Mamo, why are you crying?' Henry asked immediately.

'It's Luke, we think he's been found,' she blurted out.

Henry punched the air.

'You were right, you knew he was still alive!' He got off his chair and gave her a hug.

'Really?' Alice's eyes were like saucers.

Rob spoke and gave the same outline I'd given him. All of the commotion distracted me from the shock of it all, and a little bit of me allowed some joy to seep into my veins. I filled them in with all the details.

'Are we all going to Lisbon?' Henry asked.

'No, just me,' I answered. 'It would be too overwhelming if more than one person went. It also might not be him.' I cautioned.

By now they'd seen the photocopy of the photocopy Stuart had given me.

'It is,' Henry and Alice almost said in unison. They'd only ever seen the meagre collection of photos from when he was little to fifteen.

Only Tyrel was quiet.

'You alright mate?' Rob asked.

'I'll have to leave now you've found him,' he replied.

It shocked us all. We'd been so caught up in the moment we'd forgotten Tyrel wasn't part of the years of longing and hope.

'No!' This time, Alice and Henry were in unison and looked horrified.

'We found you Tyrel, first. You're not going anywhere,' Bernadette said.

He shuffled on his chair. I picked my words carefully.

'This is your family now Tyrel, if you want us. We'd hate to lose you. We've lived with Luke missing for years. This is a surprise development. One we'd always hoped for, but never knew if it was anything more than just hope to be honest.'

'Mate, you are not going anywhere. It's even with you around, otherwise it would be three against two,' Rob added.

Tyrel began to relax a little, and I immediately made a note in my head to speak to the foster team for advice. Then Bernadette sealed it for him. She reached across the table and grabbed his right hand.

'I couldn't bear to lose you too.' She squeezed his hand. He squeezed hers back.

More questions and more speculation carried on as everyone had finished eating or given up. Bit by bit, we moved from the table and cleared things up. No one went to watch television, no aimless flicking through the channels.

'Alexa, play *Happier*,' Alice suddenly said.

'Playing *Happier* by Marshmello featuring Bastile.'

She grabbed her mamo and made her dance with her, holding hands. Before long, we were all dancing around in the kitchen as Tyrel and Alice chose tune after tune.

'Was that the f word?' My mam exclaimed at one point and carried on hopping from side to side. There was gaiety in her voice and her movement.

Rob pulled me close to him. We were side by side.

'We've got this,' he whispered. Finally, I smiled, really smiled.

TWENTY ONE

The morning sun fell heavily onto the bed. My face felt red from the warmth. I must have snorted myself out of my slumber. The next moment, my feet were being held and Rob attempted to pull me down the bed under the duvet.

'Arghhh, stop it!'

'Someone is chirpy this morning. This is your punishment for jumping on me when you got home last night.'

'I didn't!' More in hope.

'You did.'

I groaned, crawled back up to the pillows, and realised today was the morning after the night before...

...'What have I missed?'

My opening words as I joined Caroline and Ursula on our evening out. The bar was already full at six-thirty in the evening. It was definitely a Friday night crowd. The twilight point where some groups of mothers were still there. Their meal finished, and yet there they were still chatting with an almost finished bottle of wine, their children fixated on their iPads, apart from two feral boys who wished they'd had a ball to play with instead of napkin chucking. Then at the actual bar, the middle-aged lads on their pints, starting to hit the guffaw stage. The spectacle of the known, the usual Friday night, on the night before I flew out to Lisbon.

'Not much, unless you count Ursula telling her John story,' Caroline winked.

'What?'

'You sure?' Ursula looked fed up about having to repeat it.

'Go on.'

She sighed and said, 'I heard Stuart calling John 'The Pope' when saying goodbye to him a couple of days ago.'

'And?'

'Well, it turns out John's middle name is Paul, and of course, he was a graduate trainee in the height of John Paul the Second being Pope. When his colleagues found out his middle name, it became his nickname.'

I laughed; it was funny.

'Did you laugh?' I asked Ursula.

'I did then, it was funny the first time. Only John could have had Paul as his middle name.'

'Cheers to the Pope of Surrey Police.' I filled my glass from the bottle of prosecco. Caroline always ordered prosecco; she only drank Italian alcoholic offerings, despite being half French.

'How did it go?' She asked. I knew she was referring to my afternoon of interviews.

'We have two new recruits. On a freelance contract basis initially. They both already do gardening work and are happy to be our hardcore gang.'

Ursula giggled.

'Fiona! Well, who are they?' Caroline rolled her eyes.

'One's called Jay, and the other fit lad is Steve. They are keen and obviously hit the gym at four o'clock every day. They're both really nice and up for the work, what more can you ask for?' I was triumphant. Caroline poked me in the ribs.

'Ouch.'

'As long as they do a good job, I don't care, but it will be good to meet them. I'm not sure HR will approve of you calling them fit lads, and you need to give me their details.'

'Funny you should say that, but I might have mentioned we were out tonight. I sort of invited them to meet us if they wanted to. I'm sure they've got better things to do after their gym session on a Friday night.'

'I don't think they'll want to hang around with us,' Caroline said and pulled a wry face. 'What made you ask them here? What were you thinking?'

'Not much, other than their muscles,' Ursula laughed.

'Ha ha! Not entirely true, I must say, before madam from HR berates me again. I accept I can be accused of favouring looks, but truthfully, they were the only candidates who didn't stink of weed. One guy was missing a tooth and a joint fell out of his shorts' pocket when he got his mobile out. He told me he started the day with one. At least he was honest.' I shrugged my shoulders.

'Blimey!'

'Yes, blimey Caro, I'm pretty sure Jay and Steve won't be joining us, but they were decent and seemed competent. If they are not any good, they are contractors, so no complications if it doesn't work out.'

I reached down to my tote bag that I'd dumped on the floor and pulled out two packs, one for each of them.

'These are the new business details, and my handover to you both while I'm away. Did you think I'd lost my control freak touch when it comes to work? And while we are at it, can we order some food?'

Whilst Caroline and Ursula read through my business outline, I ordered food for us. The pack contained the new business name *Serene Spaces* and detailed the bespoke solutions the customer could choose. I'd broken the offerings down to *Classic Cottage*, all flowing flowers, colour and meadow elements. *Totally Tranquil,* which was water features, grasses and shrubs, and finally, *Form and Function* focused on the outdoor kitchen, eating and barbeque area. Then a list of all the garden maintenance options after landscaping makeovers. I briefed them on my vision.

'The goal here is to franchise the business in the same way those lawn ones have been. No one knows how to choose a gardener. It is all word of mouth, and you don't really know what you are getting. This cuts out the faff, in the same way the looking after your lawn lot do.'

Caroline and Ursula read through my pack. I sipped my drink in a bid not to guzzle and realised my anticipation about Lisbon was building.

'I really like it all, Fiona.' Ursula beamed at me, bringing me back to the evening and not tomorrow.

'Good, because I'm relying on you to plan the launch event.' I didn't have a creative bone in my body. I'd already pulled in a branding favour from an old colleague for the names and positioning of my idea for the business.

'I've already got an outline idea prepped for tonight based on our previous conversations.'

We were interrupted by the food arriving. After a few mouthfuls, we managed to resume chatting about the business launch event.

'Come on Ursula, we are all ears now.'

'Okay, but do not react immediately.' She drew breath, 'I'm planning a hoedown.'

Silence.

'I'm taking the silence as you not reacting.'

Caroline and I nodded our heads.

'The plan is to hire The Barn, you know, the place at Malden Rushett. It's where we did the Tyrel handover. It has plenty of space and gives us an opportunity to showcase the proposed garden spaces, plus we can use bales as seating and have a band doing country songs, mainly Dolly Parton, and line dancing.

Now you can react.'

I took a swig of prosecco.

'Bloody love it, Ursula.'

'My only worry is, and it is just a worry as they do have weddings there and other parties, is it too upbeat an event for the brand name you've come up with?'

'Good grief, no. It's totally awesome. We are selling a concept, not expecting people to have a miserable time when they come to the launch. Will the press come?'

'Can't see why not. Most of them live around here now, and it *is* still London, however much on the edge of it, it is. Phew, managed to get that out, the fizz is going to my head. Can we get some rosé now?'

'I'll get it.' Caroline got up and went to the bar.

Ursula and I carried on talking about the event, and Caroline came back with a bottle of wine and glasses. She took the finished prosecco out of the cool bucket and plonked the rosé bottle in it instead.

'You didn't have to go to the bar,' I said

'Oh, I had a message I needed to reply to and didn't want to be rude at the table. Honestly Ursula, I can't wait to do the line dancing. I mean what a hoot!' Caroline responded.

'Will you be alright to do the planning for the garden landscaping and plants while I'm away?'

'Yes. You're only away for a week anyway.'

'I know, but I am doing a dump and run.' I didn't want to think about my trip, but I couldn't avoid it.

'Oh gosh Fiona, less about the business and more about what you are going to do in Lisbon. How do you feel?'

Caroline grabbed my hand and held it. Always her touchy-feely self. I didn't want my hand to be held, but I controlled the urge to pull it away and attempted to relax into her thoughtfulness and caring.

'You don't have to say anything, Fiona.' Ursula could read my thoughts at that moment.

I hesitated some more. What could I say? I had a plan, but was it a reasonable one? Would I actually find him, and would he talk to me?

'I'm winging it. I'm booked into the hotel he works at. Although I got Rob to do the booking in case he read through the booking names. I've no idea what he does there or if he is still there. I've read up on disappointment about five hundred times. I'm there for a week, but can come back earlier if I need to as I bought a flexi ticket. Mammy is beside herself with excitement, expecting him to return with me. I'm not sure it will happen. Basically, watch this space.'

Either the drink or my talking out loud fuelled a rising panic about the trip. I wish I smoked. I could pretend to have to go outside for a cigarette and then hyperventilate.

'Fiona, go and get some fresh air, you've gone pale. Paler than your normal paleness. Sorry, alabaster Irish skin.' Ursula winked and shooed me with her arms. Caroline looked guilty for asking in the first place.

'Five minutes, okay? I do need a moment.' I felt relieved.

Outside, I drank in the not-so-fresh high street petrol-filled air, but the air and space stopped the momentary anxiety. After a while of suffering from the outside vaping filling up my nostrils with repellent, sweet, sickly smells, I turned to go back inside. Two spruced-up men walking towards the bar on the pavement caught my eye. I took a second look.

'Alright, Fiona?'

'Alright, Jay?' And then I nodded at Steve.

'Hi,' he replied, also nodding.

'You both came.'

'Yes, it is Friday night. This place makes a change from our usual haunts.' Steve delivered this with a massive grin.

I laughed. Tonight really was taking a turn.

'Come on, I'll introduce you to the other oldies.' With that, I linked both my arms through theirs and we squeezed through the open door. It was completely satisfying to see Caroline and Ursula's mouths drop. I stood at our table and made the introductions.

'Steve, meet Caroline and Ursula.'

'And I'm Jay.'

It was handshakes all round and a massive effort to get them sat with us by pinching a couple of chairs. I asked them what they wanted to drink and they opted for red wine. My mood had elevated to party. My impending trip was downgraded from being utmost in my thoughts. Now I was focused on the evening. Returning to the table from the bar laden with two bottles and a new cool bucket, I plonked everything down, interrupting the flow of conversation.

'This is why I never used to drink on a works night out, I'm too much of a control freak to want to be missing out on conversations.'

'Come on Fiona, you can only sack yourself now, and if you are that fascinated by small talk, I suggest you ask a totally inappropriate question.' Ursula had a giddy edge as she raised her glass for me to fill.

'I was asking Jay and Steve about their current projects,' Caroline added.

Ursula rolled her eyes which looked slightly pissed. Maybe I shouldn't have got another bottle of lady petrol.

'Right, so Jay, and Steve, we might as well get all our cards on the table,' I said, although this was driven by slight inebriation.

'Go on mate, this sounds interesting.' Steve nudged Jay in

the process.

Ursula shook her head at me.

'No, it's too late now to back out.' Jay laughed.

'Thanks, Fiona.'

Having everyone's attention, I took a deep breath, a swig of rosé, and proceeded.

'Might as well be honest here. I'm about to hot-foot it off to Lisbon to hopefully find my brother who's been missing for over thirty years.' I paused and was gratified to see them both look taken aback. I carried on.

'She,' I said and pointed at Ursula, 'is recently divorced and loved up with the detective who is dealing with the dead body we dug up.'

Mouths hit the table at this point.

'Whilst Caroline is the only sane one amongst us, working towards doing something at the Chelsea Flower Show.'

'No I'm not, Fiona. I'm doing all the qualifications I can possibly muster to be good at my job, which I happen to love. Despite the fact that you forced us to do it. Don't take any notice of her, she's a big softie and has recently fostered a lad who was in a terrible bind.'

'Fuck me,' Jay said.

'Too much?' I started to squirm inwardly.

'No, sounds all very reasonable, but I can only counter with single and fed up. Lover boy here,' he said and pointed at Steve, 'is about to become a runaway groom if his fiancée asks him what colour the wedding napkins should be. But all good otherwise.'

Maybe it wasn't the wisest of ice breakers, but before I knew it, we were all discussing what colour the wedding napkins should be and trying to put a playlist together for the evening do. The bar music was turned up, and as diners left, we had room for some moves.

'Oh, I love this song,' I said as I heard the words *Sweet Sensation.*

Next thing I knew, I was raising my arms to the song, and Jay was also up on his feet.

'Didn't have you down as a Chase and Status fan,' he said as we both shuffled.

'I know not the most danceable tune outside of a sweaty jumping up and down mosh pit.'

'Tell us a bit more about the dead body?' he asked.

I carried on with my moves and then signalled to go to the bar. 'Shots?' I asked.

'Alright, tequila or a cheeky sambuca?' Jay laughed.

'Tequila.'

As we waited to be served, I gave him a brief and as coherent as possible outline of the events at Mr Etheridge's. We finally returned, and everyone was dancing to Cedric Gervais' *Do it Tonight.*

'Tune!' I said as I barged next to Ursula, who was flinging her arms in the air whilst doing the looking down head shake thing. Jay and I handed out the shots, and Caroline announced she was off to the DJ to ask for ABBA.

'Stop her!' I heard Steve shout as she went off.

I'm not sure I remember much after that apart from lots of dancing, laughing, and last-minute dashes to the loo...

'You have to get up soon, you've got a plane to catch.' Rob was smoothing my hair. I sat bolt upright in the bed.

'Ouch.'

'Head hurting?'

'A bit. Not sure if due to dehydration or lack of sleep,' I answered. Both probably.

'Well, I let you fall back to sleep, but Alice is fretting you'll miss the plane.'

'What more than my mother? Surprised she hasn't appeared and thrown a bucket of cold water over my face and forced me to eat.'

'I've prevented it so far, but unless you show your face soon, you are toast.'

Reluctantly, I got up and showered. I noticed I had a few bruises from last night appearing mainly on my legs. Good grief, what was I thinking? Talk about peaking too soon. I was meant to be fresh and ready for Lisbon. After breakfast, which was nearly lunch, I called Ursula.

'Mate,' was how she answered the phone.

'That bad?'

'We were a bit wrecked. Not sure John is speaking to me. He's certainly rolled his eyes at me a few times today,' she said.

'I'd better phone Caroline and check she is okay.'

'I wouldn't. You might have suggested she took Jay home with her last night. In front of Jay.'

There was silence.

'No! Did I?'

'Yep. Totally cringe, but leave it and everyone will have forgotten in a couple of days. Text her when you get to Lisbon to let her know you've arrived,' Ursula suggested.

I thought I'd best take the advice in this instance.

'Will do. Was I really dreadful?' My voice faltered.

'Of course not. We were all a bit 'Friday night fever', I would say. Don't think about it, and also text me when you get there. And...' she said, followed by hesitation 'If you need to call, please do, no matter what time.'

'It's the same time zone.'

'I know that silly, but if you need to talk and can't get hold of Rob, then I'm fine to call,' she said.

'Thanks Ursula, look, I'd better finish packing and get going.'

I hesitated before I said goodbye as I wanted to say 'love you' but it wasn't my style, but at that moment, aside from my family, Ursula and Caroline felt like the most important people in the world to me.

In a haze, I managed to finish my packing. It was particularly painful to say goodbye to Mammy. The hug was crushing, she held me so tight with all of her hope bound up in it. Even Tyrel looked genuinely concerned. His absorption into the family had enriched us. We felt fuller and more of a unit. I made a mental note to buy him a tin of sardines on the way back. Alice had already given me a duty-free list, although she did look a bit sheepish when she handed it to me. Rob cajoled me into the car and off we drove to Gatwick.

The journey was silent. I knew he wanted to give me advice and a mini Ted talk –

the strain of saying nothing was playing out as cursing all other drivers – but he didn't. My stomach did multiple somersaults as we arrived at departures.

'It's costing me a fiver to drop you off and give you a hug,' Rob said as he pulled into a space.

It was a very heartfelt hug.

'You're crushing my ribs, like Mammy did.'

'Don't exaggerate.'

He stepped back, holding me, and gave me a rueful smile, ruffled my hair and a final kiss goodbye on my forehead.

I was alone. Coffee was required. I dragged my head, along with my body, through all the mechanics of getting through departures, the glare of duty-free, and to the lounge. Thank goodness I had lounge access on this ticket, as I had no ability to deal with ordering food from anywhere. The hangover had a solid grip on my coordination. Everything I was doing required focus. Thanks to my stupidity last night, I didn't even care when they announced the plane was delayed by an hour. I had nothing left inside me to get indignant with. When I finally boarded, I slumped into the seat, head leaning against the window, and I was asleep.

TWENTY TWO

'Passport, please,' a smiling man in a grey suit with a name badge asked me after he'd found my reservation. I leant on the hotel desk, partly due to tiredness but more to keep my head down. It was late and I needed to go to sleep to be fresh for my enquiries about Luke. My surname didn't seem to beget curiosity. It looked a lovely international hotel and, in fact, there seemed to be an opticians conference taking place, judging by the banners and a few people sat in the bar with lanyards.

'May I have your credit card?'

I handed it over and tried to look engaged in the mini bar explanation and breakfast information. I gave a nod to the receptionist and politely declined someone bringing my case up to the room. The lift, with its view of the street, whisked me to the eighth floor. Despite being utterly shattered, I unpacked my suitcase, put all my toiletries out, and had a shower. Then fell into bed and a deep sleep immediately.

My alarm went off and I snoozed it. Ten minutes later, it went off again, and I forced myself up out of bed and opened the curtains after pressing them the wrong way several times. My view was of a road, some buildings, and the hotel bar below. It looked very warm and sunny outside.

'Come on Fiona, stop stalling, you've got to do this,' I said aloud.

Saying it out loud helped me to remember why I was here. It felt unreal. I felt very unsure of everything right now. I wanted to call Rob but texted him instead to say '*Morning xx*'. Another shower and I was washed and dressed for the day ahead. I packed my bag to take with me to breakfast so I didn't have to come back up to the room. I certainly hadn't listened to the guy last night as I had to go back up one floor to get to the breakfast restaurant. I must have looked so dodgy as I kept looking to see if I could spot Luke. But no one seemed to be particularly interested in me.

The restaurant was busy and I was directed to a table for four. The other set places were swiftly cleared. I ordered coffee and was asked if I wanted anything, but I wasn't particularly hungry and could help myself to the breakfast buffet spread anyway. I forced some yoghurt and fruit down me, then picked on a pain au chocolat. I checked my watch and it was quarter to nine. I don't know why I was waiting until nine o'clock to go to reception, but I was.

Of course, reception was busy checking people out, and I couldn't ask my question in a crowded environment. I wandered aimlessly out of the hotel and walked up towards the peak of the hill the hotel was on. I passed a static, iconic yellow Lisbon tram next to an actual tramline where I had to stop and wait for the tram to pass. Instead of continuing to walk towards what looked like a shopping centre, I followed the tramline down the hill. It led me to a small park on the left where there was a kiosk serving coffee and food. I got myself a coffee and sat down at a table. The metal chair had some residue of morning dew generated by the shade of the trees which I hadn't noticed when I sat down. I nearly cried about this, although I didn't really care about my now damp shorts, it was the being alone. I felt lost and alone in a strange city with nothing to connect me to its being other than hope. After years of never crying or shedding a tear, my newly acquired emotional flare-ups were exhausting. I tried to watch the people around me and take in the surroundings, but the pressure of my question kept building. After twenty minutes or so of fidgeting, I got up and retraced my route. This time, I did venture towards the shopping centre. Everything was opening slowly. There was no urgency. I'd forgotten it was a Sunday but decided to kill more time peering at shop windows. When I could bear it no more and everything was very much open, I left to go back to the hotel. Outside, the sun was higher and the morning warmer, and I could no longer put off the inevitable.

'Hi, can I speak to the manager, please?'

'May I ask the nature of your enquiry?' was the very polite response.

I hesitated.

'I'm trying to make contact with one of your team.' I swallowed and then forced his name out. 'Luke Riley.'

'Luke?'

'Yes, Luke.'

The man at reception turned to his female colleague and spoke to her in Portuguese. She shrugged at the mention of the name Luke. He turned back to me.

'Can you please write this name for me?'

I did as requested on the paper with the pen he passed to me. One of the doormen wandered over and looked at the name. He spoke rapidly to them both and said the name 'Luca'.

'Sim, sim.' The guy was nodding now.

'Ah, my colleague has pointed out you are asking about Luca.'

Am I? I didn't know what to think, so I said yes.

'He is not here.'

'Oh. Has he left?'

'No, he has his day off. I think he is back tomorrow.'

I was crestfallen. Another day of waiting.

'I'm his sister.' The words came out. Was I his sister? Was

this the same person.

'Go to the beach,' he replied.

'The beach?' I didn't know why he said that.

'Yes, he'll be there with his partner Andre. At the bar.'

I had a vision of a drunk Luke with his boyfriend. Was this who my brother was?

'Which beach?' I gathered my thoughts and became focused. 'I've not been here before.'

'It is called Praia do Guincho, it is near Cascais. You can get the train to Cascais, then a taxi, or get a taxi straight from the hotel to the beach. We can book for you?'

'Yes, I'll take a taxi, please. I'll go back to my room and be back down shortly.'

'Okay, that is no problem. When you come down, go to my colleague, the doorman, and he will arrange a taxi straightaway.'

'Thank you.'

'You're welcome.'

When I got to my floor, I practically ran to my room. I couldn't remember what I had packed. Then I had an internal meltdown because why on earth was I fussing about what to wear when I had no idea if Luca was Luke and if he was there anyway. I phoned Rob.

'I can't breathe.' I didn't even say hello back to him.

'Talk me through it,' he replied.

I garbled everything out.

'It is fine. You are allowed to have a mild panic over what to wear. Just take a few breaths in and a long exhalation out.'

I did as instructed and slowly felt the panic subside.

'How are you feeling?' Rob asked.

'Bit better. Less spaced out.'

'Good, what have you got with you?'

'A week's worth of clothes but no beach clobber. I didn't

think about the beach.'

Are you planning on going into the sea?'

'No,' I responded.

'Well, don't stress. Wear what you want, you live in flip-flops anyway. Charge your phone before you go and call me when you get there.'

'I will. How's Mammy?'

'She's chewing her fists and dusting skirting boards. She can't eat, but I've made her drink water.'

I sighed. The pressure returned and I took in a deep breath.

'I'll go now, and love you, Rob.'

'Love you too, Fiona.'

With renewed faith, I managed to get my act together. I changed out of the damp shorts and into a tiered short sundress with pockets. I kept my flip-flops on and put sunglasses, sunscreen, my purse, and some lipstick into my shoulder bag. I gave my phone another five minutes to charge before I left the room.

I stood on the cobbled pavement outside the hotel, waiting for the taxi. I'd read in the hotel information that the pavements of Lisbon were covered in these distinctive small, handcrafted limestone or basalt stones arranged in intricate patterns. My eyes concentrated on their smoothness, and picked out the ground-in daily dirt. The doorman interrupted my thoughts.

'You haven't seen Luca for a while, huh?' he asked.

'No. Not for a long time.'

'It'll be good. You will like. Here is your taxi.'

He opened the back passenger door. He leaned into the front passenger seat and I caught the words Guincho and *rapido*. The driver spoke back, and with a tap of the doorman's hand on the roof, we were off. I'd like to say the journey afforded me time to relax, but I spent the whole journey praying not to crash. If the taxi driver wasn't changing lanes suddenly, someone was drifting into ours or pulling in. Only the slowing down to go through a toll booth allowed me a moment to release my clutching of the seat and the seat belt. Thirty-five euros later, I staggered out onto a dirt track with the driver gesturing to a path leading to the beach.

There were cars parked everywhere and people meandering down towards the beach. Halfway down there was a shop, and below there, a beach bar. Then the wooden path ran down to the beach, surrounded by sand, pointing towards the sea which stretched blue to the horizon. Even with sunglasses, the sun glared all around. I went into the shop and bought a towel, bikini, and a basket. I looked at the bar area. It was already full, and I couldn't see any sign of Luke. Faltering, I approached and asked for a table. The young woman took my name and suggested I return in half an hour. I made my way down to the beach, found a spot on the hot sand and awkwardly changed into the new bikini, gripping the towel covering me with my teeth. I wrapped my dress around all the contents of the newly purchased basket and ran down to the sea.

It was freezing. A very blue, clear and cold Atlantic. Bit by bit, I waded in, and when my stomach was covered, I flung the rest of me forward, deep into the incoming wave. The rush of cold was exhilarating. Standing up, I brushed my hair back and allowed the sun to warm my face. Reluctant to leave my belongings for long, I took one more plunge and headed back to my spot. I lay down on the towel and allowed myself to dry in the sunshine. I realised this was the first time I'd truly been on my own for over fifteen years. I wasn't in reach. No one could demand anything of me, and I couldn't rush back home if I wanted to. It was bliss. For a brief moment, my reason for being here was forgotten as my body relaxed lying down on the towel and sand.

The timer went off on my phone. I got up and shook out my towel. I rubbed the sand off my legs, and although my bikini was still damp, I put my dress over the top. I walked barefoot back to the bar.

There was a table ready for me. The outside area was nicely shaded and I sat down on the chair with the sea view. Which I immediately regretted as my back was to the rest of the bar area. I looked at the menu and turned my head around to see if I could spy anyone resembling Luke. A lithe, beautiful young lady with the greenest eyes I had ever seen came to the table and initially spoke to me in Portuguese.

'Do you speak English?' I asked

'Yes.' Her response was almost as bored as any delivery from Alice. I suppressed a laugh.

'Okay, do you know a Luke Riley?'

Her face changed. I wasn't sure if she looked alarmed or puzzled.

'Sure.'

'Is he here now?'

She turned, walked off, hung over a rail, and shouted to what looked like a stack of surfboards. 'Papa,' I heard her say. The rest I didn't catch, but I stood up and looked in the direction she was facing. All of a sudden, I heard a voice, a voice I knew immediately. I ran to the spot, and there, looking up, was Luke. He was a bit taller than I remembered. His still wavy hair was tucked behind his ears and was peppered with grey. The man before me was muscular and tanned. He saw me and ran up to the restaurant where we were standing.

We were both facing each other. Tears were streaming down my face. I was shaking, and before I knew it, the young woman had grabbed my hand and had put her other arm around my shoulder.

'Please, are you alright?' I heard her ask.

'Luke,' was all I could say.

The next moment, he was there, holding me up, and I collapsed into his arms. All I could hear between my sobbing was a voice saying 'Fiona, Fiona' over and over again. Eventually, I lifted my head up and looked at him. His face was as tear-splattered as mine. I started to laugh.

'What? What's so funny.'

'We both look like a pair of snotty eejits.' I then promptly began to cry again.

Luke guided me to the table where my basket was, and we both sat down. I couldn't let go of his hand. I'm sure everyone was looking at us, but I was absorbed in the moment.

'Papa!'

'Sorry Ines. Ines, this is my sister Fiona.'

'Oh, she is my aunty.'

The next moment, Ines flung her arms around me and kissed both my cheeks.

I looked at both of them.

'Yes, this is my daughter, Ines. She is seventeen and normally at school, but they have finished their term exams.'

I wasn't really interested in his explanation as the questions I wanted to ask flooded into my head.

'But Andre is your partner, they said at the hotel?'

'Yes, my business partner, Fiona.'

'Are you married?' I heard a bit of anger in my voice as I asked this question.

'I am, to Ines's mother. Her name is Carla.'

It all brimmed over.

'How could you? I couldn't get married because you and Dad left me!'

Both Ines and Luke exchanged looks, and Ines took off.

Luke grabbed my hand.

'I'm sorry Fiona, I am.'

He hung his head.

'I know about everything.' With Ines gone, I couldn't stop myself from saying it.

It was his turn to display a flash of anger. I saw it in his face, and then I regretted it. I regretted my anger because it was all my pain, lashing out for no reason. I took his hand this time.

'No, I'm sorry. I've missed you, and we've been looking for you forever. We never gave up hope. Well, Daddy did, it killed him, the hope.'

'That's not fair, Fiona. He had prostate cancer.'

'How do you know?'

'I had my ways, and I came to the funeral.'

'You came to the funeral? Why didn't you come home?'

He sighed. 'Look, let's not go over everything right now. I was still caught up in a lot of shit at that point.'

There he was, my brother. He was alive, and he had survived.

'Luke, I really do know. The police know, and I haven't told Mammy, but you weren't the only one,' I said.

He leant back and took in a deep breath. Before another word could be exchanged, a woman was pulling me to my feet.

'Fiona, oh it is you, my *querida,* finally I can hold you.' Although she was slightly smaller than me, I was again being crushed.

'You tell your brother off. I have been telling him this for years, no.' She looked at Luke with a sense of satisfaction.

'Fiona, meet Carla.'

He gestured his hand in her direction. She took absolutely no notice of him and focused all her attention on me.

'What can we do? Where are you staying?'

It was a barrage of questions, all of which I answered. Then suddenly I felt hungry. Before I knew it, Carla had read my mind and told me I was so like my brother and ordered lunch. While we were waiting for the food, she insisted that Luke show me around.

'You two need some time together.'

Both she and Ines looked so happy. Of course, Ines had our daddy's eyes. No wonder they were so green. Luke and I had our mammy's blue eyes. Luke directed me to the shop, then down to the surf school.

'Is this all yours?'

'It belongs to Andre and me, plus a couple of investors who love to surf.'

'I need to tell Mammy, Luke.'

'Can it wait? Can we have some time? I'm in a bit of shock.'

'But it is your mother. She has been clinging to this forever.' A note of impatience crept in.

He stood there. I wasn't sure if it was defiance or distress. I decided to capitalise and led him towards the sea.

'Come on Luke, we'll be eating soon, and I can't be all happy and jolly knowing Mammy doesn't know.'

He nodded his head, and we sat down on the sand. I pressed FaceTime. There was no answer. Then the phone rang.

'Fiona,' she said, breathless, 'I was upstairs when I heard it.'

'Mammy, I...' I couldn't go on. I handed it to Luke.

'Hi Mam.'

'Oh my boy, my boy,' she said.

I was crying all over again. She didn't stop. She told him she loved him, she'd missed him, and she was so happy to see him. All Luke kept saying was 'Sorry, I'm sorry'

'Tsk, don't you worry about that, you silly boy. What matters is we've found you, my love.'

Both of us were teenagers again, sat expecting to be marched off to Mass. We both managed a wry smile. Before we knew, it we'd all agreed for her to fly out as soon as possible, and Rob, Henry and Alice had said hello.

'No Tyrel?' I asked.

'He's got a football match. John has taken him,' Rob said. I'd totally forgotten with everything going on.

'Three?' Luke looked at me.

'No, two, but long story. Not for now.'

I somehow managed to finish the call despite Mammy's attempts to touch Luke through the phone. At the end of the call, we were both sat on the beach, emotionally exhausted, looking out to sea.

'This isn't a happy ending, Fiona,' Luke said as he held my hand and looked into my eyes.

My eyes were full of tears, and my left nostril was leaking. I nodded.

'I know, but it is a new beginning.'

CAROLINE

TWENTY THREE

'Mum, what's for dinner?' I heard Ruby shout from the living room. How hard would it be for her to walk to the kitchen and ask? I ignored her as I was flat out with Fiona away and was in the middle of getting the garden plans ready for the business launch. Sure enough, she appeared in the doorway not long after.

'Didn't you hear me?'

'Yes.'

'Why didn't you answer then?'

I turned my head towards her, took off my glasses and smiled.

'Darling, I'm busy and you've interrupted my flow.'

Ruby pulled a face at me.

'Right cheeky, let's make dinner then.' I abandoned my pile of drawings and laptop, and got up from the dining table.

We decided to make pasta with pesto and use up the leftover chicken from Sunday's roast. Ruby made the salad and happily told me about her day at school.

'Did you know Mrs Allen is leaving at the end of this term, so we'll have a new English teacher for the last term of our A levels.'

'How do you feel about that?'

'I don't mind, and Georgie and I are hoping for a hot male teacher.'

'Ruby!'

'Don't stress mum, it's not going to happen at our school. I don't think the Catholic teacher pool is strong enough.'

'Not all your teachers are Catholics, are they?'

'Think a lot of them are. Mrs Allen is going to a private girls' school.'

'More money, probably. Is there a collection?'

Ruby shrugged her shoulders. I thought I'd wait to see if anyone emails or tells me. I hardly have any contact with the school these days, other than to drop off or occasionally pick up. I removed my work and laid the table for us. I still sat down every night with her, except if she was out on a Saturday or we had a takeaway in the living room.

My whole focus had been Jack and Ruby for as long as I could remember after my divorce. Dealing with a drug addict had drained me, and I could only function day to day for years. A modicum of guilt as well. I had chucked Paulo out. He didn't really disappear from us as I told the children, his family, and my friends. I drove him to Reading one evening. Parked outside the station, I gave him twenty pounds, made a vague gesture in the direction of a shop outside the station concourse and then drove off. He was so out of it when I took him there. For a few days, I was on edge, waiting for him to come through the door, but he never did. He disappeared. I keep that bit quiet. Along with a couple of other things.

'Gosh Ruby, this year in June it will be your eighteenth birthday,' I said.

'Durr obvs,' was her response.

'Have you thought what you want to do?'

'Well, Nonna wants me to go to Milan, which I do want to do, but really I'm not that fussed about being eighteen.'

'You must do something.'

'Yeah, but no, naff parties. I'd quite like cocktails and dinner.'

'You have such expensive taste.'

'It is because I am a little bit French and a big lot of Italiano,' Ruby said, putting on an Italian accent.

'Hmm.' It was my turn to pull a face.

'Will I get a trust fund like Jack, do you think?'

The guilt for me lay with Paulo's family, their generosity to me and the children. With Paulo out of the frame and not able to spend any money on drugs, they used their wealth to support us. I was grateful after years of struggling to become so comfortable. It meant I didn't have to carry on as a PA in the city. No more hauling myself into London every day on the rammed commuter train and the constant pressure of childcare. I missed my lunches, when we grabbed them, with Fiona, but my part-time teaching assistant job with school holidays and no responsibility was bliss.

Of course, it was Fiona who put paid to that with the gardening gig. Although I have to admit, less school breaks with cakes, and now more exercise with gardening, has meant I've lost some weight and started to tone up nicely. Even *he* has noticed. Not that my fulsome size 14 body was an issue or not appreciated. The thought of him made my stomach do a dance. The illicit nature of our relationship had, until recently, been my favourite element of it all. I was softening, warming to the idea of being with him. I hadn't figured out how to make it happen, but I would.

'Mum!' Ruby's voice brought my thoughts back to her question.

'I'm sure Nonna will let you know. But maybe Italians only give the males money.' I couldn't resist teasing her.

It worked, there was a moment of annoyance.

'That would be sexist, and anyway Italians loooove women,' Ruby said.

'Alright, enough chitter chatter. I've got to do some more work, and you need to finish any homework you've got.'

We cleared the table, stacked the dishwasher, and I resumed

creating the landscaping details and planting for *Serene Spaces*. My hand drawings were a reminder I needed to learn some more CAD design skills with the level three part of my diploma. Although land management and production wasn't my favourite element of the course, I had pushed aside doing any work on the module for the moment. The challenge for me right now, was the creation of bespoke solutions or a 'to do kit' to choose from the three franchise business offerings. *Classic Cottage* is flowers with lots of colours to be set in pathways and a meadow area. *Totally Tranquil* would provide a water feature and shrubs. The water feature had to come from a small disguised rainwater butt and I was still investigating solutions which were not based on tapping into the water supply. Fiona had stipulated no artificial grass nor anything Monty Don disapproved of.

Finally, the *Form and Function* element was easy. The barbecue and outdoor kitchen area. This would require recommendations and agreement with suppliers. The planting revolved around creative solutions for herbs and bay trees in pots. I wanted to create a hanging display of ferns and creeping jenny as we would be setting *Form and Function* in the shadiest part of the garden or outside space.

As I tried to meet the deadline and juggle the day-to-day management of our gardening clients, I had less time to think about him. I picked up my mobile and nearly sent a message but quickly changed my mind. No point. We were both busy, and I wasn't really in the mood for phone sex later. There'd been a lot of phone sex lately due to missed opportunities to meet up. It was inconvenient, his move to London. Ruby was calling me again. This time, I got up and walked to the living room.

'Mum, have you washed my...' I stared at her, stopping her

in mid flow.

'Ruby, you know whatever it is you want is either in your room or in the airing cupboard.'

'Oh yeah, I forgot,' she replied and went back to her phone and messaging.

Honestly, my grandmother would be turning in her grave. Malory, my father's mother, was a stickler for all things. From a young age, she instructed me in all manner of household jobs and personal vanity. I had to make sure all washing was pressed and folded or hung daily. Rarely did I miss a day. None of my habits had taken root in Jack or Ruby despite their years of helping out. I still had to instruct or request. Nothing was done willingly. Only I observed the requirements of the house. My own mother's approach to life, especially housework, was more haphazard. She found it a chore and employed a cleaner. Her work as a solicitor was far more important to her, but I found comfort in the routine of the home. It was always a rock for me, not a whistle-stop tour.

As the youngest child, my time after the age of eight was spent on my own within the house, as my eldest brother and sister were much older than me. Both were more like our high-flying mother and were very focused on studies and university. Instead, I had my father to chat to about my day when he came home from work, and my grandmother to instruct me in life. Firstly on my visits to her own home, and then when she moved into ours. Malory understood the importance of filling one's time not only with books and television, but order and certainty.

My fridge and cupboards were organised and, without fail, stocked with the basics for any necessary meal. Although, unlike Ursula, I didn't bake cakes. I had two simple throw-together cake options in my repertoire, one plain, one chocolate, and neither required icing or adornment of any kind. Everything without fuss.

'No one likes fuss Caroline, ma chere, especially not men. Of course, you fuss over them and for them, but with a smile, with a sense of pleasure. An unwritten contract not to squander time with trivial 'humeurs'. No huffing or puffing, eh.'

My fond memories of *grand-mère* Malory and her notions of order and purpose renewed my approach to the required designs. I started to draw triangles and plot the options for layouts within that space. I was in full creative flow when a text message interrupted.

'*What you up to, sexy?*'

How annoying. When I didn't want to see him, he was a pest. Typical. My flow ebbed. Oh well. I sent him a clown emoji. He sent me a donkey one back. It carried on like this until we ran out of steam. I gave in and phoned him. He answered immediately.

'Well?'

'I was working.'

'Me too. Late one at the office. What you got for me?'

'I'll need to pop out for some milk.' It was my code for either Ruby or Jack being at home.

'How long will you be?'

'About fifteen minutes,' I replied, thinking it was all too much effort.

'Get your skates on then. Are you sure you can't pop over?'

'No.' I had no intention of getting on the train to Vauxhall. I knew he was on his way back to his flat, otherwise he'd never have agreed to fifteen minutes, and would have badgered me to have a bath.

'Ruby-love, I'm popping out to get some milk. Anything you want?'

'No thanks, Mum.'

'Won't be long.'

I parked the car, paced it into the store and grabbed a milk carton. Thank goodness for self-service checkouts to allow for whizzing in and out. In the corner of the car park, I pushed my seat back and submerged myself as much as possible. Not too obvious. More like a cheeky nap than the reality of attempting to talk filth in a supermarket car park on a Tuesday evening. I called him. He was breathless.

'Ah, you don't need me then,' I whispered, more with hope than he knew.

'Oh, I need you to sort me out. Today has been stressful and demanding. I'm not sure who annoys me the most, our hugely successful podcast team, the advertising media team or our breakfast presenters.'

I laughed. I knew him all too well. He needed to be soothed. But somehow, a dirty phone call in the car park, any car park, was not going to end well. Fuelled by my desire to get out of this situation and also keep him happy, I quickly changed tack.

'Actually, you are filthy. You need a shower. You'd better scrub yourself clean.' My voice was bossy and stern. I knew he'd love it. With the phone on speaker and the sound of hasty undressing, I repositioned the car seat, started the engine and began to drive home.

As I stopped at a pedestrian crossing with cinema goers flooding out, I was telling him to clean his nether regions. My exact phrase was 'exfoliate your butthole if you want any licking with my tongue.' I was smiling as the crowd finished crossing. The shower afforded me enough time to get home, pop my head round the living room door, put the milk in the fridge, and get up to my room. I asked Alexa to play some Chilled Ibiza and firmly told him to dry himself with his towel, otherwise I'd spank him.

At some point, my mind was transported back to Paulo and me running for the *vaporetto* crossing from Venice to Punta Sabbioni. The water bus passed by the north part of the lido. I remember being cross we weren't going there, but Paulo insisted we had a better chance of a night out on the mainland spit beaches. We wanted to be out in the open, away from the suffocation of the family apartment in Venice where we were staying. His grandmother kept fussing over him and his sisters kept fussing over me, or were they trying to annoy me in some way? We had sleeping bags, some wine, and cigarettes.

I vaguely registered my muttering 'you are so hard' to him, but in reality, I was thinking of the excitement and lust Paulo overwhelmed me with. His touch, his smile, and his gorgeous, thick dark hair I loved to run my fingers through. I almost arched my back at the vivid memory of him deep inside me. I gasped at the memory of his sweat and hot body.

'He's Italian. His father is a Count and probably knee deep in bed with the Milanese mafioso, because who wouldn't be? I'd marry him.' That was my grandmother's blessing.

Of course, she didn't have to suffer the pain of his demise and the worry of the two children who needed food on the table. There was no spare money then, otherwise he'd have snorted it all up his nose. It's why I had two bank accounts. One in my maiden name, and our joint one, which at first had been healthy and replenished not only by my salary but his family and his work. Paulo did work. He had been a computer whizz. Always contracted by various businesses for his programming skills until the missed days, the mistakes and eventually the obvious outward appearance of an addict.

I sighed.

'Babe, that was great.'

'Uh huh.'

I'd totally forgotten about him. All done on autopilot.

'I know we'd planned to meet up this weekend babe, but I've got a huge board meeting coming up and I'll be working. Do you mind if we postpone?' he asked.

'No, of course not. We'll do it another time.' I was tired now and wanted to chivvy Ruby to bed.

'You're a star. Goodnight, Caro.'

'Goodnight, Ed.'

TWENTY FOUR

It was official. Fiona and Rob were getting married. Ursula and I were all ears as we sat in her kitchen. She looked exhausted and exhilarated at the same time. Bernadette had sobbed over the pair of us as we arrived to catch up on everything. The house was in a heightened state of emotion, apart from the youths who were either asleep or lounging around with AirPods in.

'How did it happen? Was it a surprise?' Ursula asked.

'Well, it was for Rob because he has waited so patiently. Although he hadn't expected me to insist he proposed at Gatwick North car park.'

We looked suitably stunned.

'The car park!' Though in reality, I needn't have said it. My face said it all.

'I know it sounds gross, doesn't it?' Fiona had the decency to admit 'But all these years I have refused to marry until I knew Luke's fate. When we got to the car, I insisted he ask me again. I was more than ready to give my answer.' She smiled.

'Oh Fiona, we are so happy for you.' Ursula was right, we were, despite the circumstances of sealing the deal.

'At least you are true to your word and refusing to live an Instagram life,' Ursula added.

'Talking of which, we need one for the new business launch.' Fiona was right back into her comfort zone, work.

'Hey missus, you don't get to change the subject just yet. Come on, tell all.' I opened my eyes as wide as possible to emphasise the point I was making.

After a moment of hesitation, a tear rolled down her left cheek, which she brushed away. Ursula uncharacteristically put her arm around Fiona. John had certainly improved her touchy-feely side. We sat patiently, without interrupting, and listened as she explained the initial meeting, the emotion of it all, and how, upon coming home, the family had endured a range of emotions with happiness, trepidation and anger. Tyrel had been very quiet until he spoke to Luke on the phone, and Fiona had organised a specialist therapist to have a few sessions with them all, and separately.

'Anyway, I need you both to help me plan a fairly low-key wedding, either here or another venue to be decided.'

'Beaverbrook,' Ursula exclaimed.

'No,' Fiona responded firmly. 'I'm not doing anything extravagant. It's not my style. I'd rather do Oxshott Village Hall. It needs to be a no-fuss occasion. I know I don't especially want a pub reception, but I don't want the works either. Something genuinely lovely and easy. My brother's beach restaurant is the perfect place.'

We sat in silence.

'Something to think about then,' Ursula ventured.

Fiona nodded. I decided to change tack.

'Right, the concepts. Are you ready to have a look?'

Both of them cheered up and looked interested as I laid my A2 papers on the kitchen island.

'Don't forget these are first drafts,' I reminded them. Whilst they were poring over the designs, I began to dwell upon the forthcoming wedding. Perhaps it would enable me an opportunity to hook up 'unexpectedly' with Ed.

'These look awesome,' Fiona exclaimed, interrupting my thoughts. She genuinely looked pleased at the designs.

I gave them a few more moments before I made a point.

'My only genuine problem is the sustainable water feature. I think we'll need to offer three different options depending on cost. There are lots of new solar solutions coming onto the market, so it will be price and customer preference driven.'

I showed them both the circular solutions with or without the solar-driven pump, the trough style, either sunken or standing, with foliage in different pot heights around the trough, and a seating option with it.

'I know we can't make them choose something that isn't pump-driven from the mains, but I still think we push the sustainable solution as well as being clear on no artificial grass or foliage,' Fiona said.

'What is this?' Ursula asked and then added, 'Sorry'.

'A hammock.'

'Where did you get the idea?' Ursula said.

'How do you know I didn't spontaneously think of it for the *Classic Cottage* area?'

'Well, you've never mentioned them before, and shouldn't it be hung from tree to tree?'

'I realised we need to provide solutions for all spaces, and the one on a stand is perfect. But you are right, I read some woman's tweets on Twitter, she was banging on about them.'

'It's X now,' Ursula replied.

'Does anyone actually say X?' Fiona asked.

'No. Well probably, but everyone, as we like to say, is on Bluesky or nothing these days,' Ursula said. 'Social media ain't what it was. But the hammock is genius, I can Instagram the life out of a hammock. From the idea of lazing in your garden, reading a book in the hammock, to lounging early evening with a chilled glass of something.'

'Perfect, and it can go in other zones. We should source our own supply,' Fiona said, then, 'What are these?' She was pointing to cascades of trailing plants in the *Form and Function* design from a shelf next to a barbecue.

'This one is called *creeping jenny*, it is a perennial and easy to take cuttings from. The one with the dots of blue and purple is a trailing *rosemary*. It will smell divine and be useful as a herb,' I replied.

We carried on chatting about the designs and I relaxed. I wanted to show them the reason for triangular designs and put my final A2 on the island. On this were nine grids in three rows. On the first row, each grid featured one of the designs with different compass points. The second row showed two of the designs combined, and on the third, examples of all three in different combinations. I took a deep breath.

'If we are seriously going to franchise, then the main website needs to allow prospective customers to be able to mix and match according to the size and aspect of their garden. We'll have to provide examples of every amalgamation and scales for small to large gardens.'

My face was flushed. I felt my cheeks burn.

Fiona looked pensive, and Ursula's mind was whirring as she was twitching her nose.

'Blimey,' Fiona said. 'I mean it, Caroline, when I say I had no idea how good you were. This is incredible, the level of thought and creation. I'm stunned. It is more than I expected.'

'Well, you were rather preoccupied.' I laughed but my redness subsided and was replaced with a warm inner glow. I felt proud of my work, but to hear someone else say it validated my effort. It was worth crying off Ed's demands and putting this first.

'Gosh, to think only a few weeks ago we were in a bar before I went to Lisbon.' Fiona exhaled. 'We'd better get our skates on. What about the launch event, Ursula?'

'Ah,' Ursula pulled a face, 'I've changed my mind about a hoedown.'

‘Oh,’ Fiona and I both said.

She fidgeted on the stool.

‘When I went to chat to the owner of The Barn, he looked a bit crestfallen about the hoedown. The place they’ve created is quite a brand in itself. I thought about their ethos and our objectives and have another plan. Mind you, the band I auditioned were incredible. Loads of Dolly Parton, Garth Brooks and some ceilidh numbers.’

Fiona’s ears pricked up.

‘Did you say ceilidh?’

‘Yes.’

‘And they do weddings?’

‘They do, but they are pretty booked up with events,’ Ursula said.

We both knew where Fiona was going with this. I was in favour of a ceilidh. What better excuse for dancing and getting carried away? I could blame it all on the wedding. I could even ask Ursula if she minded if I had a dance with Ed. My mind wandered on this point as Ursula carried on explaining her new plans for the launch event.

‘We’ll have three zones to reflect the three bespoke options, and the tranquillity space will be set outside of the hangar for meditation and a sound bath session. Only fifteen minutes, which will allow for three sessions for people to join. The cottage garden area will be where we meet and greet everyone, with the food van being set in the outdoor kitchen zone,’ she said and drew breath.

‘Sounds like a boss business launch event,’ Fiona said. I nodded.

‘We will need to crunch the numbers. Events aren’t cheap, Fiona,’ Ursula said.

Fiona smiled. ‘Exactly why I don’t want to go crazy on a

wedding. The business is really important.'

'So is getting married!' Ursula exclaimed.

'I just want a nice day of fun after everything. Which is why I'm thinking of booking here as well. It doesn't matter which day or month. Can you organise it for me Ursula, please?'

'Of course. Caroline and I,' she said, hesitated and looked at me, I smiled back, 'will get the ball rolling.'

'Thank you. I've got to prep first for Luke coming over. Mammy is beside herself. You can imagine how she is?'

Fiona looked rueful, and I could only imagine how exhausting this emotional reunion was. I preferred to keep emotion out of things despite the perception people had of me. The fact I refused to discuss my love life despite being bubbly and bouncy in everyone's eyes garnered me an emotional aspect I neither had nor deserved. I mean, come on, being the mistress of one of your best friend's husbands for years requires an amount of unemotional steeliness. I'm not proud of this fact, merely accepting.

Malory always spoke about relationships as contracts of knowledge. My grandmother believed you were either the wife or the lover. If you were a girlfriend, you were neither. You were an option before being the wife or lover. It is why Paulo married me. I told him he was my lover whilst I waited for a husband. Now I have to negotiate the challenge of changing my mistress status.

'Caroline, do you agree?' I heard Ursula say.

'What? Sorry, I was miles away.'

'Fiona is suggesting you, Steve, and Jay build the spaces for the event.' Ursula looked at me quizzically as she spoke.

'Fine, should be no problem. I was thinking back to Paulo, which is why I wasn't concentrating.'

Both of them were agog.

'Don't look so surprised. He was a total catch and I utterly adored him until it all became too much,' I said.

Fiona touched my arm. 'We forget.' She gave me an apologetic look.

'I understand,' Ursula said. 'It's not the same, but I sometimes think about and miss Ed even though I'm deliriously happy with John. We had the boys together and I mind the fact we fell apart. But you lost Paulo even before he died. How you managed with his addiction and the children, I'll never know.'

I decided to say nothing. To dismiss this moment.

'Well, anyway, I'll be using our fab muscle crew to get the zones ready. What is the budget?' I turned to Fiona as most of the funding was still via her and not the business.

'I'll work it all out and let you know. It does mean if the business model is successful, the business will be paying me back first and then us, is that okay? Of course, the wages will still be as usual, but any excess from operation costs will pay back this investment loan.'

Ursula and I gave our agreement. We fully understood this was Fiona's pet project and the risk was all hers. She liked the risk and the challenge it presented.

'Absolutely, Fiona. I can't believe we are having this conversation. Everything has changed since we started this. It's incredible.' I truly shook my head in amazement. I felt different. I had a new skill, and more, I had a future I liked. My only conundrum was to sort out Ed one way or another.

'I must dash,' I added. 'Got to go into central London to meet an old secretarial college friend.'

'It's only two o'clock.' Fiona looked hurt.

'Early supper, need to go home, glam it up, and get on the train. I should have said before.'

'You go and enjoy.' Ursula smiled at me. 'I'll let her boss me around for a bit.'

Fiona rolled her eyes, and I'd like to think I felt a bit guilty, but I didn't. After all, a woman has needs. It's not as if Ed wouldn't be doing it with someone else if something hadn't happened between us. I'd bet money on him having had other dalliances.

TWENTY FIVE

I didn't set out to become involved. He propositioned me. Of course, I declined, but the opportunity had permeated my thoughts. I was flattered. I swerved the thoughts for a while, but it had been a long time since anyone had piqued my interest or been interested in me.

I also observed Ed and Ursula for a good six months. Ed was too needy and demanding for Ursula to cope with. She wanted to be seen and adored, yet Ed drank in the limelight of his world. His first love was himself. He seemed fairly tender and interested in his boys, but Ursula, he'd tired of her years ago. Her status was assured as long as I kept him occupied, and he needed a wife in his position.

Two things put paid to their marriage. The pandemic and DCI John Smith. The norms shifted during and after the pandemic. Post 2021, half the country had some sort of epiphany, breakdown or pulled themselves back from the precipice of priggishness. Hello, the indignation felt when a runner jogged too close with their heavy breathing! Whilst it robbed many of their senses, some pressed a reset button on what was really important. Turns out not a lot of stuff is that important. When I met John, I knew he was perfect for Ursula.

It was obvious they'd both fallen for each other immediately. All I had to do was hasten the inevitable. It was easy to push them together, despite Fiona's party outburst nearly jeopardising everything. Ultimately, she hastened their relationship. Fiona did see Ed kissing an unknown woman in the bar that night, but what she didn't know was that I paid her to deliver Ed a message and suggested she get a bit saucy with him. Of course, he'd loved the unexpected attention of an attractive young woman. He wasn't going to hold back, which I'd betted on.

We were in a bar, and luckily, I saw Fiona as I came out of the toilets. I retreated back in and considered what to do. I really couldn't think of a plausible reason why I would be in a Soho bar with Ed. What the heck was Fiona doing in Soho? Normally, she never strayed from the city, or only went to the latest 'it' restaurant if it was work-related and she had to push the boat out. It was a work night. Out of the cubicle came a slightly tipsy but gorgeous young woman in a delightful short dress. As she applied her lip gloss and shook her mane, admiring herself in the mirror, she smiled at me. I took the opportunity and told her the truth, minus my name. I quickly wrote a note, gave her twenty quid, and she happily undertook her mission. Fifteen minutes later, Ed was outside, joining me down the alleyway and by my side.

'You could have mentioned it was Fiona. She nearly slapped me across my face,' he fumed. 'I told her the woman started it and I was messing around back, but she wouldn't have it. Great.'

I soothed him.

'Didn't you like the little surprise I organised?'

He turned to look at me.

'You utter minx.' He grinned and grabbed me.

However, I'd caused a rift between Ed and Fiona. A rift which has never healed, hence the outburst at the party. Here I was, all those years later, sat in a tapas bar in Soho, and here he was arriving. Now we had some time before I needed to get back home.

'Watcha, gorgeous.'

Ed pecked me on my raised left cheek as he sat on the bar stool next to me. He clinked the bottle of lager I'd already got him with my glass of Cava; they had no prosecco. We grabbed something to eat and happily chatted about our day. Although he was less keen on my work stuff, for obvious reasons. Being together like this, I imagined we were a couple. Suddenly, I started to find myself a little bit in love with him. Until the whole divorce scenario, it had been about snatched company, passion and a distraction. Little by little, I'd imagined moving from lover to wife.

'Right Caro, when are you going to stay over at mine?'

Maybe he felt the same.

'Why are you asking? You know my circumstances. Ruby and Jack will be off for a few weeks to Italy soon and I'll be able to stay then,' I replied.

'I want more. I want more company.'

'Oh, I'm company, am I?' I smiled and sipped some Cava.

'You know what I mean. Come on babe, you and me?' He slid his arm round my waist and drew me closer. My stomach lurched.

'What about Ursula?'

'What about her? We are divorced now. It's been ages. A man has needs.'

'That's my line.' I pulled a face. 'Let me have a think about how to sort it out. Don't you be hasty, Ed.'

'Alright, I get it.' He turned to signal to someone behind the bar for another bottle of lager. 'Do you want another drink?' he asked me.

'No, I'm fine. Maybe grab a bottle of something on the way back to yours?'

When we got to his flat we'd barely opened the bottle of red, let alone had a drink of it, before he'd turned me round and begun to push up my dress and pull down my underwear. His hand found my clitoris, and he briefly touched me before withdrawing and running his fingers up and down inside my right thigh. His left hand was on my breast and he pressed hard against me. I fumbled with my right hand to undo his trousers, slightly twisted and without much success. He touched me again. Repeatedly. I moaned. He then finished off undoing his trousers and pulling down his underwear himself before positioning to enter me. I was pushed up against the unit and had one hand on the counter to steady myself as he moved within me. I pressed into the motion.

After a while, we stopped and moved into the bedroom, taking everything off on the way and leaving a trail of items. Then I was picking my way back to the kitchen after it was all over. I grabbed two glasses, filled them up, and brought them back to the bedroom. Ed had switched on the television in his bedroom. He took a swig of red wine and went into the en-suite. He quickly showered. I joined him as he was finishing. He generously lathered me with shower gel, paying particular attention to my breasts. We had a mini soap suds fight. I tried to create a beard, and he tried to do it back.

'Oi matey, don't try and win by grabbing my dick.'

I laughed.

He left me to wash the suds off.

Wrapped in a towel, I joined him on the bed.

'I've got to hot-foot it and get the train in forty minutes.' I snuggled up to him. I could feel the tension the moment I mentioned leaving.

'Yeah yeah, I'll walk you to Vauxhall.'

'It's okay, I can go by myself.'

'No, I don't like the thought of that.'

'But it's the summer and the evenings are lighter.'

'I know, but I'll see you to the station and then I can come home and relax. I'll probably fall straight to sleep. Early meeting tomorrow. I don't want to have to check you got back alright.'

He changed from the news to sport. I sighed. It would be nice to stay. After a moment of sentimentality, I shook my head and got real. I got dressed, drank some more wine, sorted myself out, and before I knew it, we were having a quick hug and a kiss goodbye on the concourse outside the station. As Ed walked off, I gave him a quick wave and turned to see John looking at me and in the direction of Ed. Fuck.

'Oh, hi John.'

'Hi Caroline, getting the train home?'

'Er, yes.'

We were both walking together now. My head was hurting, and my heart was beating fast.

John said nothing.

Next thing we were stood on the platform as the train pulled in. I got on first and found a seat. He sat next to me. I waited. It took two stops.

'You and Ed. How long has that been going on?'

I honestly didn't know what to say. I couldn't say how many years, but what to choose? I felt hot, clammy and sick. John spoke again.

'On second thoughts, don't answer that, the less I know the better,' he said and paused. 'All I can say is you need to sort it out. End it or tell Ursula. It's not an ultimatum, it is advice. I'm not going to say anything, but you might not be so lucky next time.' He looked really stern.

'I'm sorry. I truly am. I don't know how it happened.' My voice faltered. I couldn't trust myself to say anymore.

Two more stops passed in silence between us. I had to ask him why he was in London. It broke the fear I was feeling.

'Interview, then a drink with an old colleague.'

'Are you leaving the police?'

‘No. An opportunity has come up in the National Crime Agency. A more strategic role and less shift work, which would be nice. Did I mention more money?’

I shook my head and then looked out of the window. What had I been thinking? I wasn’t sure what I wanted. Being rumbled like this made me uneasy and doubtful of everything. The rest of the journey passed in silence. My head hurt, and when I got off at Epsom, I decided to undertake the long walk home to clear it.

TWENTY SIX

There he was. Luke. Stood tall and a little uneasy in Fiona's kitchen. He was flanked by Bernadette and a woman I'd never seen before, but who I assumed was his wife, Carla. She seemed very at home in the circumstances and was happily being directed by Bernadette in putting things out on plates. I was scanning the room for Ursula and, of course, John.

'Hi Caroline,' a voice said behind me. I jumped.

'Geez, you've given me a heart attack.' I drew breath and gave Ursula a hug. 'No John?'

'He's on his way with Stuart. Fiona invited him as well, as he helped locate Luke. It's all a bit nerve-racking for poor Luke. I feel slightly dizzy with it all as well. Big family occasion.'

'I've got Ruby with me, but she's sloped off with Alice and Tyrel.'

'Fiona said Alice was disappointed Ines didn't come.'

'Classic teenager.'

'She will be coming for the wedding, which will make up for it. Poor Luke had his police interview yesterday. Must be awful having to dredge up the past and then…'

Another voice came from behind us.

'He's fine. He wanted to do it and also wanted to get this over and done with. It's for Mammy. She wants to say thank you to John and Stuart.' Fiona gazed at our faces.

Ursula shuffled.

'Oh, I didn't mean to…' she started before Fiona interrupted.

'What, chat about it? Come on, I wouldn't want you talking about anything else apart from my wedding.'

We all laughed.

'Honestly Fiona, I'm really pleased for you and Bernadette. Luke looks just like you. Well, a bit older and more tanned,' I said.

She grabbed and squeezed my hand. I patted it with my other hand. Was I always the tactile one? Was it me always hugging and touching? Both my grandmother and father had showered me with affection. My brother and sister resented this, which added to the pleasure of it all. I was such a spoilt brat. My mother had on one occasion cautioned me against taking pleasure in receiving such advances and to display more humility. I hadn't grasped her advice until now. Maybe she had a point. Why had I accepted advances from Ed? My face flushed.

Carla was thrusting a glass of champagne into my hand.

'Take.' She smiled and briskly gave one to Ursula.

I was about to say something to Ursula when I noticed John come into the room with a slightly taller and bulkier man. Judging by the biceps outlined under the shirt he was wearing, he was used to lifting weights.

'Ah, just in time,' Ursula murmured as John came to join us.

'Caroline, this is Stuart Johnson, and Stuart, this is Caroline.' He nodded at me. Stuart gave me a very, very firm handshake and smiled with his eyes.

I managed a tentative smile back, trying not to wring my hands to get the blood flowing again. Still, it was a good handshake. John gave me a sideways glance. I quickly stared straight ahead. Fiona was calling the errant youths into the living room where we'd all been directed with our glasses in hand. Within a few moments, the small group of us were stood with Bernadette facing us and clearing her throat.

'Can you all hear me?'

'Mammy, it's the living room, not an auditorium.' Fiona

rolled her eyes. Luke started to laugh. Carla stared at him.

'I'm not used to this sort of occasion and I'm not going to say much. I wanted you all here today as Fiona and me reached the end of a long chapter when John and Stuart came into our lives,' she said and hesitated. Both John and Stuart kept neutral faces, but I saw Stuart clench and release his fist. '...Because they made an effort to help us. They've helped not only Fiona and me, but also our newest addition to the family, Tyrel.'

We all looked at Tyrel and beamed. He didn't keep a neutral face, and also didn't know where to look in such embarrassment.

'Mammy, come on, will you?' Fiona was getting impatient.

'It's fine Mam, take your time.' Luke was by her side now.

She nodded and the tears fell. She wiped them away.

'This is a happy occasion because Luke came home. He came home, and that is all that matters. I never thought I'd be able to say this, but welcome back Luke.'

Bernadette let out an enormous sob. Carla produced a tissue and Luke gave his mother a hug and a kiss on top of her head.

'For goodness sake, raise your glasses you eejits, and drink,' Fiona said.

Fiona was in fierce form, but I knew it was to keep her own tears from falling. We all raised our glasses and proceeded to take a sip. I nearly glugged mine down but caught John's eye, and it stopped me in my tracks. I turned to Stuart.

'How long have you worked with John?' I asked him.

He looked taken aback.

'Oh, I hope I'm not prying.'

'No, not at all, I wasn't expecting the question.' He smiled at me. 'No idea on actual years, but it feels like a lifetime.'

'Oh, tell me more?' I found myself being flirtatious.

'Nothing exciting. The demands of the job. But these last few years, since his wife Jean passed away, have been interesting.

Mainly because he threw himself at everything. That's why we are here today, because he worked harder and longer than he should, to get the results.'

'You did as well, from what Bernadette said.'

He grinned and shook his head.

'Well yes, but only because John made me. I've enjoyed doing it as well. It's nice to get a result. Especially a result like this.'

I nodded. Gosh, he was a nicer person than I was.

'What do you do?' He asked.

'I work with Fiona and Ursula.' I looked to see if he ran anything through his mind, but I couldn't detect anything. 'We have the gardening business.'

'The dead body team.' He laughed.

'I know. It's how it all started.'

'Well, I wasn't on it at the start, but I am now. We are nearly there on the case.'

This time, he did reveal his mind. He looked like he'd said too much. 'I'm sure John will be in contact soon about it.' He hastily closed the conversation down and offered to get me a refill. I was left standing there and looked around the room. Everyone except Alice, who was on her phone, was chatting. The doors at the end of the living space were open onto the garden. The room was beautifully decorated. Soft beige walls with vanilla-shaded porcelain floor tiles housed two large, very designer sofas and a snuggle chair, all in a glorious olive green fabric. My eye for design had increased since the gardening and landscaping course.

'What are you thinking about?' Fiona appeared by my side. 'Stuart gave me this to give to you.' She handed me a fresh flute of cold champagne.

'I was admiring the room and the soft colour palettes. I've

never noticed it before, mainly because we are always in the kitchen.'

'Well, it wasn't me. I briefed a design place on the Fulham Road. My only criteria was not Essex grey or anything vibrant. Mammy said we got the County Sligo look in this room.' She laughed.

'What's that?' I asked, puzzled.

'She thinks it's the same colours as the stones and grass there. The kitchen/living area is County Galway, based on the oyster colour of everything. It's all too fancy for her taste and she'd like it all to be more colourful.'

I changed tack.

'What does Luke think of it all?'

'He's been really relaxed considering. Carla is a big help. Don't you think she is a livelier version of my mam? She's like Bernadette on steroids.'

We both started to laugh. I couldn't have agreed more.

'I bloody love her,' Fiona added. 'But it is exhausting. I swear the two of them have got a 'who can tidy the most' competition going. It leaves Luke and me with lots of time to chat or sit in silence. We seem to do a lot of that. Weird, huh?'

I nodded, but I was too caught up in my dilemma to be a better friend and ask her more. Instead, I squeezed her hand.

'I'm going outside to get some fresh air before we embarrass our children,' I said.

'Oh yes. I'd forgotten we needed to do that. Alice is going to think it is cringe, but I want Tyrel to be the centre of attention. You get some fresh air, and I'll get the gifts ready for him and Ruby.'

I breathed in the warm air deeply. My mind was whirring about Ed. On the one hand, I was thinking about how to out us as a couple, and on the other hand, the folly of it all. This time, Ursula appeared next to me. Was there no opportunity to be left alone?

'Whatcha,' she said in typical Ursula fashion. I had to smile.

'Did you bake a cake?' I asked her.

'Of course I did, duh. Although the way Carla looked at it, you'd have thought it was a supermarket number. She said something about the cakes in Portugal being bigger and better decorated. She's lucky Bernadette was there to tell me how 'grand' it was and how it would taste divine.' She rolled her eyes.

'Fiona loves her.'

'Of course she does. Everyone does, even John. She is wonderful and has embraced this family's life to the full. I'm merely amused by it all and prepared to defend my meagre cake offering.'

'It is funny for us both, after years of being bossed about by Fiona, we've now got the next level bossiness.' I laughed.

'Please, can I take your glasses?' We both jumped as Carla came out with more fresh glasses. 'You need this chilled always.' Her smile was incredible. She departed as quickly as she'd arrived, striding across the lawn in her espadrilles and perfectly fitting cream trousers, her hair bouncing.

'Her hair bounces more than yours,' Ursula commented. 'No wonder John likes her, it's like having Penelope Cruz in your midst. She really does exude European chic. Luckily, Ed is not here, his hands would be attempting to be all over her.'

I bristled at the mention of Ed. Instead, I managed to mumble, 'Lucky Luke.'

'I'm wondering where she got that brown shirt from, and when did brown look that good?'

Ursula pulled a face and then took a gulp of the freshly poured and perfectly chilled champagne before asking me,

‘Anyhow, what do you think of Stuart?’

I wasn’t expecting this question, so I could answer honestly.

‘I’ve not given him any thought. Why do you ask?’

Ursula shrugged her shoulders.

‘No reason. I saw you both chatting earlier. He’s single, by the way. Messy divorce apparently.’

‘Cheery. It appears, Ursula, we are at the stage of life when death and divorce can be graded. Oh look, that’s Stuart, messy divorce. See John there, recently bereaved. Caroline here, widowed years ago and so on.’

Ursula pulled another face.

‘Alright point taken, but in the event of a nuclear war Caroline, would you shag him?’

Before I could respond, Bernadette was tapping a glass with a spoon. ‘Come on in, everyone.’ She was beckoning us as well.

‘That had better be the champagne talking, Ursula,’ I countered and winked.

‘If you let your hair down, it’ll be bouncier than Carla’s.’ Ursula grabbed my hand and pulled me back towards the house. I could see John looking at us both. I lowered my eyes. I couldn’t read his face. There we all were, the adults and the four youngsters, all back in the room. It was Rob’s turn to give a speech.

‘Okay everyone, here we are again. I’m not going to take long but…’

The doorbell went.

Bernadette dashed off to answer, and a few minutes of us all shuffling on the spot later, Ursula’s James and my Jack were with us all in the living room.

‘We’ve just finished work,’ James said as he and Jack did a half wave at us all. I smiled at Jack. They were both so grown up now. It seemed years ago when they were small boys running around, now we'd put them both to work with Steve and Jay for the summer holidays.

'Are either of you driving?' Rob asked them.

'No,' they both replied.

Carla was up and off to the kitchen immediately. Once they had glasses in their hands, Rob continued.

'As ecstatic as we are to have Carla and Luke here, we have more good news to share. I'm going to go alphabetically to avoid any charges of favouritism. Ruby,' he said and halted. All eyes were upon her. I could see her squirming from the attention.

'Ruby, we've all known you for years, and it will come as no surprise to you that I can only do this in English, while you can probably do it equally well in French or Italian. Which is just as well, as huge congratulations are in order for your three A stars at A level, and your place at Oxford University to study French and Italian.'

All of us whooped, cheered and clapped as Ruby blushed the colour of her name. Bernadette and Carla nearly squeezed the life out of her, but when Ursula ruffled Ruby's hair and Ruby hugged her, I felt duplicitous tears welling up. My friend. My friend who had Jack over when I was still juggling the commute. I brushed them away. Fiona was grabbing me.

'Don't forget Ruby's present.'

'Oh gosh, yes.' I walked towards Ruby.

'Darling, we all thought you'd need this.' I handed her the wrapped item.

Her eyes lit up, and then she looked a bit downcast when she opened it and saw a bicycle bell.

I couldn't help but laugh. I loved how she didn't hide her disappointment.

'Come on Ruby, aren't you curious about the bell?' Fiona asked her. Ruby looked puzzled.

'Why have I got a bell for a bike?' Rolled eyes and a bit of a bottom lip pout accompanied her question.

'I'll put you out of your misery,' I said as I grabbed her hand and led her out of the living room, into the hallway, and then onto the drive. Everyone followed. Rob stood proudly holding a baby blue coloured bike with white tyres and a basket.

'You'll need this in Oxford.' I said.

Ruby beamed and Alice was pointing at the basket.

'Look Ruby, there's something else,' Alice said.

She eagerly opened the huge package that had been sat in the basket and squealed when it revealed a beautiful oak-coloured Mulberry Bayswater bag.

'Oh my days!!' Ruby danced around with her bag.

'We know you have Gucci tastes Ruby, but this is quintessentially British and a present from your Granny, read the card.' I handed her an envelope. My mother had managed to write somewhat shakily, due to her Parkinson's, how proud she was of Ruby. My sister had sent nothing other than a text to her and an email to me, pointing out she'd had to help order the bag for our mother and didn't I think it was too expensive for a bag. I knew I'd have to go to visit shortly, bearing suitable gifts and a smile. But this was Ruby's moment, and for once, this moment had nothing to do with anyone but her. Rob then reminded us there was someone else to mention. Ruby stood next to me, hugging her bag. Fiona went and stood next to Tyrel. We were all outside still, with the late afternoon, early autumn sunshine on us.

'Tyrel, it is your turn now,' Rob continued. 'I cannot emphasise how proud we all are of you. It feels as if you've been a member of this family forever, and that is no mean feat. And what you have achieved is certainly no mean feat.' He hesitated, and I could see him welling up. Fiona was stood with her arm around Tyrel's shoulder. 'To get all seven GCSEs you sat, and only really studied for for less than a year, is in itself massive, but to get three 8's, A's in old money...'

Most of us laughed.

'... is incredible! The rest were 7's, again B's in old money, and you now have a place in the sixth form at Alice's school. I also want to give you this.'

He handed Tyrel an open envelope. Tyrel pulled out the letter and read it.

'What does it say?' Alice asked before snatching it off him. He was beaming. 'Sick! You've got a football scholarship!' Alice threw her arms around him and they both jumped in joy. Henry joined in immediately.

Even I brushed a tear away. John walked up to him and extended his hand to Tyrel to shake. Tyrel gave John a hug instead.

'Speech!' James shouted. Ursula nudged him.

'I'd like to say a few words if that is alright with you, Tyrel?' John waited for his reply, which was a nod of the head. I could see how choked up Tyrel was.

'Thanks Ty, when I first met you, it wasn't ideal circumstances. You didn't know me, but I always hoped that I could know you. I have no idea why I felt your circumstances were beyond your control, but I did. I want to thank Mr Etheridge and Fiona for helping me in my mission, I couldn't have done it without their support. It's a shame he's not here today, but when he gets back from Hong Kong, he will be over the moon at this news. But this isn't about me or anyone else. Tyrel, you are incredible. You took an opportunity, and with minimal fuss, you have worked your socks off and look where you are. You start in sixth form this coming week. I know you'd give anything to have your family back, but I think I'm right when I say we are all family and friends now, and are always here for you.' John broke into a smile. Tyrel grinned back.

'You ain't bad for a fed,' he said, and we all laughed.

'Present time again, Tyrel.' Fiona stepped towards him with a holdall. 'This is the school sports holdall, but look inside.'

We all watched as he opened the bag and pulled out football boots and some wireless earbuds. Tyrel immediately hugged Fiona.

'Thanks.'

'You're welcome, and next I'll be making sure you study hard, so milk this moment.'

She beamed while looking at him. I glanced at Alice, but she was equally full of happiness for Tyrel's moment. How different from my siblings, who were diffident and uninterested in each other's existence. Jack, Ruby and James surrounded Tyrel to look at the earbuds and boots. I walked away and went into the kitchen, where I found Bernadette and Carla tidying up.

'Let me help.' I said.

Carla immediately handed me a tea towel.

'You dry, please.'

Bernadette winked at me.

'Your Jack and Ruby have grown into fine specimens, Caroline.'

'Aww, thank you.'

'You must be so proud of Ruby.'

'Yes, I think she gets her brains from my mother. I didn't even do A levels.'

'It is the same with my Ines. Where she got her brains from, I do not understand. Maybe it is you, Bernadette?' Carla added a shrug for further effect.

'Ah, her daddy Luke was always a good student.' And at this, Bernadette burst into tears. I prevented Carla from smothering her and took her hand to lead her to the seating area outside.

'I'm sorry Caroline, I'm truly happy to have my boy back but I can't help minding. All those lost years. All the worry and pain.'

'Have you managed to have some time alone with him?' I gently asked. 'I mean real time alone without Fiona or Carla.'

'No, not really.'

'Let me get him while you sit out here to relax for a moment. You've been non-stop. Let Carla carry on. I'll get the youngsters to do a final pour and sweep of the glasses so you can rest here.'

She patted my knee.

I found Jack and asked him to get James and Ruby to help Carla.

'Maybe the others as well?' he asked.

'Sure, get Ruby to organise them. There is a bit of tidying up to do, not much, but let's not outstay our welcome,' I replied.

I found Luke looking at a picture.

'Hey, do you mind if I have a word?' He turned round.

'We've probably not really been fully introduced, and you obviously don't know me from Adam, but your mother is outside and she's a bit teary.'

He looked upset. I softened it by putting my hand on his forearm.

'Not your fault with Fiona monopolising everything.'

'Carla is a bit all over my mother as well, isn't she?' Luke gave a rueful smile.

'Which is adorable. I'm sure Bernadette is lapping it up, but she needs some time with you. Some time alone with each other. I doubt she even wants to talk. She is aching for all the missed time with you.'

I thought for one minute I'd gone too far, after all, he had his reasons for going away. Instead, he said, 'Thank you.' We both stood there for a moment.

'I'm going to see her now. Can you make sure we aren't interrupted?' Luke asked.

'Will do my best.'

He walked off and side-stepped Fiona, who was talking to John. Stuart came up to me.

'All going well?' He asked.

'I think so, considering I'm only the mother of the super clever child. Currently, my new role is making sure no one gets near Bernadette and Luke if you fancy helping me.'

'Mission accepted. What is the brief?'

'The youth are on kitchen duties and I need you to get Carla sat down with a glass and keep her talking.'

'Yes Ma'am.'

'Off you go.' I hesitated before adding, 'And I expect a good result.' I saw him grin as he went in search of Carla.

'I've heard the sirens for the nuclear attack.'

There was Ursula interrupting my thoughts again.

'Oh, give over. I'm helping Luke and Bernadette have a bonding session. You are now part of the operation.'

'Willingly.'

'What are you two up to?' Fiona asked from across the room.

'Nothing!' we replied in unison.

Two hours later, we were in a taxi on the way home. Ruby was sat clutching her bell and bag.

'Mum, I could have ridden the bike back.'

'You've got no lights and it's too far.'

'She'd have had to get off and walk up any hills,' Jack said, to which Ruby elbowed him. I left them to it. I was too tired to care about young adults squabbling. I took my phone out of my bag and saw there were three missed calls from Ed.

TWENTY SEVEN

'Over there.'

I pointed to the far right corner of the hangar. Jay and I were working to bring the vision of the designs to life. Stuff was strewn everywhere. The plants were neatly grouped, but the bigger pieces were less organised. The hangar was dwarfing our areas, but I could see Steve laying hay bales strategically to create zones. The warm sunlight was either giving my face a glow, or I'm due a hot flush.

'Caroline, don't take this the wrong way, I'm not perving, but has something changed recently? You've lost weight.'

I could see the panic on his face as he said that.

'In a healthy way I mean, sort of slim, strong and toned,' he said and paused. I didn't say anything. 'You look different.'

'In what way?'

'More relaxed.'

'I haven't been joining those lads who start their day in the Stew Pond car park with a morning joint, I can assure you.'

We both laughed. Every time we'd had an early morning rendezvous there for convenience, lo and behold, there was another gardening van. From it, there was a huge stench of weed at eight o'clock in the morning. It seemed to be a thing. It was either the gardeners or the guys turning up to fish.

'Reef expectations as I call them,' Jay replied.

'Thanks for the compliment anyway,' I said as I passed him with a few plants to put in place. 'I've no idea why I feel different. Maybe I've relaxed now that Ruby is off to university, despite her extensive demands.'

Or perhaps it was the stress of John knowing. I hadn't been

able to eat much for weeks. Also, I'd reduced my anti-depressant dose to next to nothing as the HRT kicked in. Then my mind wandered off briefly to Ed. We'd hardly seen each other in the last few weeks, which I'd found pleasantly surprising. No demands made of me, no need to put him first. Less guilt.

'No one in the picture?'

'I could say the same to you.'

Jay looked in the distance.

'I can't click with anyone. I've met some lovely women, but no one who I feel at ease with. Am I being too fussy?' He sighed.

'No! If you don't feel it's right, that is all that matters. You can't force it. I've been seeing someone on and off and...' I didn't get to finish.

'Reporting for duty, ma'am.' There was Stuart smiling at me. I introduced Stuart to Jay and then asked him, 'Haven't you got a proper job to attend to?'

'Her majesty Fiona has requested all hands on deck. Who am I to deny?'

I laughed. Fiona had certainly demanded help. I looked around and Ursula was frantic with a list and checking the catering. Fiona was being interviewed by a journalist, leaving Steve to work on one section on his own.

'I think Steve needs some help.'

'I'll go over with him.' Jay smiled and didn't give me a chance to stop him. I had meant to send Stuart.

'Looks like you are stuck with me then.' Stuart looked pleased.

'Okay. I need you to help me plant these, and then we have to rearrange the installations.'

We worked silently and quickly. I found him easy to be alongside, and he followed my lead. Midday came, and we took a breather. Steve and Jay joined us. We sat on the hay bales at the edge of the hangar. I lay down to drink in the warmth of the sun. It was more fun than I'd anticipated, lying here looking up at the blue sky. The event was hard work, but it felt like such an achievement. I lifted up my head and peered to find Fiona. I couldn't see her, so carried on with my rest. Ursula flopped down next to me.

'I'm pooped and I've got the styling to do still,' she said and groaned.

'Haven't you got any help?' I asked.

'No, because I've got hired help this evening for drinks, canapes and welcoming. Fiona was strict about it. Classic event and PR budget. Oh, this is nice lying down here. Don't let me fall asleep.'

We all seemed to lie there for an age. I heard Ursula sigh, and I looked towards her, but she had her eyes closed. I couldn't tell her about Ed. I knew it would be the end of our friendship and my current life. The voice of my grandma Malory entered my thoughts, *'Most people are disappointing.'* My actions were disappointing. As much as I justify the fact that Ed would have been a serial philanderer without me as an outlet, was it a wise choice? I did fall for him, and I do know Ursula left him not because of Fiona's revelation of the woman in the bar, but the realisation that her marriage was over. It had been one-sided, but still. My plan to dance with him at the wedding was the best option. Get permission, take it from there. I shoved guilt away. Pointless to dwell.

'Come on, lazy bones.' Stuart's voice penetrated my mind.

Ursula groaned. 'I've got to get back to it. Thanks for the siesta, Caro.' She hauled herself up.

'I've got to be off in an hour,' Stuart said. 'What do you want me to do until then?'

'Can you help Ursula?' I suggested.

'No, I'm fine, honestly. It takes too much time explaining things. See you in a bit.' She dashed off before I could say anything else. I must have looked a bit crestfallen.

'Anything the matter?' Stuart asked.

'Gosh, no. Probably need Fiona to give me some input,' I answered.

'And here I am.'

Fiona stood right next to me and looked across at the *Totally Tranquil* area I'd been working on. The sunlight shone into the hangar, and the installed pond twinkled in a kaleidoscope of colour. Even the enveloping grasses seemed glossy with the light reflection.

'Wow. I'm genuinely impressed. The way you've brought everything together is glorious.'

'I think the sun did a PR job for me right then.' I laughed. It did look good.

'I do wish it was summer and I could add some lychnis to add some grey to tie in with the eucalyptus in the outdoor kitchen area,' I replied.

'*Form and Function* area, Caroline.'

'Alright Fiona, CEO.'

She poked me in my side.

We laughed. It was incredible to think we were about to launch a business. A long way away from me inadvertently digging up a dead body. I crossed myself.

'What was that for? Fiona asked.

'You know, dead body moment. Gives me the shudders.' I shrugged my shoulders.

Stuart was stood there shuffling his feet.

'Are we going to do some more? I can go now if not needed.'

'Sorry,' I said immediately. 'Of course you are needed. We'll be quick, only a few more things to move and plant.' I smiled at him and he stopped looking so bored.

'Alright, I've got half an hour now.'

I winked at Fiona, who managed a thanks to Stuart.

'Rob is coming soon,' she said as she walked off.

I grabbed my can of *Forza* and sprayed a few circles for us to dig and then plant.

'How come you got divorced then, Stuart?' I asked him.

'My wife, or rather my ex-wife, decided.'

'Okay.'

He laughed.

'Did I sound bitter? Honestly, I'm not. It's just I disappointed her and I'm sad about that.'

I thought about asking him if he still loved her, but decided against it. I didn't want to sound as if I was interested or cared. But he carried on regardless.

'It was my job. The time spent away, the shifts and the fact I was often very distant.' He sighed.

As I patted the soil with my hand around the plant I'd put in, I changed tack.

'What is the funniest thing that's happened to you at work?'

He paused and I could see his eyes lifting up as if searching within his mind.

'During your probationary training, you get your first dead body shout. My supervising officer took the call and told me we were going to have to enter a property. I was really nervous and also really hyped up. The neighbours are outside the property, an ambulance is on its way, but we have to enter. The door opens after a few shoves and I almost fall in with my final push, and there is a body of a man, lying face down, halfway across the hallway, with the rest of him in the other room. The other room turns out to be the downstairs toilet, his trousers are down around his ankles, and his bare backside is sunny side up. The supervising officer has tears rolling down his face and he's shaking with laughter. Even the ambulance crew crease up when they get there. I did find it funny a few days later. The poor old boy had had a fatal heart attack whilst having a dump.'

I did laugh because he looked as horrified as when it happened.

'I expect you'll find your dead body story funny in a few years,' Stuart said with one eyebrow raised.

A rather unreasonable flash of irritation ran through my body. I'd pushed the memory of the unfortunate incident away. It wasn't done on purpose, and I hadn't actually killed the person. Why would he bring it up? Men. I carried on planting and refused to look at him. We continued working in silence until all the plants were in position.

'Right, I need to get the hose and water all these now.' I finally broke the atmosphere with my work mode voice.

'I'm off anyway. Hope it all goes well tonight.' He smiled at me.

'Oh, okay, and thanks.' I was taken aback by his pleasant tone. I was used to Ed being petulant and needing reassurance. It was a relief not to have to explain myself for reacting or not talking. Stuart patted me on the shoulder and was off.

Watering the plants, I had some time to myself. To think. Was I a terrible person? I certainly was a terrible friend and had failed as a wife to a drug addict. The latter was understandable, it was a choice to save my sanity, what little money I had left, and protect the children. But Ed? What was the excuse for him? *'Caroline, people are disappointing. Très très décevant.'* Grand-mère penetrating my consciousness again. Did Malory live in my subconscious? I physically shook my head. The water was suddenly over my foot and I had managed to soak my Crocs and socks. Forgive me, grand-mère. I was mainly thinking about her look if she'd seen the Crocs I was wearing. I started to giggle.

'Are you sure you haven't been on the weed?' Jay asked as he came back with some bark to put down.

'Nope. Daydreaming.'

We both scattered the bark where required and stood back to admire the area. The cottage garden plants looked lovely, especially the out-of-season hollyhocks we'd managed to get from a supplier who grew them indoors. Most of the plants were out of season, but arranging them in clusters with a gravel walkway to the next zone helped to recreate the feel. Our hammock had a beautiful pot of red flowered salvia next to it, and Ursula had 'dressed' the area with a couple of mismatched cushions, a blanket in the hammock, and some books on the floor with a mug and magazine.

'Not bad for a toker.' Jay laughed.

'Ha ha! Don't give up the day job, mate,' was my retort.

We stood there, again in silence, to evaluate our handiwork. I did feel proud and as I looked around, the whole hangar was nearly finished, ready for this evening's launch. Jay interrupted my thoughts again.

'Before Fiona makes us do a final walk round, was that the new fellow you were with? The one who's...' He hesitated. 'Well, you know.'

'No, I don't, and no, he isn't. He's John's colleague. That is how I know him.'

I almost snorted with indignation. How had Jay thought that about me and Stuart? I'd barely looked at the guy. Jay shrugged his shoulders and didn't say any more. My indignation was interrupted by Fiona calling us all to the right-hand side of the hangar. We almost lined up behind her on the path which led from the farmyard block to the hangar. Almost. Ursula and

I tentatively muscled our way alongside her.

'Okay, fresh eyes everyone.' Fiona was in full command. 'Walk through, take it all in and let's regroup to discuss.'

The few helpers we had left shuffled awkwardly on the spot. I suspected they'd rather be off and had no view on anything, it was job done as far as they were concerned. I tried to give an encouraging smile, but Ursula pulled me forward so my head spun back to walk forward with her.

'Come on Caro, let's get this over with. I need to get home and change. Especially as Ed is coming.'

'Is he?' I replied.

'Well yes, because of media and advertising. Fiona insisted. I'm just glad John is working tonight so I don't need to worry about them being in the same space.'

Ursula plumped a cushion on the seats in the outdoor kitchen area. Not to be outdone, I rearranged some herb pots. I didn't realise Ed was coming. I hadn't spoken to him for a few days, and not given him much thought with this event taking place. Now I needed to get home and spruce myself up as well. Honestly, what a pain. I did a mental flick through my wardrobe and realised I had nothing to wear. Most of my clothes were too big for me now and I hadn't bought anything new for ages.

'I've got nothing to wear,' I said aloud before I could stop myself.

'Me neither,' Ursula responded. 'Right, we've got no option but to hot-foot it into town and dive into M&S.'

'Really?'

'Yes, let's go.'

She marched up to Fiona, told her we were happy but needed to make ourselves presentable, and would be back at six thirty. She didn't wait for the response. I waved and followed her to the car.

'Book an Uber or taxi for later as it'll be impossible to park here. I'll drop you back at yours after shopping.'

Ursula started the car and, in her customary fashion, made sure she had music on coming through the CarPlay. Dexy's Midnight Runners came blaring out, *Seven days too long.*

I looked at Ursula.

'I'm having a nostalgic teenage bedroom playlist phase. *Mirror in the Bathroom* is next.'

I laughed. Before I knew it, thanks to the music, we were parking up and making a dash for the store. Thank goodness Ursula was so stylish, she grabbed things almost out of fresh air, and before long I was in the changing room with a pale blue shirt on and olive green trousers. Ursula was folding up the sleeves.

'Stay there.' And off she dashed. As if I was going anywhere.

She returned with an ivory chunky knit.

'It will get colder later once the sun drops, and you can put this on. Do you have any decent trainers?'

'You sound like Ruby. She adds 'decent' and raises an eyebrow when she asks me about any item of clothing.' I smiled.

'Oh gosh, sorry, I'm doing it all in a rush. Have you?' Ursula winked.

'No.'

'Fuck's sake.' And she was off again.

I liked the pale blue of the shirt. My highlighted blonde hair was enhanced as the curls fell on the shoulder. I did a twirl.

'Quick, put these on. Luckily, they've got loads of shoes and trainers in stock. Size 6, yes?'

I nodded. As I put them on, Ursula was quickly trying on her items. There we were both dressing for the same man, for different reasons, and I was trying not to think about it. Ursula had the same trousers as me, but in navy, and a white shirt with a grey chunky jumper.

'I've got some green New Balance trainers, I'll wear them with this look even if they're not in anymore, no one will know,' she said as we both admired ourselves.

'Ruby would.'

'Of course! Well, we both look on point and sort of on brand in our newly created *Serene Spaces* uniform.' She laughed.

I gave Ursula a hug. She'd done a marvellous job at breakneck speed. We paid for our items and then she dropped me off at home.

'Make sure you add some lippy.' Her parting remark as *Down in the Tube Station at Midnight* was heard loud and clear through her open window as she pulled off. Less than an hour later, I was on my way back to the event.

'Is this the right place? You sure, love?'

The taxi driver wasn't happy to be turning off the main road onto a track. It was a concrete one, but there was quite a lot of mud in various places.

'Drop me where you can turn around just up here, please.' I ignored his whinging as I bounced out of the car.

I wasn't sure what I was more excited about, the event, or unexpectedly seeing Ed. I'd resisted the urge to text him, especially as I'd had such a lovely time with Ursula. It felt wrong, and also, I needed to let it all build up naturally to the wedding. I decided to chat pleasantly with him tonight, safe in the knowledge that John wouldn't be there.

There were already a lot of cars parked in the farm's parking area. A sign pointed the way to the hangar. There were fairy lights along the pathway, and I got a real buzz before stepping back into the hard work of the day. The whole space looked amazing and I was handed a glass of fizz as I walked into the hangar and our business launch. How had we got from arguing with Fiona at Ursula's house when she insisted on our gardening business, Cultivating and Co., to this? A huge launch party for *Serene Spaces*, a gardening franchise business. I stood there in wonder.

'Quick, come with me,' hissed Ursula as she grabbed my free hand and pulled me in a direction towards the Portaloo area. 'Avoid Fiona, she actually frigging air kissed me. She's with city types. I need you, Jay, and Steve for a photograph for a magazine photographer. Let's find them.'

We found them sat in the outdoor area, *Form and Function*. They were at one of the tables which Ursula had decorated with thyme plants in ceramic pots, and next to their table was a rosemary bush and olive trees, all in white planters. I'd not seen either of them out of their work clothes since our night out ages ago. Both of them were wearing white shirts and had jeans on.

'Great, you've got the white shirts on.'

'Hello Ursula, nice to see you too.' Jay winked at me as he said it. Steve was grinning.

'Oh, okay, sorry, but no time for pleasantries. You both look great, by the way, I'll give you that. Right, come on, photoshoot.' Ursula pointed towards the *Totally Tranquil* area.

'Lots of shrubs and the palm trees to pose in,' she explained.

The photographer was all set up, and he took some light meter readings whilst his assistant repositioned what looked like a lamp and a big square of tin foil on a tripod.

'It's a reflection thing,' Jay whispered to me, reading my quizzical look.

But I noticed he was looking at the assistant. She was too busy moving the equipment to notice his staring. I nudged him and did the fake throwing back of my head and laughing. We were both then doubled up.

'What?' Steve said, looking confused.

'Only Jay looking at the equipment,' I replied and did a side head movement in the direction of the assistant. As I was doing this, I saw Ed in the distance. He was talking to Fiona.

'Can you guys move together more, please?'

The photographer signalled he wanted us closer with his hands as well. He kept gesturing until I was almost squashed between Steve and Jay.

'He's going to ask you if you are wearing a bra next,' Jay muttered, and we started laughing again.

'What now?' Steve exclaimed.

'Charlie Dimmock.' Jay was pointing his finger down at my head. Steve raised his eyebrows and did an eye roll.

'Actually, can we stand behind the bed of *lychnis*?' I said to the photographer. 'This area of pink.'

I suddenly wanted to look good in the photographs. I wanted to maximise my posing with Jay and Steve. I knew Ed would see us. After a quick reshuffle and lots of poses with me mainly leaning forward, smiling, with my arms around the waist of both Steve and Jay, we got the shoot out of the way. Ursula seemed happy, and the photographer was looking through the photos. Jay had made a beeline for the assistant, and I put my hand on Steve's arm and suggested we go find Fiona together. Ed wasn't with her. She was being interviewed by a journalist. Ursula was standing nearby. I walked over to her.

'How is it going?' I asked.

'All good, Well, I've managed most of my list. There are a few no shows, and Ed has left already, so he won't be here for when we do our speech thing, thank goodness.'

'I didn't see him.'

'He wasn't here long, some other meeting he had to go to,

but the main thing is he did the FT interview with Fiona about how advertising on home improvements is seeing an increase again in his sector, particularly on outdoor living. He did say something brilliant about ice baths and Wim Hof. Fiona immediately mentioned the *Totally Tranquil* element of the *Serene Spaces* business. It might be a new option.' Ursula was beaming despite being focused on getting everything done.

I tried not to look crestfallen. Why hadn't he mentioned ice baths to me? Had we talked about my designs? I couldn't remember. Why would he go without even a momentary catch-up? Then my phone pinged. I checked my messages. Sure enough, it was Ed. He was in his car. He wanted me to come and see him. I made some excuse and wandered off, checking no one was with me and was watching where I was going. Of course, he was being driven. The back door of the Mercedes was open. I got in and shut the door quickly. He practically pulled me on top of him. His nose was buried in the top of my head.

'I've missed this mop,' he said as he lifted his head off mine and leant back into the door he was leaning partly against.

'I can't stay long, I've got to go back.'

'More fooling around with hot younger men on the cards?'

'Oh, give over Ed. That was work.' Although I was secretly pleased he minded. I knew he would have seen me.

'Well, I've got some work for you.' He started to unzip his trousers.

'Ed!'

'What Caroline?' He looked taken aback.

I scrunched up the left side of my face and pointed my head in the direction of his driver. He stuck his tongue in my right ear and pulled me on top of him. Tempted as I was, I used my free left arm to push myself back up and then completely sat up on the back seat.

'Ed, I can't. I've got to go back. Come to mine later.'

'I'll see.' His voice sounded a bit sulky.

'You know I want to, but the business event is so important.' I tried to sound disappointed in an attempt to soothe him. I opened the door, leant back towards him, and gave him a quick kiss and squeezed his balls as I backed out of the car. As soon as I shut the door, the engine started and off the car went. I smoothed my hair, tucked my shirt back in properly, and stood there for a moment. No one else seemed to have been there, so I breathed a sigh of relief. That was too close a call. The sun was setting, and I needed the jumper chosen by Ursula. I wanted to be with her and Fiona. As I walked back to the hub of the hangar, I could hear *Jolene.* I smiled. Of course, Ursula hadn't dropped the whole of her plans, she'd kept the Dolly Parton tribute singer. I ran, filled with pride, instead of walking; I didn't want to miss another moment. This was our night.

TWENTY EIGHT

The weeks had flown by since the launch, and I'd been nonstop with alternative designs and sourcing new products for the franchise. Fiona's business acumen had struck home, and we had four companies in different parts of the country becoming a *Serene Spaces* franchise. It's why I had to undertake a few alterations to our recommendations. It seems Cheshire is a hot spot for ice baths.

I grudgingly had to acknowledge to Ed that he had come up with a great suggestion. I decided not to ask him why he hadn't mentioned it directly to me. I suspect he was trying to score brownie points with Fiona. It is also why he's given her rock-bottom media rates to run some adverts. We still weren't back to seeing each other as much as we had been, but with driving both Ruby and Jack back to university, the business planning, and actual gardening work, I didn't really mind. I was being patient. As long as Ed came to the wedding as an evening guest, I could start to pave the way for us being together properly.

Today was not different in terms of work, but interestingly, we were having a meeting at Mr Etheridge's house. I hadn't had time to think too much about it as I had a client meeting of my own with a hotel venue. Fiona had abandoned the idea of The Barn as it would be too cold for December. Ursula had managed to steer her away from settling on the local pub, despite it being a very nice pub, to a nearby hotel.

I was enjoying the late morning drive with the trees bowing over the road and creating a headdress of copper, red, yellow, and green. My life was a million miles away from being a teaching assistant and the drudgery of photocopying. The hotel venue had been happy to indulge Fiona in a tentative chat about gardening needs. I knew I needed to have a wander around the grounds first and propose something useful, but not attempt to take over their landscaping contract. We weren't in the business of treading on anyone's toes, well, I certainly wasn't. That thought led to a pang of guilt and John's words ringing in my ears. He'd kept his word and not said anything all this time. I was nervous about how he would react at the wedding, but I was counting on him not spoiling Fiona and Rob's big day.

The hotel looked resplendent, covered in ivy, as I approached it on the driveway. It was very much a country-style place, and I was surprised it was located here. I hadn't expected such a place on a main road towards Leatherhead. I swung the car into a parking place off the main drive and switched off the engine. A quick reapplication of lippy before I got out, and made my way to reception. Once there, I explained my visit and asked if it was okay to have a wander around outside before meeting with the general manager.

To my eye, the aesthetics of the landscaping were classic and bold, if not a little dated. The grounds, being beautifully kept, were proliferated with trees and shrubs. A dewdrop fell from one of the trees and splattered away. I explored behind the tree, and it was there I spied an opportunity for our *Classic Cottage* option. Full of confidence, I walked back to the hotel.

Before I knew it, I was at Mr Etheridge's house.

'How was the meeting?' Fiona was sat on a huge, comfy green velvet sofa, so I joined her.

'Oh, this is rather nice.'

'Less about sofas and more about work, please.' As soon as she said it, I moved because I knew she was going to try and tickle me.

'We are too grown up for that, Fiona.' I couldn't help but smile. I quickly told her everything while Ursula was helping Mr Etheridge to make some drinks in the kitchen.

'Do you think they are interested?' she asked.

'I think they liked my *Classic Cottage* idea the most. It fits in with the style of the place, but it was the idea of creating it as an almost hidden nook with a hammock that they liked. I might have said it was a place to retreat, within a country retreat.'

'Whatever works for them. Best no one disgraces themselves at the wedding,' Fiona replied as Rob came into the room. I wasn't expecting to see him, and nor, by the look on her face, was Fiona.

'Oh, hello Mr Clarke. What are you doing here?' Fiona got up to give him a hug and a kiss.

'John called me earlier and suggested I come. I forgot to let you know.'

'Rob, would you like tea or coffee?' Ursula asked.

'Tea, please.'

Rob went over to shake Mr Etheridge's hand.

'Hi David, how's tricks?'

Only Rob could pull that off. Fiona and I pulled a face at each other as we'd never quite mastered calling him David. I glanced around at the lovely space and light in the room. Everything was white, olive green or wood. It all looked very Italian. For a moment, I was transported to Milan and Paulo's parents' apartment, not their one in Venice nor their house at Lake Como. The apartment was extremely modern, and at the time, it was very white, something vastly different to the floral wallpaper and heavy furniture my family had at home. How I loved that apartment for its cosmopolitan vibe. How I had loved Paulo then, and how innocent that love had been. My memories were dispensed with immediately when Ursula handed me a cup of tea.

'You okay, Caroline?' she asked.

'I was deep in admiration of the interiors in this place.'

'Isn't it the best? I love it so much.' Her gaze left me and took in the room.

The tranquillity of the moment was undone with the arrival of John with Stuart and another colleague. I wondered what this was all about. It had to be the body. Why else would we be here? But then, Rob had come too, and he had nothing to do with it. Stuart smiled at me. I nodded back. He did look nice in his suit. I had thought he was a bit burly, but I realised now it was simply his stature and muscles. I dismissed any further observations from my mind. It wasn't as if I was interested in him, but he kept well...being there.

We were all sat down when John got up and started to address us all. He loosened his tie a bit and thought for a moment before he said, 'Right everybody, I should let you all know what we are here for today.'

He paused and we all seemed to move forward on whatever item we were sat on. There was total silence in anticipation of his next words.

'I've never done this before, talked about a case in such an informal setting. However, with the coroner's and my boss's permission, I am going to explain to you our work and identification of the body discovered here over eighteen months ago. This, I think, is my Hercule Poiret moment when I do the reveal.' He smiled.

'More like Death in Paradise,' Stuart said.

'Thanks DC Johnson, who I did think of as my Captain Hastings until the heckling.'

We were all laughing, but I think it was more out of light relief from the trepidation of what he was going to say. Ed would have hated it if he were here, with John commanding the room in this way, all of us mesmerised about what he was going to tell us.

'Right where was I? Oh yes, the work on identifying the remains of a decomposed body at this very location. I've been rude and failed to introduce DC Duncan Bennett, who along with myself and comedy Stuart there, has been working on the case. No one from the forensic team could join us today, nor the forensic pathologist, but they will be at the coroner's formal inquest.'

He took a sip of water.

'There is going to be a formal inquest, but it really is a formality with routine processes to be completed. However, the body will be released after this date, and I'll come back to this point.'

The room continued to remain silent. We were transfixed, and I couldn't remember the last time my mind was this empty and waiting for the next sentence.

'You'll all be pleased to know no charges are to be brought for the initial discovery, and the concealment is omitted from our submitted report to the coroner.'

'Flipping heck, John.' Fiona exclaimed, looking a bit cross. I think he was enjoying teasing us, and Stuart winked at me. Ursula rolled her eyes.

'It's okay Fiona, I couldn't resist that. You are off the hook and have been for ages, but you know, formalities. Back to business. Okay, so we really didn't have much to go on as there didn't appear to be anything significant or that stood out from analysis of the body. We knew she was female, we knew she had multiple low-level injuries consistent with harsh living conditions and taking drugs. There were no broken bones or impact to the skull. The reconstruction was able to pinpoint residue toxicity impact on her bones from heroin use, bruising from needle use, bruising on the knees and legs from falling or climbing, and the fact she'd had a full term pregnancy due to the pelvis position and what could be identified as muscle or womb lining. Very little of the muscles were still covering the skeleton, but the team had enough tissue to identify organs, tendons and other parts of the body in their reconstructive analysis. But enough of the forensics.' He drew breath. 'We knew we had to identify a female roughly aged twenty-five or younger. We did a huge trawl of missing people within the location and slightly further afield, but drew a blank.'

He picked up a glass of water from the sideboard next to him and had a sip before carrying on.

'It was when we did the Tyrel handover at The Barn coffee area that I noticed the close proximity of Mr Etheridge's house to the farm. Duncan then went back there and was able to establish reported burglaries at the farm and time stamp them. We painstakingly went through all convictions or all incidents where the suspect was unable to be convicted.'

Again, John took a sip of water and drew breath.

'This is where it gets interesting. We were able to identify one individual who committed at least two known burglaries and possibly a third. He was a known drug user, a petty offender to sustain his drug habit, and he was linked to a few women who were his on/off girlfriends. For some reason. he was quite the flavour.'

John shrugged his shoulders and gestured by raising his lower arms.

'We identified the man as Gary Reid. Now, Gary Reid died in a fire at a flat in Wallington over fourteen years ago. There was one other body, which at the time was identified as a Lynette Wilcox. In looking further into Lynette, we discovered a couple of key things. Firstly, she was fostered by the Etheridges as a teenager. She was with them for nearly two years before she ran away at fifteen. After that, she was put into a care home, and it was there she first met Gary.

We suspect Gary got Lynette into drugs, but we also know there was a period of a few years where she was working full-time at a fashion store in Croydon and was drug free. We know this because during this period she gave birth to a son. But not long after the birth, it seems she went off the rails again. It is a complex story, and who knows what went wrong, but even us police officers know enough today about post-traumatic stress and post-partum depression having horrific impacts on people.

Everyone thought Lynette had died in that fire. The police files were extracted from the Met, and the identification was due to documentation pertaining to Lynette, including personal possessions.' He stopped. 'But she didn't. And it is likely she also may not have gone off the rails, but was lured back or absconded to assist in a burglary for Gary Reid. Most of what we can piece together though, is supposition in terms of how she ended up being buried in the garden of this house.'

Ursula had grabbed my hand by now and was holding it. All of us were stunned. There was a sense there was more to come. The poor thing. At least we had a name now and a person. It was no longer the dead body. I felt a bit nauseous. Again, John hesitated to speak and looked across at Stuart and Duncan. Duncan stood up, and John looked relieved.

'To carry on from the DCI, I have liaised with colleagues in the Met as to our discovery and given them all the information we are sharing with you now, because it would mean Lynette's death occurred earlier then when her known family were informed, and it also leaves a question mark over the flat fire. Namely, was there a third victim who died at the scene?

This is why the coroner is opening and closing the recording of the death and the verdict swiftly, so we can pass all the documentation over to the Met for them to reinvestigate the incident at Wallington. We are fairly confident the death of Lynette will be recorded as an open verdict, either accidental or by misadventure. As the DCI, er, John said, we really don't have any reason to suspect foul play, but we do believe her previous known relationship with Gary Reid contributed to the circumstances leading up to her death.'

He nodded at John and Stuart and sat back down. I think we were all gawping by now, and Fiona was on the edge of her seat. I saw Stuart glance at Mr Etheridge before he rose. Mr Etheridge cast his eyes down, and he suddenly looked very sad.

'Right, it's over to me,' Stuart said immediately. 'And I'm afraid it is a mixed bag for you all to take in. I do want to say it has been a pleasure to have worked on this case, and like John, I am really pleased we can tell you this today, without you having to traipse to the coroner's court. David, I am sorry, I know this is upsetting for you as Lynette was in you and your wife's care at one point. It does seem that around 2011, she helped or had to assist Gary with a burglary on this property. Mr and Mrs Etheridge were away for some considerable time in Hong Kong visiting their son. Their alarm did go off on several occasions, but the neighbour with the key never saw or noticed anything suspicious. Probably because nothing was out of place, but after a chat with Mr Etheridge, he was able to recall some small details which fit with our supposition. David, perhaps you'd like to mention it rather than me.'

Mr Etheridge nodded his head. He didn't get up and stayed seated. Ursula moved to sit next to him.

'Well, there's not much to tell really, other than Eleanor, my late wife, remarking she felt the house had been disturbed.

She insisted somebody had slept in one of the bedrooms, and a couple of friendship bracelets she used to make with the foster children had gone. There was no money to take, and there were no valuables missing. I mean, I am fairly minimalist and actually all the decent stuff is in my study, but unless you are a keen artist or draughtsman, you wouldn't know the value of any of it.' He paused and brushed something off his right trouser leg.

Gosh, he was such an engaging and elegant man. Now I knew why Ursula was always popping over to see him and mooning about the house. John had confidence and authority, but David had a voice that rested any thoughts or soothed you. It reminded me of my father. I don't know where that came from, but suddenly my eyes were filling rapidly with tears and I used the sleeve of my jumper to dab them away. I tried to wriggle my nose, but it didn't help. Stuart got up and came to give me a tissue. I was embarrassed, irritated, and thankful in equal measure. My emotions were ridiculous at the moment. I tried to concentrate on the exchange that had just struck up between David and John.

'It's fine John, I'm happy to continue. Of course, once I knew about Lynette, it seemed Eleanor was right. We came back a couple of months after the event, and apart from what my wife said, I never gave it another moment's thought.' Mr Etheridge paused. John spoke immediately.

'I've already explained to David that Gary was an excellent burglar and would most likely have picked a lock of a door or managed to open a window. What it suggests is he got the valuable items from the farm and needed to bunk down somewhere, before he either got picked up or made his own way to transport. We did do a cross-check with any stolen vehicles, but that drew a blank. Sorry to have interrupted.' Again, the charm and grace of Mr Etheridge shone through as he smiled at John.

'Interrupt me all you like John, this is not an easy or palatable story really. Despite clearing out my wife's clothes and quite a lot of other stuff months after her funeral, I couldn't bring myself to touch her sewing and making table. Her chest of drawers was neatly packed with material, wool, patterns and all manner of things. I gave one of the old friendship bracelets to John and his team. Forensic analysis confirmed the same thread as one found, either on the skeletal remains or the surrounding debris. I didn't ask for details, but was told it was pink. Eleanor loved to make pink and orange plaited bracelets. It was a favourite colour combination of hers.' Another pause. 'But I digress, Lynette was very close to Eleanor during her time spent here. I was still working and really only spent evenings and weekends with the children we had over the years. A couple of them are still in contact, but Lynette wasn't one of them. Anyway...' he really hesitated, and for one moment I thought he was going to break. 'I think it's better to hand back to you, John.'

John stood back up.

'Thanks David, I know it isn't easy to talk about this, but it helps, and you've been a great help on our investigation. In some ways, once we'd pieced everything together, we were able to rule out foul play, although I'll maintain Gary Reid would not have been decent to Lynette. She was in poor health, and it is likely her heart just stopped. Reid would have panicked and buried her here, but ultimately, we have effectively solved, to the best of our knowledge, what happened and why her body was here.'

John stood there wringing his hands and took off his already loosened tie. As he was wrapping it round his hand to put in his pocket, Fiona spoke.

'What is it?' she asked.

'Brace yourselves.'

I drew in a sharp breath, and I could see both Ursula and Fiona looking very apprehensive.

'I couldn't leave it at that. We knew she had had family in the area, so I decided, well, we decided as a team to inform them properly.' John continued. 'Duncan applied for hospital records and we managed to get the baby information and birth date. It took a while because we had to apply for access to certificates. Lynette had married and her surname was now Perera.'

Fiona shrieked. Rob looked as if someone had shot him, and I was wondering why the surname sounded familiar.

'As you may have just realised, Fiona and Rob, Lynette is Tyrel's mother.'

'Good grief!' Ursula exclaimed.

'Does he know?' I asked.

'No, he doesn't,' John replied. 'I'm not sure how we tell him, but we must. He has a right to know, and however difficult the circumstances and information are, he will be fine.'

There we all were, sat in comfy sofas and chairs, stunned into silence—except forJohn, who stood with his arms folded, staring into space. The high ceilings with skylights had clouds floating over. I stared at them to raise my eyes. I couldn't look at anyone. Poor Lynette and poor Tyrel.

TWENTY NINE

It was a bright and sunny, crisp November day, a month after the news of Lynette. There was a chill in the air, alerting one and all to the oncoming winter, but today I enjoyed the dry, sunny optimism of the sunshine. I always used to hope for winter to never come, but now I love the seasons for my work, for the gardening. As I put the finishing touches on the bed, the last of the autumn leaves began to fall. The layers of yellow and brown were spoiling my effort as they dropped and blew over off the trees in Mr Etheridge's garden.

'Cup of coffee or tea, Caroline?'

'Not at the moment, thanks David, I'm nearly done.'

'What have you done here? It looks lovely.'

'It is a crescent style, sloping back, raised bed, and at the tip of each crescent is rosemary. I've put a hazel border in at the back as I could bend it, and I've planted ferns and slow-growing ivy. Then at the front of the crescent, I've put in snowdrop bulbs, as well as these early snowdrops I got from the wholesaler's greenhouse for decoration today,' I said, pausing and pointing. 'In the middle there, I've sunk a hardy frost-resistant plant pot so Tyrel can come and put flowers in, if and when he wants to.' I took a breath and stood back. I had one dilemma. 'Shall I put these couple of hostas in the bed as well? It was when I was planting them over there…' I pointed further along, deeper into the back of the garden bordering the field, 'that we found her.'

Mr Etheridge thought for a moment.

'Yes, plant them. They did give her a better ending than she had. This moon shape you've created is a wonderful gesture. Hang on a moment.'

He was off immediately, back to the house. I planted the hostas and put a big pebble I'd got years ago from Brighton beach in the bottom of the pot so it could be filled with water. The pebble had a faint 'K' painted on it. It must have been Jack's.

'Here we are.' In his hand, Mr Etheridge had a handful of crystals.

'What are they?'

'Moonstone crystals. Rough ones, but I thought they'd be nice for this bed. Here, take them.' He handed me some small, green, oval stones.

'Are you sure?' I asked

'Yes. Please use them. I had them once to inspire me with the colour palette for interiors on one of our building projects.' He smiled.

I put three of the stones next to the sunken pot. There were about ten centimetres of pot showing above the freshly laid soil. I placed them in the middle.

'Only three?' Mr Etheridge said.

'I thought they could represent Tyrel, his mum and his dad.' I glanced nervously at him.

'Splendid. Exactly right.'

There we were, stood looking at a bed created for a memorial ceremony in a couple of hours, for the body we had discovered all that time ago. Me, Fiona, Ursula, and Mr Etheridge, all bound by one body. Our fragmented lives were completely joined up. Living jigsaw pieces melding into a new picture.

'Caroline, look at the stones and the veins coursing over elements of brown and green. It's like it is joining all the fragments of our lives together.'

Stunned.

'You took the words out of my head. I was thinking exactly

the same!'

We linked arms and I had a sudden urge to unburden myself on Mr Etheridge. I wanted to ask him his opinion, but I knew what the answer would be.

'Caroline, ignore your grandmother, she fills your head with fanciful ideas. It is better to be clever than liked. Study hard and don't worry who likes you, otherwise you'll do foolish things for attention.'

'But Papa, grand-mère is right, people are very disappointing, n'est ce pas?'

'Yes Caroline, people are disappointing and life is disappointing. Study hard, find your channel and swim in it.' My father's voice filled my head. I took a deep breath. Mr Etheridge patted my hand.

'Are you feeling alright?' he asked. 'It is all a bit emotional, isn't it? I'm rather glad we've had this maudlin moment before later. We need to stand strong for Tyrel. Come on, let's get back to the house. I'm expecting Ursula to help get things ready, and you can shower and change. Eleanor trained me well.'

He smiled. Gratitude filled my every cell. With Fiona and Rob's wedding two weeks away, the tension about Ed had risen. We'd hardly seen each other lately, but he'd promised me he'd be coming to the evening party. We'd planned to meet tonight but I'd called it off because of today.

After I'd showered and dressed, I towelled my hair and left it damp with my natural curls bouncing a bit higher because I couldn't dry and straighten it. Ursula was in the kitchen. She had baked a cake, and it was incredible. It was heart-shaped and covered in pale green icing with what looked like garlands of flowers at the top and bottom. Five butterfly decorations were added to sit amidst the flowers.

'Ursula, this looks too good to eat.'

'Thanks, Caroline. It is the decorating that makes it look good. It's a really plain but light Victoria sponge inside. I didn't want to make anything heavy in case no one was in the mood for eating. Help me with putting these sandwiches on this board.'

I opened the pre-bought handy sandwich platter and we arranged them on a big wooden board. Ursula put grapes in a bowl and passed me two large packets of crisps to fill a much bigger bowl.

'That was my cheapy fruit bowl from IKEA years ago, but it's great for crisps. I always used to buy wooden so Dan and James couldn't break them.'

'Oh gosh, yes, I don't think Jack and James could be trusted at mine when they were younger with anything. Always a breakage or spillage scenario.' I laughed at the memory.

'Weren't we lucky they got on and were such good friends?' Ursula looked equally as wistful.

'All grown up and left the nest now.'

'Fingers crossed!' she said, and we both laughed.

Then, almost before we'd finished wiping down the counter, everyone had arrived. We made a solemn gathering in the garden. Bernadette was with Tyrel, her arm around him. Rob and Fiona stood alongside him. Alice and Henry, myself, and Mr Etheridge stood on the other side. Ursula was with John, Stuart, and Duncan to Bernadette's right. I didn't know what to expect, but knowing what we did, it felt worse than attending a funeral. I couldn't begin to imagine what Tyrel was going through. The mother he had no memory of. Mr Etheridge cleared his throat.

'Thank you all for coming today, and thank you Caroline, for this lovely memorial patch in memory of Lynette. Tyrel, when your mother came to stay with us, I know she had never had a stable home life. I wish Eleanor were here to tell you all the lovely things they would have done together. I can tell you she was no trouble, but also, she was sad and lacked confidence. Your mother loved this garden because of the space to run around in, but it wasn't enough to hold her, and I'm sorry about that.' He faltered.

Bernadette looked up and interjected.

'Tyrel, whatever troubles your mammy had, she had you. She was married to your daddy, and you had a wonderful life with your family. Your Nana did everything right by you under the circumstances. I know a lot about pain and loss, and you are a grand lad, and you need to say thank you to your mammy for having you.'

With that, the mood changed. John and Stuart started to clap, and we all joined in. It was such a good move, otherwise, there would have been silence. I picked up the bunch of flowers I'd prepared and gave them to Alice. Fiona was too absorbed for me to hand them to her. Alice walked to Tyrel, took his hand, and they both put the flowers in the pot. Henry knelt down with them. We stood patiently watching. Fiona stepped forward and picked Henry off from the ground. She brushed the knees of his trousers. She got Tyrel to stand up and gave him a hug. There they were together, both comforting each other in their sadness. Ursula gestured with her head towards the house. We walked back and were joined by Stuart and Duncan.

'Let's get the kettle on for tea and coffee.'

It was the only thing anyone said until the others came back to the house a little later. Then it took on the trajectory of a wake. The mournful beginning, when no one wants to say anything, then bit by bit, the conversation warms up, usually aided by alcohol. There was no alcohol today. Fiona didn't think it was appropriate, given the whole drug thing. We all stood around chatting.

'You what?' Fiona shrieked. 'That's awesome.'

The room was silent. Ursula was beaming.

'Are you getting married?' I immediately asked her.

'Good grief, no,' she replied.

'Worse, a ruddy mortgage together,' John said. All of us wanted to know more and he knew it, but for some reason, he looked at Mr Etheridge.

'David?'

'Well, now is as good a time as any, I suppose. I am reluctant to say it because it makes it real.'

I felt a real panic. Was he going to say he had cancer? Please no, not Mr Etheridge.

'I'm moving to Singapore to be with my son who has recently moved there from Hong Kong.'

Phew.

'And?' said John.

'That is your news, you tell them.'

Ursula interjected.

'John and I are buying this house. We are moving here. You can come any time you want, Tyrel,' she said.

'We don't want you to go,' I said to Mr Etheridge, which everyone else echoed. I knew he wanted to be with his son, and as much as he was part of our jigsaw, we could never be enough.

'Thank you, Caroline. Who knew when Fiona persuaded me to let you be my gardeners, we'd all be here together like this? It's been quite an event. I think I'm going to Singapore for a well-earned rest.'

We all laughed. He was right, it had been a roller coaster, and next it was the wedding. Suddenly, Tyrel rushed over to Mr Etheridge and gave him a big hug. I needed a tissue again.

We all cleared up after Fiona and Rob left with their tribe

and then said our goodbyes to Mr Ethridge.

'See you in a couple of weeks at the wedding.' I had to give him a hug, too. I didn't like to leave him on his own, but we were going to the pub across the road. Ursula and I walked up the lane to the main road.

'Oh, it's quite dark, isn't it?' I put my arm through hers as I was slightly disconcerted.

'Yes, but peaceful and a new beginning.'

John, Stuart, and Duncan were already at a table when we walked in.

'Duncan is driving, so what will you have?' Stuart asked us both.

'A blooming large glass of chardonnay for me, with ice in it, please.' I plonked myself down next to Duncan. 'What a day!' He nodded.

THIRTY

After all the events of the last few weeks, the day of the wedding came quicker than expected. Apart from the evening at the pub after the memorial event, and surprisingly, one quick drink with Ed last Friday night, I'd not been drinking and had made sure to watch what I ate because I had to fit into the dress and look hot. Luckily, my dress was bottle-green in colour, so very forgiving. The style was very Dior's 'New Look'. Super glamorous and 1950s Hollywood. All I had to do was arrive at the venue, as dress, hair, and make-up were all happening in a room.

'Jack! Ruby! Come on, we need to go now,' I shouted from the bottom of the stairs. Ruby came out of her bedroom.

'Mum, James is picking us up, otherwise we'll be hanging around for ages. We'll see you there.'

'Okay.' I decided not to fuss about the legitimacy of these plans, I was sure they would get there on time.

I drove to the venue, safe in the knowledge I was crashing there. Fiona had booked both me and Ursula in for the night, as well as her and Rob's family. I was really excited. Reception showed me to my room, and Ursula was a few doors down. After I'd unpacked my holdall, I knocked on her door.

'Coming!' I heard her shout. As soon as she opened the door, she pulled me in and was jumping up and down. 'Let's have a pillow fight!'

'Are you that excited?' I asked, laughing at her bouncing around.

'Of course I am. This is such a great day. Finally, they are getting hitched.'

It was true. The culmination of quite a lot of drama, all ending in a celebration and hopefully some great dancing. Ursula got our dresses out of the wardrobe. Her dress was exactly the same, except in burnt orange.

'With Fiona wearing white, we really are the walking Irish flag.'

I shook my head. 'I know, and she's coming in to the music of *The Quiet Man*, well, the fight scene music,' Ursula said.

'What?'

'Yep, really. Edited version. Bernadette loves that film and watches it every year without fail. It's a family joke and she wants to make Luke laugh,' Ursula explained.

'Please tell me Rob is not dressing in the colours of the Barbadian flag, because that would be an unholy clash with our dresses.'

Ursula laughed. 'He's not. He's wearing a tuxedo, as is Luke. Very smart, nothing garish. And look what else I have.' Ursula pulled two shoe boxes from the wardrobe.

'This is your Kate,' she said as she handed me the Christian Louboutin shoebox containing a nude high-heeled pump.

'Do not tell me how much they cost because I'll be afraid to wear them.'

'Caroline, they are just shoes, expensive ones, and actually not too bad to walk in. I went for three-inch heels, not the four-inch version.'

'Thank goodness for that. I'm hoping I can get my trotters in these.' They were surprisingly a good fit, and although a lot higher than I've been wearing, I could walk in them.

'I can't remember the last time I wore heels,' I confessed.

'My last time was at my house party, you know, before Ed and I divorced. I think I remember not because of Ed, but because I hardly ever wear heels anymore. Do you think it is an age thing?' Ursula asked.

'No. Ruby lives in trainers and loafers. But I do believe she is wearing heels today, so perhaps we've just been to less weddings and going-out things that require heels.' I suggested to her.

'Good point. Anyway, I need to check on the hair and make-up people. I found this great Bobbi Brown pro make-up artist for us today and booked Fiona's hairdresser. I have told them both that glowing skin, enhanced eyes, and glossy hair is the brief.' At this, she did a twirl.

There was a knock on the door. I opened it to Fiona.

'Thank Christ for that!' She said.

'What?' For the second time since I'd set foot in the room.

'Mammy and Carla are driving me nuts. I need you, Ursula, to get them out of my room, and you, Caroline, to find a babysitter to make them stay in their rooms, or downstairs, I do not care. Here.' She handed me a bottle of champagne. 'Open this first.'

Ursula pulled a face which meant say nothing, do as instructed. We both knew this was the best way to get through the next couple of hours before the ceremony. I didn't want to be drunk though, not in the heels I was wearing. Imagine! I opened the bottle and used the two room glasses and the one for toothbrushes in the bathroom. I took the hit on the bathroom one.

'I had nice glasses in my room.' Fiona sighed. I took a sip and put mine down.

'Why don't I go and talk to them, and Ursula can stay with you?'

Fiona nodded.

I wasn't sure I could do it. Not Bernadette and Carla, but Ed. Did I really want to be with him that much? Well, one dance with him tonight wouldn't hurt, and I could tackle the rest afterwards. I knocked on Fiona's door. Carla opened the door with her hair in big rollers. In fairness, she looked a million dollars and definitely like Penelope Cruz.

'Carolina!' she said, followed by air kisses, and for the second time today, I was pulled into a room by my hand. Bernadette was sat there looking a bit lost, which gave me an idea.

'Ladies, Fiona is a little bit stressed, and Ursula is just sorting out the hair and make-up, so this room needs to be clear of anyone else. I think Bernadette, you should be helping Luke get ready as there is no one to look after him, and Carla, would you make sure Ines is ready so you can introduce her to Jack, James, Dan and Ruby as they are her age.'

Bernadette's face lit up. Carla looked pensive for a moment and then, luckily for me, acquiesced and agreed. Phew. From then on, it was a complete whirlwind of primping and preening. Champagne was drunk, champagne was spilled, and in my case, champagne was poured down the sink or left untouched. We finally wriggled into our dresses, and immediately Ursula had us practising catwalk walks down the corridor. We didn't stop laughing until the moment all three of us were stood outside the door with Luke, waiting to walk into a room full of family and Fiona's selected friends.

'Stop now,' Fiona hissed. 'We've got to be serious.'

She put her right arm through Luke's left one. He put his right hand over her right hand and said, 'Ready, my gorgeous sister?'

Ursula almost sobbed, but caught it in her throat and sounded as if she was having a hiccup. I breathed out as Fiona gave a gentle knock on the very slightly ajar door. Dan was primed to start the music. He'd bought his JLB party box, and immediately the room was resounding with Victor Young's score for *The Quiet Man*.

Luke burst out laughing as he led Fiona into the room; the pair of them had the biggest grins on their faces, and Bernadette was caught between dabbing her teary eyes and laughing with them. The ceremony, conducted by the registrar, passed without incident. There were no fluffed lines, and Alice, Henry, and Tyrel all read short poems or passages beautifully.

Well, I say passed without incident, but Dan, instead of playing the carefully selected and gentle *You and Me* by the Cranberries so everyone could chat and congratulate the newlywed couple, he managed to hit Ursula's playlist by mistake and out blared Dexy's Midnight Runner's *There There My Dear*. Before the registrar could process the change in the atmosphere, Rob had decided to do his best Ska dancing, and before long, we all joined in. I caught Stuart doing fake trumpet playing, and Carla stood open-mouthed at the unfolding scene. I'd never seen chairs cleared to the side so quickly. Rob gestured for everyone to get behind him and Fiona, and we followed their moves as best as we could.

'Dan mate, top move,' Rob said as Fiona flung her arms around him at the end and went in for the snog.

'Mum don't, er, gross out.' Alice was pulling a face at her parents.

'Fiona, Rob, you need to thank the ladies,' Bernadette interjected.

The registrar and her assistant were making their way out of the drawing room.

'It's alright Mammy, I've got this.' Luke went up to them to thank them and gave them both an envelope. The registrar declined immediately, her colleague hesitated. I joined Luke while everyone else was busy chatting.

'It's a thank you card and a small token because you do not know what we have been through to get to this point,' Luke said. I stood alongside him and smiled at them both.

'Well, I'm very much a public servant. It is not a tipping service,' the registrar said.

'The priest would have cost more.' Luke laughed.

'Please accept the token,' I pleaded. 'It really is part of this day. Fiona and Rob want to be generous. If you feel it is not acceptable, then donate it to the charity Missing People. All of us have done this in lieu of a wedding present.'

The registrar relented and thanked Luke. We walked with them to reception and said goodbye.

'I didn't think she was going to accept it, and I was going to have to pocket the card and the money.' Luke laughed.

'I reckon her colleague might have snatched it out of her hand before she gave it back to you,' I said.

As we were walking back, the photographer was leading Fiona and Rob out to the front of the hotel. Fiona rolled her eyes at me and Luke.

'We are not doing this for long.'

She looked beautiful in her white, crepe-back, satin sheath dress, her hair pulled back into a chignon bun, with some ivy cascading from it, and daisies dotted in different places in the bun. Her deep ebony hair glistened in the December sunshine. Ursula came rushing out with a white faux fur stole.

'You'll be freezing otherwise,' she said. She also had some mince pies, which she handed to me and Luke.

'This is something I haven't eaten for years. The smell brings it all back. A proper Christmas,' Luke said.

The three of us stood watching the photos being taken for a few minutes, until Fiona pulled a go away face. We walked back in silence towards the bar area of the reception. I felt quite nauseous again. The stress of this evening was beginning to play on my mind.

‘Are you okay?’ Luke asked.

‘I’m fine, honestly,’ I said. ‘It’s all been a bit emotional. Ursula nodded her head in agreement.

‘I definitely need a drink,’ she said

We went to the bar room, which then led into the room where the wedding reception would be. There were a few tables with canapes on, I grabbed a couple and then went to the bar. John was there.

‘What you having, Caroline? Not that I’m paying,’ he said, grinning. Of course, it was all on a tab.

‘Mine is a gin and tonic, please.’

John asked one of the bar staff for my drink, and after a few minutes of polite chit chat, I had my gin and tonic.

‘Give Stuart a chance,’ John said.

‘What?’

‘Look, we both know you have a choice, and I’m offering you an alternative perspective. Stuart is single and reliable. He won’t let you down,’ he continued.

‘Understood,’ I replied, loath to acknowledge or commit to his suggestion.

When we finally sit down, there are only two round tables and an oblong top table in front of them, where Fiona and Rob will be seated when they escape from the photographer. To the left is Rob’s aunt, Veronica, and her husband, Noah. On what will be Fiona’s right is Luke, then her mother. On one of the round tables are all the offspring. I notice Dan, James, and Jack all paying far too much attention to Ines. Ruby, Alice, and Tyrel are deep in conversation, and poor Henry is sat silent, taking it all in. Luckily, James notices and swaps with Dan, who is oblivious, and starts chatting to him. On our table are Ursula, John, Carla, Mr Etheridge, Stuart, and me. Then we are joined by Rob’s cousin, whose name escapes me, and John’s daughter

Amy sits at the other table.

'Where have you two been?' Ursula asked, leaning over her chair to talk to Amy.

'Rehearsing,' Amy replied.

'For what?'

'Ah ha!' Amy tapped her nose.

Ping, ping, ping went a glass from somewhere, and one of the hotel staff says, 'Please be upstanding for Mr and Mrs Clarke.'

As they walk in, we all stand up and cheer. Amy and Rob's cousin start singing a calypso song in unison. Their voices fill the room, and this small, intimate gathering is once again stirred with emotion. I can't help but look at Luke as he is beaming, and Fiona turns to him and they embrace. Her dream came true. Rob then shakes Luke's hand.

'Thank you everyone, and thank you, Amy and Delfina,' Rob says, then gestures for us to sit down.

We all give them another round of applause, and then everyone sits down. Once we are all seated again, the starter of the meal is brought to the table, and we all start eating and carry on chatting. It is a really pleasant afternoon. John is right, Stuart is reliable. He is attentive, chatty and good fun, even Jack gives me a knowing wink. To which I shake my head.

More food, more drink, and then it is the speeches. Rob thanks his mum's sister, Veronica, and her husband Noah for coming and mentions his departed mother and father. He pulls Fiona's leg by suggesting he had to have his arm twisted to get married, and then gushes about how wonderful she and his wonderful children are. Luke manages to mention his father, his lost years, and how happy he is to be here to see his sister married to Rob. There are a lot of tears. He finishes his speech with a nod to Dan, who gets the song right this time.

'It was this song that kept me going,' he says, looking at Fiona. 'And it is this song that I can now play here today, to promise my mammy, and Fiona, that they will never walk alone without me again.'

The room filled with Gerry and the Pacemakers' *You'll Never Walk Alone.* All of us stood during the chorus and waved our arms from side to side. Even Veronica and Noah. Noah mouthed 'John Barnes' at Rob, to which he grinned and said 'Yes'.

At the end of it all, Rob picked up Fiona and gave her a twirl. Then there was quiet, and we all sat down, exhausted from emotion, food, drink, and exertion. I honestly had never been to such a buoyant and carefree wedding celebration.

Geno!..

'Dan!' Ursula exclaimed. He hurriedly grabbed his mobile phone and stopped the song.

Everyone was laughing and smiling. I finally noticed there was a photographer snapping us all. Fiona had insisted on no group photos, only ones capturing the day. Then at five thirty in the afternoon, we were sat back in the drawing room, remade from the wedding ceremony, back to comfy chairs, sofas and a roaring fire. Tea and coffee was being served to give us all time to rest before the party began at seven. It was going to be a big bash, and we'd finally meet Steve's fiancée. For now, I was glad of the rest. Ruby came and snuggled up with me on the chair.

'Bit of a crush,' I said

'I know, but can I sleep on your shoulder?'

'You can always have a lie down in my room, darling.'

'Can I?' she said. 'I really need a snooze.'

I gave her the keys and continued to sit contemplating. As lovely as Fiona and Rob's wedding day had been, I felt a bit of a spare part as the single friend. It was my own fault, but surely my time had come. I understood why I couldn't be with Ed. I knew it was complicated and could cause ructions. Was it worth it? Suddenly, I realised over the last few months I'd seen him less than when he had been with Ursula. Then I met up with him regularly once or twice a week. Now it was very sporadic.

'Penny for them?' Stuart had joined me on the chair opposite.

'Ha! I don't think there are any. This is the look of being worn out from a fabulously long day.'

He smiled.

'It has been a long day and I am actually honoured to be here, especially with Luke. When John and I started the investigation, I never thought we'd be successful and find him. Not at all.' He shook his head.

'Look, Stuart...' I didn't get to finish.

'Caroline, I know what you are going to say. Don't take any notice of wishful thinking by others. I enjoy your company and I like you, but there is no pressure or moves coming from here, okay?'

I nodded. I felt much better. The next moment, Fiona was practically on top of me.

'Come on Caro, me, you, and Ursula, outside right now.'

'It's dark.'

'Oh yeah, but anyway, right now.' She grabbed my hand and pulled me up out of the chair.

Stuart waved goodbye to me. With Ursula in tow. we went outside into the cold December evening. The photographer had set up lighting in front of the hotel entrance and was on a step ladder. James was helping him.

'Right, stand there, ladies.' The photographer directed us to shuffle together. 'Now look up and smile at me. That is great,' he said as his camera clicked. 'Couple more, please.'

'James, I want the hoes, and you two, legs out please,' Fiona said. Then James handed us each a hoe. Ursula couldn't stop laughing.

There we were flashing a leg and our high heels, each with a hoe in one hand.

'Mad,' James said, laughing at us goofing around.

It was mad. Mad fun.

'Right, we've got to go back in for round two and the hoards arriving,' Fiona said. 'Including Ed, cos Rob insisted. Are you alright about that, Ursula?'

'Yes, why wouldn't I be? Water under the bridge. I'm glad the house is sold and I'm moving out. It is all done and over.'

Fiona squeezed her hand.

'Still, he is a chuffing dickhead,' she said.

As we were about to go back in, Jay and Steve arrived with Steve's fiancée, who he introduced us to. It was nice they'd come so early. We were all a real team now. Back inside, the bar room and the room we'd had the wedding reception in were all opened up. There was a DJ and lights to get us in the mood to party. Mind you, my feet were starting to feel a little achy.

'No changing shoes,' Ursula said. 'We've got to style it out.'

'How did you know?'

'I saw you wince, and I feel the same. If we take them off, then we'll never get them back on and have filthy feet at the end of the night.'

We both pulled faces, and then Jay asked me to join him on the dance floor, so I obliged. It was good fun dancing and chatting with different people. There was a good crowd, although no sign of Ed. I grabbed my clutch bag and went to the toilets to freshen up. As I was applying some make-up, Ursula burst in.

'Quick, I need the loo.'

I got out of her way as she was hoisting up her dress before closing the door. We were both laughing when a few minutes later she said, 'Relief!'

'Did you leave that to the last minute, Ursula? Bit dangerous at our age, don't you think?'

'I know! I was dancing with your Jack and had to dash. I'm going back out now to get my lippy.'

'Oh, use mine if you want to.'

'Thanks, Caro.'

She deftly applied a smidgen and dabbed the rest around her lips. She was flushed from dancing and looked so happy. I was glad for her. She handed it back and gave me a hug.

'What are you doing in here, Caro?'

'I'm touching up my face and contemplating life in the toilets of a wedding, as you do.' I laughed.

Ursula winked at me.

'Well, don't be too long. It is a bit of a surprise, but Ed has turned up with his new girlfriend. James said she is his divorce lawyer, but who knows?' She shrugged.

My face barely concealed my shock.

'I know, it is a turn up, isn't it?' she continued. 'I don't mind, it is all fine. Are you okay?'

I forced a smile.

'Bit tired. You go, I'll see you in a moment after I've finished here.'

The moment she left, I banged the cubicle door open. I went in and stuffed my mouth with some toilet paper and screamed. I felt sick to the core. I put the lid down and sat down. Think, think. I took a deep breath. Exhaled. Then another one. Probably five minutes or more passed before I walked back into the party. The band had started playing. I put my bag down on the table next to Ruby and looked for Stuart. Found him. Deep breath again. I leant in and whispered into his ear. He replied and smiled at me. I made sure I did a throw back of my head, all smiles, and took his hand, pulling him onto the dance floor.

EPILOGUE

Standing outside a congregation of gleaming glass buildings, he lifted his head up to the sky. A very blue London sky. New job and new location. Who'd have thought it? The blue sky warmed him.

Rather than enter the building immediately, he sat on the wooden plant border, designed to also act as a bench. He was surprised at the quality of all the buildings and the landscaping. They were all very modern, and it did rather feel like a different city here with all the space. The space allowed you to breathe, and it was a deep breath he needed with his new role tackling the impact of county lines. What did his first wife, Jean, used to say? He racked his brains.

'Look for the opportunities.' Her voice, her lilting New York tones, popped into his head. It was true, the opportunities, it's what the gangs did to recruit their foot soldiers. Gave them an opportunity. Well, it was now his responsibility to figure out a way to stop and stem those opportunities and make other ones more attractive. Of course, the current Mrs Smith didn't think he had a hope in hell unless the law changed and drugs were decriminalised. The current Mrs Smith. He smiled. Ursula loved to describe herself this way.

They had picked a wonderful day in June to get married at Chelsea Registry Office on the King's Road. It was that or the Elvis chapel in Las Vegas, and he'd vetoed that option, much to Ursula's disappointment, given she wanted to walk in to *Suspicious Minds.* Instead, the nearest cool celebrity music option for her was the King's Road and a joint decision to have Paul Weller's *You Do Something to Me* as their wedding song. The best part of it was the two of them with only their offspring, no one else. No Fiona, and certainly no Caroline; they'd had a hen weekend all together instead. He'd insisted on just family, the only way not to cause offence or have to explain his reasons to Stuart. Though it was all done now. Forgotten. But he kept one eye on Caroline now that she was with Stuart.

It was magical, the long walk down the King's Road to Sloane Square and then to Pavilion Road. All of them chatting, and Olivia joking it was like they were in 'The Split', which went completely over Ethan, Dan and James's heads. It had been a joy to surprise them all with the private dining at Three Darlings. Amy Instagrammed everything. The lunch went on well past the afternoon. When they finally stepped out into the cool, early summer evening, the best part for him was Ursula tucking herself next to him for warmth, and he pulled her tight.